McNally's Folly
is the ninth Archy McNally novel

'For those who prefer their crime in very funny doses.'
Mike Ripley, *Daily Telegraph*

'Archy McNally is a wonderfully unlikely character,
the Bertie Wooster of private detection . . . suspend
belief and sit back and enjoy.'

Guardian

'Sanders writes smoothly about characters complex
enough to care for, deftly suggesting the grimace
behind the grin.'

Cosmopolitan

'Fluent and confident, urban and urbane intelligence.'
The Sunday Times

'Lawrence Sanders has honed a voice for Archy
McNally that is wonderfully infectious. You can't
help falling for him.'

Washington Times

D1151889

About the author

Lawrence Sanders, one of the world's most popular novelists, wrote twenty-five international bestsellers including the Deadly Sin and Commandment series and the eight Archy McNally novels.

The publishers and the estate of Lawrence Sanders have chosen Vincent Lardo, author of *The Hampton Affair* and *The Hampton Connection*, to create this novel based on Archy McNally and his fictional world.

McNally's Folly

An Archy McNally Mystery by Vincent Lardo

Lawrence Sanders

NEW ENGLISH LIBRARY
Hodder & Stoughton

G. P. Putnam's Sons and the estate of Lawrence Sanders
have chosen Vincent Lardo to create this novel based on Lawrence
Sanders' beloved character, Archy McNally, and his fictional world.

First published in Great Britain in 2000
by Hodder and Stoughton
First published in paperback in 2001
by Hodder and Stoughton
A division of Hodder Headline

A New English Library Paperback

10 9 8 7 6 5 4 3 2 1

A CIP catalogue record for this title
is available from the British Library.

ISBN 0 340 79360 0

Printed and bound in Great Britain by
Clays Ltd, St Ives plc

Hodder and Stoughton
A division of Hodder Headline
338 Euston Road
London NW1 3BH

1

What could be nicer than holding the hand of a beautiful young lady with the lights turned low? Why, holding the hand of a beautiful young lady with the lights turned off, that's what. And when the young lady is none other than Elizabeth Fitzwilliams – 'Fitz' to her intimates, whose number, according to Palm Beach gossip, is legion – the experience can be quite uplifting, if you get my drift.

I was restrained, literally and figuratively, from joining the ranks of Fitz's intimates by that pillar of Palm Beach society, the formidable Penelope Tremaine – 'Penny' to her intimates, whose pedigrees make up for their numerical paucity – who was holding my other hand.

Penny's hand that wasn't holding mine was attached to that of her husband, Vance Tremaine. Vance had a serious predilection for pretty young ladies, so it's always wise to know exactly where his hands are with the likes of Fitz in the immediate vicinity.

Vance, in turn, held the hand of the charming Mrs

John Fairhurst. If Penny was a pillar of Palm Beach society, Emily Fairhurst was the concrete in which the pillar was embedded.

Moving right along, Emily held the hand of her secretary, Arnold Turnbolt, and to complete the circle, Arnold and Fitz played bookends to Palm Beach's current diversion, Serge Ouspenskaya.

Me? I'm Archibald McNally – Archy to my intimates, whose number can be counted without going into the higher mathematics of double digits – of McNally & Son, Attorney-at-Law. Father is the attorney and I, having been expelled from Yale Law, am the son and director of a small department (employees: one) at McNally & Son assigned to Discreet Inquiries. We represent some of the wealthiest residents of the Town of Palm Beach, whose problems often require private investigation rather than the assistance of the local police. The very rich like to keep a low profile, especially when a spotlight might reveal them to be as foolish and sinful as lesser folks who don't have a portfolio to call their own.

By now, those of you who are ardent readers of Conan Doyle, Dashiell Hammett and Dick Tracy know that on this (may the PB Chamber of Commerce forgive me) chilly January night we had not come together to play ring-around-the-rosy, form a daisy chain to protest the pollution of our planet or pray. We were, in fact, in the midst of Palm Beach's latest craze – a séance. And lest you think that I have taken leave of my senses (and there are those, whose number is myriad, who would say that one cannot take leave of what one never possessed) I am here not as believer, agnostic or neophyte, but in pursuit of my duties as a discreet inquirer.

As we sit, emptying our minds – with this crowd a feat easier done than said – I will recapitulate, for those who do not have ready access to a crystal ball, the events that got me from home to here (in my fire-engine red Miata and not upon a flying carpet).

My office, in the McNally Building on Royal Palm Way, is slightly larger than a duplex coffin. I can only assume that my father relegated me to this minuscule closet to show those he employs that he, Prescott McNally, is not an adherent of nepotism. Though deprived of a window, he did permit me an air-conditioning vent; he has not, as yet, installed a razor-sharp pendulum in the ceiling, swinging in an ever widening and descending arc. Father is a devotee of Dickens, not Poe, and I am thankful for small blessings.

When my phone rang I picked it up after the third ring giving the impression, I hoped, that the caller was intruding upon a business conclave of paramount importance. It was Mrs Trelawney, my father's secretary, who knew better. 'Mrs Trelawney,' I cooed, 'I was just about to call you.'

'Meaning you have completed cooking the books, as they say.'

'I don't know who *they* are, Mrs Trelawney, but if

you are referring to my expense account the answer is, yes, I have just completed reconstructing last week's expenditures.'

'I hope you're not billing us for yet another lunch at the Pelican Club, Archy.'

'As a matter of fact I did not,' I assured her, then added, 'However, now that you mention it, I do recall lunching there on Tuesday last in the line of duty.' I quickly added fifty bucks to my paltry list as recompense for a meal I had shared with my lady friend, Consuela Garcia. It had not been a business lunch, in the strictest sense, but Connie has so often aided and abetted me in my duties that I saw nothing wrong with advancing her a lunch in expectation of future assistance. And besides, my father could well afford it.

'You're a con artist, Archy.'

'I've been called worse, Mrs Trelawney.'

'And all deserved, I'm sure.'

'Mrs Trelawney,' I sang, 'you make a sunny day cloudy.'

'Well, before it starts raining, put away your wish list and get yourself down here. Your father is with a client and for reasons known only to my boss and God, your presence is required.'

If I was required, the client with pater was not in need of legal counsel but of the services of Discreet Inquiries. 'Anyone I know, Mrs Trelawney?'

'A Mr Richard Holmes. He's new to me and I've been here since before the flood.'

McNally's Folly

Assuming she meant the biblical flood and not an ambitious leak in her basement, that would put Mrs Trelawney's age somewhere between classic and antique. The name Richard Holmes rang a distant bell – more of a faint tinkle, actually – but I could not connect it with a face, occupation or previous encounter. This was as frustrating as encountering a familiar face and being unable to assign it a name. I chalked this memory lapse up to my hectic schedule and not an early onset senior moment.

I took the elevator down and entered my father's outer sanctum, where Mrs Trelawney eyed me from head to toe before exclaiming, 'Tennis anyone?'

I was wearing a pair of white summer flannels with a navy blazer emblazoned with the Pelican Club's crest: a pelican rampant on a field of dead mullet. I gave her weary cliché as much time as it was worth before answering, 'Would you please announce me, Mrs Trelawney.'

'As who? Andre Agassi or Pete Sampras?'

'Touché, Mrs. Trelawney. Touché.' I love sparring with my father's secretary, who is one of my favorite people in spite of, or perhaps because of, our mutual delight in pelting each other with verbal abuse. She is a charming beldame with an ill-fitting gray wig and a penchant for risqué jokes. As she buzzed the inner sanctum, I slipped my expense account on her desk and ventured into the lion's den. Here begins the latest adventure of Archibald McNally, aged preppie, who is not licensed to kill.

The McNally Building is a modern edifice of glass and stainless steel. The office of the man who commissioned it is oak-paneled and furnished in a style that is more Victoriana than art deco. One of its treasures is an antique rolltop desk boasting thirty-six cubbyholes and four secret compartments – that I know of.

A major drawback of such a museum piece is that the owner cannot converse vis-à-vis with visitors while seated at his prize possession. For this reason, a more conventional desk is also present in the guv'nor's suite but I suspect, when alone, my father sits at his rolltop and examines the contents of its secret niches. Ladies with hourglass figures in black silk hose and corsets? I believe that in a former life my father, Prescott McNally, was the man who left Miss Havisham waiting at the church.

'This is my son, Archy,' the sire introduced me as I entered the office. 'Archy, this is Mr Richard Holmes.'

'How do you do, sir,' I said, taking the hand Holmes extended toward me as I again rummaged in vain through my mental Rolodex in search of a card that bore his name and profile. Richard Holmes was a portly man but the excess adipose tissue, except for his rather prominent jowls, was solid rather than flabby. Here was a man who refused to deny himself that second helping of *mousse au chocolat*, but made up for this indulgence by regular visits to the gym and sauna. I drew a picture of a good-time-Charlie with the soul of a penitent.

I put his age at sixty, give or take a few years, which was about forty years older than the Lilly Pulitzer jacket he wore atop a pink polo shirt. Ms Pulitzer's men's line was all the rage in Palm Beach a quarter of a century ago, when her famous flower-print fabrics had her faithful looking like walking hothouses. Mr Holmes's heirloom was a bouquet of daisies, carnations and pink rosebuds. I drew a picture of a man who clung to the past and would wager that he donned his plus-fours to play golf.

'Mr Holmes and his wife are here for the season, Archy,' my father was saying as I took the other visitor's chair, 'and have taken a place on Via Del Lago. He was recommended to us by Bob Simmons.'

Modest but not a bad address, about a block from the ocean. Simmons was a longtime client of McNally & Son and a man of great wealth. *Mein papa*, no doubt, was hoping Richard Holmes was in the same tax bracket as the guy who sent him our way.

'They may decide to purchase a home in the Town of Palm Beach, and if they do we will advise and act on their behalf via our real estate division,' father continued. 'However, Mr Holmes is here on more urgent business that I think is more in line with your expertise than mine.' With a smile, father passed me the proverbial buck.

No surprise to this Jr McNally. If Holmes was merely looking for a house, Simmons would have introduced him to his realtor. As we had rescued Simmons's son from an embarrassing situation involving a lady of the evening and a controlled substance, Simmons had directed the man to Discreet Inquiries for a more pressing matter.

'How can I be of help, Mr Holmes?' I began my usual spiel.

'We speak in confidence?' he answered, in my clients' usual spiel.

'Discreet, sir, is our name.'

With a nod that put his jowls in high gear, Holmes said, 'Are you familiar with a man who calls himself Serge Ouspenskaya?'

'No, sir, I am not.' But I was familiar with the European character actress, Maria Ouspenskaya, who made a name for herself on this side of the Atlantic in a role that was more kitsch than camp as the mother of a werewolf. I hoped Serge was not one of her offspring.

'He claims to be a psychic,' Holmes informed me in a tone that implied Ouspenskaya was anything but.

'A resident psychic is de rigueur for Palm Beach, Mr Holmes. They come and go like the rise and fall of the fairer sex's hemline, some achieving more fame than others, but few survive more than one season. We had the Ouija board craze, the crystal craze, ESP, EST and reincarnation, when every gentlewoman along Ocean Boulevard claimed to have been Cleopatra, Josephine or Mona Lisa.' Only my father's presence deterred me from adding, 'and we had the Lilly Pulitzer craze.' Instead, I ended the lecture with, 'It's a rich community, sir, and diversion is the name of the game.'

'I know what you mean, Mr McNally, and my wife is no stranger to diversions, the occult included, but this guy has caught her fancy and I believe he's milking her for every buck she's worth, which happen to be my bucks.'

Not a new scenario. I was involved with a psychic a few years back who spoke in the voices of those who have passed over, as psychics refer to the dearly departed. Her name was Hertha Gloriana and I never learned if she actually had the power or if she was a phony. What I did learn was that Hertha preferred Sapphic love to the more conventional kind and proved it by running off with the lady I was romancing at the time. My ego has not yet fully recovered. I decided not to relate this tale of unrequited amour to Mr Richard Holmes.

'Please, sir, call me Archy. My father is Mr McNally. How did your wife come in contact with Serge Ouspenskaya?'

Holmes shrugged, sending his jowls into a tizzy, and explained, 'At some social gathering or other. You know how women talk. Ouspenskaya claims to have a knack for locating lost objects. He's supposed to have told a woman where she could find a diamond clip she misplaced and gave up for lost. They say she talked her insurance company into paying Ouspenskaya a finder's fee.'

My policeman friend, Sergeant Al Rogoff, once told me that the police and insurance companies use psychics and mediums more often than they care to admit, especially in cases of missing persons and objects. 'Did your wife seek out Ouspenskaya especially for this reason, Mr Holmes?' I asked.

'Yes, Archy, she did.'

'And may I ask what she wanted him to locate?'

His jaw was set so tight those jowls remained as firm as his response. 'No, Archy, you may not.'

The pater raised one bushy eyebrow, a trick that never ceases to fascinate me, and spoke like a judge counseling a reluctant witness. 'Archy has already assured you that nothing you say here will be repeated to anyone without your explicit permission and need I remind you, sir, that client/lawyer confidentiality is sacrosanct.'

'I assume you want me to investigate this Ouspenskaya,' I came in right behind father, 'but if I don't know what your wife wants from him, how can I ascertain the validity of his dealings with her? I would rather decline the job, Mr Holmes, then proceed without knowing all the facts. Unlike Serge Ouspenskaya, I'm not on speaking terms with a higher power who's willing to share with me.'

Holmes gave this a lot of thought as father and I waited patiently for him to reply. With a sigh of what I took to be resignation rather than acquiescence he began, 'My wife was an actress . . .'

'*Desdemona Darling!*' I exploded before I could stop myself, causing father's eyebrow practically to meet his hairline. Regaining some semblance of self-control I immediately apologized for my outburst.

Holmes gave me a reassuring smile and with

unabashed pride said, 'I understand, Archy. People still respond with awe when they suddenly connect me with DeeDee, or Desdemona as you know her.'

Desdemona Darling was one of the most celebrated film actresses at a time some like to call Hollywood's Golden Age – the years just prior to and shortly after the Second World War. A photograph of Desdemona in a shocking pink maillot was a favorite pinup of our GIs and is as representative of that war as the photograph of the marines raising the American flag on the Isle of Iwo Jima.

Desdemona, it was well known, had had six husbands, three of them Hollywood idols of the moment: Her current spouse, Richard Holmes, was a self-made millionaire via the futures market, thanks for an unerring skill for buying pork bellies low and selling them high. It was no wonder that his name had struck a chord which needed only the word *actress* to inspire me to identify the key.

The Hollywood of that time had given us a Sweater Girl, a Sarong Girl, an Oomph Girl, a platinum blonde, a strawberry blonde, and a peek-a-boo bangs blonde. The ash blonde Desdemona Darling was the Golden Girl of that golden era.

So famous was Desdemona Darling that the mere mention of her name had the sire stroking his handlebar mustache, a sure sign that he was enjoying whatever immodest memories her name had evoked. When angry, he tugs at that hirsute indulgence.

'DeeDee made a risqué one-reeler early on in her

career,' Holmes told us like a man who suddenly decides to leap before he looks and to hell with the consequences.

Surprising, but not shocking. Several celebrated actresses of that bygone era had been rumored to have gotten their start in what were called 'blue' films, or 'smokers.' (But Archy, who knows all, ain't naming names; not only because a gentleman never kisses and tells, but because some of them may still be alive and a libel suit I don't need. Look what happened to O. Wilde.)

'Not as bawdy as today's porn videos, but bad enough,' Holmes went on. Had he seen the film or was he quoting his wife's rationalization of her early cinematic offering? 'It was never widely distributed because in them days you could go to jail just for looking at a smoker.'

Not to mention that in *them* days you could go to jail twice as long for starring in one. And, if his grammatical faux pas was any indication of his roots, Richard Holmes traded up when he went into pork bellies.

'The studio thought they had bought up the few that existed,' Holmes told us, 'but they missed one.'

'Your wife is being blackmailed, sir,' I stated.

The jowls shook in agreement. 'But not in the way you're thinking, Archy. The guy has never asked her for a dime. But every year, on the anniversary of the day the film was made, he sends her a reminder, telling her he owns a print and might, or might not, go public with it. I guess you could call it emotional blackmail. And it's been going on for over half a century.'

'And after all this time your wife is still perturbed by the possibility that he may go public?'

'If perturbed is a nice way of saying she's bonkers over the possibility, then she's pretty effing perturbed, if you'll excuse the English. Actresses are very vain people, Archy, and DeeDee is a classic example of the breed. Hanging on to the Golden Girl image is more important to her than life itself.'

'Do the letters contain a return address?'

'No way. They come from all over the country through some kind of mail-drop service.'

'And Mrs Holmes wants Ouspenskaya to find this miscreant?'

'That's right. And if he's dead, she wants to know what he did with that little tin can in his possession. Ouspenskaya is not the first psychic DeeDee has been to with this but he's the first to get her so bamboozled. You see, she didn't have to tell him what she was looking for. He knew.'

A good guess, I thought, or the guy did a bit of research. With a lady boasting a public record as long as Desdemona Darling's, he probably picked up enough info to make her believe he had spent the last fifty years in her boudoir.

'He charges five hundred bucks a session, Archy, and my wife has him on our weekly payroll.'

'Did it ever occur to you, or Mrs Holmes, that the threat is a paper tiger? I mean, how do you know he actually owns a print of the infamous one-reeler?'

'Because of how the letters are signed,' Holmes said.

'And how are they signed, sir?'

'Kirk.'

'And does Mrs Holmes know who Kirk is, sir?'

'Sure. He's the cameraman who photographed the one-reeler.'

2

It was time to collect on the lunch I had so generously advanced Connie a few days earlier. If Serge Ouspenskaya was the current rage of Palm Beach society, Connie could fill me in on all the vital statistics. Connie labors as social secretary to Lady Cynthia Horowitz, Palm Beach's hostess with the mostest. In that capacity, Connie was a one-woman FBI, CIA and yenta who kept an ear to our sandy ground and an eye on those who trod it. She was as vital to my line of work as Tonto was to the Lone Ranger's.

Not being the cad I pretend to be, or would like to be, I am not smitten with Connie for purely commercial reasons. She is the one steady love of my life and we have been dating for lo these many years, a relationship I prefer to marriage. However, whenever Connie plays bridesmaid to one of her numerous cousins, she never misses the opportunity to lament, 'Always a bridesmaid, never a bride.' Therefore, when I was godfather to my sister's boy, Darcy, I loudly proclaimed, 'Always a godfather, never a god.' Connie, alas, did not appreciate the witticism.

I called Connie and, happily, she was free for lunch. I told her I would pick her up at high noon and rode down to petty cash to collect on my expenses. Whoever christened that department must have had a precognition of my weekly reparation at the time. I retrieved my Miata from our underground garage, waved a farewell to Herb, our security person, and was off on the first lap of the case I would label in my journal as 'Serge the Seer.' And, were I a seer, I would have driven right back to the McNally Building and hid in my cubbyhole until the future bode more auspiciously.

Lady C, who got her title from her last husband – she had had six and the other five left her nothing but money – lived on ten acres of prime Ocean Boulevard real estate in a faux antebellum mansion that had me humming the theme from *Gone with the Wind* every time I rode up the drive to collect Connie.

Getting into the Miata, Connie gave me a peck on the cheek before complaining, 'Long time, no see.'

'We had lunch last Tuesday,' I reminded her.

'And this is this Tuesday. So where have you been for the week that was?'

'I'm a working man, Connie, remember?'

'Just make sure that what you're working on doesn't wear high heels and a little something from Victoria's Secret.'

'I know a drag queen in West Palm who fits that description.'

This got a laugh from my good-natured significant other and a pat on my thigh. 'It's been a long time since you've been to my place for dinner and . . .'

'You miss Archy's *arroz con pollo*?' I teased. Connie is more at home with a computer than in the kitchen so I prepare the meal when invited to dine at Chez Garcia. The *arroz con pollo* is my specialty.

'If that's what they're calling it these days, I miss it.'

'Why, you naughty lady,' I scolded.

Connie is no more than sixty-two inches high and blessed with a generously curvaceous figure. She sports a year-round tan and usually lets her long, glossy black hair float free. In a string bikini the lady is more impressive than the Pyramids. Today she wore a white silk shirt and white denim jeans, neither of which contained a ripple or a wrinkle. We have an open relationship, Connie and I, which works fine until I look at another woman, at which time Connie asks me if I have a burning ambition to be a male soprano. I sometimes think she's serious.

There was a goodly crowd at the Pelican Club's bar as attended to by Simon Pettibone, bartender and major domo, but surprisingly few members seated in the dining area. Connie and I commandeered our favorite corner table and Priscilla, Simon's daughter, strutted over to take our order. 'Hello, beauty and the beast,' she welcomed us.

'You can be fired, young lady,' I answered.

'If I go so does the rest of the family,' Priscilla countered.

Brother Leroy was our chef and mother Jasmine was our den mother. Without the Pettibones the Pelican would cease to fly.

'Is that a threat?' I asked.

'No, Mr Legree, it's a promise.'

'Pay him no mind, Pris,' Connie intervened, 'and tell us what delights Leroy has in store for us this afternoon.'

The day's special was our favorite grilled grouper sandwich on Italian ciabatta with spicy sweet potato fries and homemade ketchup. This came with a salad of Bibb lettuce, avocado slices, paper-thin slices of red onion and a sun-dried tomato vinaigrette. When Leroy was on, he was on, and when he was off not even little Oliver would have asked for more.

We ordered vodka gimlets to start and when they arrived I asked Connie what she knew about Serge Ouspenskaya. 'Did you get me here to gaze into my eyes or pump me for information?'

'To gaze into your eyes, of course. But in order to write this off as a business lunch I have to pump you while I gaze.'

'Did it ever occur to you not to write off at least one of our lunches?'

As a matter of fact, it had not, but intent on remaining a tenor I didn't tell her this. Instead I waxed romantically, 'You're all in white today, Connie, just like a bride.'

18

'Why Archy, whatever made you think of that?'

And I learned all I wanted to know about Serge Ouspenskaya.

Lady Cynthia had treated Palm Beach's elite to a 'who-done-it?' extravaganza just before the holiday season. She hired a theatrical agency in Miami to orchestrate the morbid gala wherein one of the guests is selected to be the murder victim, another designated the murderer. The rest of the crew have to figure out who-done-it, how-done-it and when-done-it. It's the kind of fete very popular on mystery cruises and hotels that offer solve-it-yourself weekends.

To gild the lily, as is Lady C's wont, she decided to hire a seer, allow him to exchange a few words with all the guests and then have him write the names of the victim and the murderer on a piece of paper based on his 'reading' of those assembled. The paper would be put into an envelope, sealed and opened after the lesser folks had a chance to solve the crime without divine intervention. Ouspenskaya was the chosen psychic.

'How did Lady C come to choose Ouspenskaya?' I asked Connie.

'That's the weird part of the story, Archy. He chose us.'

'How so?'

'Madame decided on the psychic show one day and the next day Ouspenskaya called us. This is not hearsay. I took the call. He introduced himself and said he was calling in answer to Lady Cynthia's need. I asked him how he knew what Lady Cynthia needed and he laughed and said, "Because I'm psychic, of course."'

'This is on the level, Connie?'

'Would I lie to the man I love?'

Love and marriage weigh heavily on Connie Garcia's mind and Mr Pettibone's vodka gimlets only added fuel to the fire. I now nursed mine, fearing that if I ordered another Connie would be asking me to name the day.

'Naturally, Lady C spread the story up and down Ocean Boulevard, more to drum up advance hype for her party than to further Ouspenskaya's career.'

'And did he name the victim and the murderer?'

Connie raised her hand as if I had asked her to take an oath and said, 'He did. Right down to the nitty-gritty of the bizarre plot.'

Anyone with two brain cells that mesh would have then stated, 'Lady C must have told the agency what she was up to and they could have hired Ouspenskaya as an extra added attraction to dazzle Madame and her guests. They had Ouspenskaya call and then they gave him all the information he needed to solve the crime they had set up.'

Finishing her drink, Connie answered, 'Anyone with two brain cells that mesh would have thought of that.'

Pereant, inquit, qui ante nos nostra dixerunt. Loosely translated, 'a pox on those who have uttered our words before us.' The arrival of our food precluded me from having to order two more gimlets, but I did ask Priscilla to bring us two lagers, which Mr Pettibone keeps on tap and draws with the pomp and circumstance of a true artist. Then we both dug into our meal with gusto. I once told Connie I liked women with hearty appetites and she's never forgotten it.

'Everyone had a good time and Madame picked up the tab,' Connie continued with her tale of Lady C's mystery shindig, 'and if the agency had supplied Ouspenskaya on the sly we just accepted it as a perk.' Connie forked a spicy fry before going on. 'But there's more to the story.'

Knowing I would hate myself in the morning, I blurted, 'Anyone with two brain cells that mesh would know that.'

Ignoring this, Connie went right on. 'A week later, Mr and Mrs Fairhurst gave a charity ball for their beloved children's hospital and, having heard of Ouspenskaya, thanks to the write-up Lolly Spindrift gave him in Lolly's gossip rag, Mrs Fairhurst hired Ouspenskaya to tell fortunes.'

When the rich want to act like common folk and have a little fun, they do it in the name of charity. Hence we have Las Vegas Night balls, April in Paris balls, costume balls and come-as-your-favorite-mass-murderer balls. The gentry get to raise a little Cain while raising a lot of cash for worthy causes, charities being the rich folks' excuse for conspicuous consumption.

'And Ouspenskaya once again astounded his audience,' I surmised aloud.

'Did he ever,' Connie said, dabbing at her lips with

a paper napkin, the linen variety being unknown to the Pelican Club. 'He told a woman that she was troubled over the loss of an expensive object. Amazed, the woman admitted she was, and the object in question was a diamond clip. Ouspenskaya told her she had forgotten to remove the clip from a dress she had placed on a pile destined for the Goodwill people. The woman went right home and guess what?'

'I can't imagine,' I said.

'She came back to the party a half hour later waving the found piece of jewelry and kow-towing to Ouspenskaya as if he were the Wizard of Oz.'

And that's just what I was beginning to think Serge Ouspenskaya was – the quintessential Wizard of Oz. But without Toto to pull aside the curtain to reveal him for the charlatan he probably was, I would have to go it alone. My pooch, Hobo, wouldn't leave his gabled doghouse long enough to assist me. 'And a star was born,' I proclaimed.

'Launched by Lady Cynthia Horowitz, who is poised for yet another launching before you can say abracadabra.'

'Now what?'

Hoisting her glass of lager in a mock toast, Connie laughed, 'Buzz Carr, the aspiring actor. Remember him? It rhymes with star and don't you forget it.'

'I hope you don't mean that muscle-brained delinquent.'

'None other. And, Archy, does that boy have muscles in all the right places.'

Why is it always embarrassing when a woman refers to a man's sexual attractions, but never vice versa? Women's libbers have a point, but don't tell my pater I said that. Phrasing it as unkindly as possible, I asked, 'Is she still shacking up with Phil Meecham's ex?'

'Really, Archy. Buzz is Madame's protégé. And he was the ex-pilot of Phil Meecham's yacht.'

'The lady draws more protégés than a hole in a window screen draws flies. There was the tennis pro protégé, the golf pro protégé, the masseur, the mystic and the maniac. And need I remind you that all of Meecham's pretty-boy employees are required to pull a double shift – pun intended. Good Lord, Connie, Buzz is twenty-five at most and Lady C is just shy of eighty.'

Looking around the room furtively, Connie whispered, 'The very mention of Lady C's age could cost me my job, Archy – and she admits to seventy.'

'Which makes her seventy-five.'

'As long as she signs my weekly check, she's seventy.'

'And just how does she hope to make a thespian out of the ex-yachtsman?'

'By buying him a theater. How else?'

'What?'

'Keep your shirt on, Archy. I'm exaggerating – but not much.' When gossiping about her lady boss, Connie is like a locomotive crawling out of the station, gradually accelerating to full speed. 'Madame has become a major patron of our community theater.

She wrote them a large check which got her elected
Creative Director. This means she can decide on what
play goes up next and who gets the leading roles,
subject to approval by the board members.'

'And if one of them gives her a thumbs-down, she'll
cut off the community theater like a disinherited black
sheep,' I said with contempt. 'What play does she have
in mind?'

'*Arsenic and Old Lace*,' Connie announced with glee.

That was a revelation. The two old maids were the
stars of the play but in the film version Cary Grant
had all but chewed up the scenery as their adoring
nephew. 'Oh,' I groaned. It was me who had once
said, begrudgingly to be sure, that in his yachting cap
Buzz Carr resembled Cary Grant aboard the *True Love*,
proving that Lady C didn't have an original thought
beneath her tinted locks.

'Indigestion?' Connie asked.

'No,' I assured her. 'I was just thinking that Madame
is in a macabre mood this season. First a "who-done-it?"
party and now arsenic in the elderberry wine and
bodies in the window seat.'

Excited, Connie leaned toward me and gushed, '
bet you'll never guess who's going to play one of the
old maids.'

Having just come from a meeting with Richard
Holmes and knowing what actress of the right vintage
was currently gracing our town, I didn't have to be a psy
chic to make an educated guess. But Holmes had made
me swear not to tell a soul, including and especially his

wife, that I was investigating Ouspenskaya on his behest or that I had even talked with Holmes about his wife. When I answered, 'Lady Cynthia herself,' I didn't know that I was indeed poaching on Ouspenskaya's turf.

'Desdemona Darling,' Connie cried. 'And I met her.'

'No?' I articulated in awe. Buzz may look like Cary Grant, but when it comes to chewing the scenery, Archy has no equal.

'It's not for publication, which means not even Lolly knows, and if you breathe a word of this I'll kill you, Archy McNally.'

And if I breathe a word of something else, Holmes will kill me. But how long can I hold my breath before an acute lack of oxygen does me in? I found myself in a no-win situation, which is the plight of a discreet inquirer in a town where 'show but don't tell' is a practicing religion.

'How did Madame snare Desdemona Darling?' I wanted to know.

'Desdemona and her husband are here for the season and she and Lady C go back to the days before the big war. They both started out as models, you know.'

Lady C was indeed a model. A unique one, so the story goes. She has a face that could scare the bejesus out of a voodoo witch doctor and a body that could safely be called the forerunner of Viagra.

'So when Madame told Desdemona about her plans for Buzz,' Connie said, 'Desdemona said she would be glad to lend her name to the project.'

'Has Desdemona Darling met Buzz?' I asked, fearing the worst.

'Oh, yes, Archy. That's when she agreed to do the show.'

I wondered if the board of the Palm Beach Community Theater was aware that those two muses of perpetuity – their patron and star – were hell bent on turning *Arsenic and Old Lace* into *Desire Under the Poincianas*.

I drove Connie back to Tara and then headed home. Our castle is a tall Tudorish affair on Ocean Boulevard with a leaky copper mansard roof. My suite is on the third floor, so I am the one blessed when the angels weep, as mother once explained rainy days to me when I was just a kid.

I parked on the graveled turnaround in front of our three-car garage, careful not to block the entrance to the left-hand bay where my father always keeps his big Lexus. The middle space was occupied by an old, wood-paneled Ford station wagon, used mostly for shopping, including numerous trips to nurseries in search of yet another variety of begonia for mother's garden. Hobo waddled over to give my trouser cuffs a sniff and, satisfied that I was a member of the household, he waddled back to his manse.

The Ford was missing and I was hoping our house-keeper, Ursi, was out with mother and not Ursi's husband, Jamie, who was our jack-of-all-trades houseman and the man I wanted to have a word with. If Connie was the doyen chronicler of Palm Beach society, Jamie Olson was

ier below-stairs counterpart. However, our Jamie was
is communicative as Harpo Marx. But he had an ency-
clopedic knowledge of local scandals, past, present and
about to occur. His informants were the Palm Beach
servants, who enjoyed trading tidbits of gossip about
those they served.

I found our Swedish-born houseman seated in the
kitchen, enjoying a mug of black coffee. 'Jamie,' I said,
taking a seat opposite him at the table, 'have you heard
of a psychic named Serge Ouspenskaya?'

'Uh-huh,' he answered.

'What do you hear?'

'He might be the real thing.'

Six words in a row. I was making progress. 'Says
who?'

'Max.'

'Who's Max, Jamie?'

'Mrs Ventura's gardener.'

'Who's Mrs Ventura, Jamie?'

'The lady who lost the diamond clip that Ouspenskaya
found.'

As you can see, talking to Jamie Olson is like playing
one-armed bandit. You have to feed it a lot to get back
very little. Having been down this road before, I kept
priming the pump.

'I hear Ouspenskaya is available for private séances.'

'Uh-huh.'

'Any idea if anyone is having one in the immediate
future?'

'Uh-huh.'

'Who?'

'Roland is preparing for one this evening.'

'Who's Roland, Jamie?'

'The Tremaines' butler.'

Eureka!

I left Jamie contemplating his cuppa and went up to my suite, which is a grandiloquent word for a small sitting room, a smaller bedroom and a bathroom that makes the other two look spacious. Here I dialed the residence of Vance Tremaine. (Yes, I still have a rotary telephone, as well as an authentic Mickey Mouse wrist watch, a Royal portable typewriter and a fountain pen – a gold Mont Blanc and don't you forget it.)

I had no qualms about intruding myself upon the Tremaines because Vance owed me big. His wife was the former Penelope Brightworth, whose father made zillions in the fast food business. The Tremaines were old guard and a good four generations removed from the Tremaine who filled up the family coffer. Unfortunately, the last two generations depleted the candy store, leaving poor Vance open to a hostile takeover and enabling Penelope to buy – excuse me, marry – Vance.

The couple moved into a 'cottage' on Ocean Boulevard and stocked it with his-and-hers Rolls-Royces, a fifty-two-foot Hatteras and three live-in servants. The only clouds on this marital horizon were in the shape of pretty young ladies in thong bikinis. Vance couldn't keep his mind off them and didn't confine his adulterous ways to impure thoughts. What Vance saw is what Vance got.

His wife finally gave him the ultimate ultimatum, 'One more bimbo, buster, and you'll be living in Pompano, driving a Chevy and traversing Lake Worth with the aid of two oars.'

Vance toed the line for an entire week and then ran into a bit of trouble in a dive in West Palm called Bar Anticipation. The bit of trouble began to make ugly noises and Archy saved Vance from a fate worse than death – poverty.

The butler, Roland, told me that Mr Tremaine was at his club. I called the Bath and Tennis and had Tremaine paged. 'Archy?' he said when he came on the line, sounding surprised.

'Who were you expecting?' I asked.

'Not you.'

Hurt but determined, I asked him if it were true that Serge Ouspenskaya was going to find Judge Crater at the Tremaine digs this evening. After a pause, Tremaine said, 'You know, Archy, some wiseguy once said that there was nothing known to man faster than the speed of light. He was wrong. The gossip mill up and down Ocean Boulevard makes the speed of light look lethargic. What's your interest?'

'Curiosity. I'd like to attend.'

'No matter where you step you always come up smelling like Chanel Number Five. We just learned that Russell Fitzwilliams came down with the flu – it's going around – and we need an extra man to partner Mrs Fitzwilliams. Ouspenskaya likes an odd number at the table, him being the odd man out, so the group

has to be an even number. We sit at ten and all we're
serving is drinks, so eat before you come.'

'Your generosity, Vance, has me all choked up. I'll
be there.'

'By the way, do you know the Fitzwilliamses' girl?'
he asked.

'Elizabeth, known locally as Fitz. We've met,'
informed him.

'She's a beauty. Do you know if she goes for older
men?'

'To her, Vance, thirty would be old, and I assume
you're going to be fifty, once again, this year.'

'You really know how to hurt a guy, Archy.'

'It's a gift, like being double-jointed or able to play
the piano by ear. Ta ta, till then.'

I like to swim at least two miles a day. Not out
and back, that's for those with medulla oblongata
deficiency syndrome. I swim north and south, parallel
to the shore and not more than twenty yards out. This
is my only form of exercise, if one doesn't count going
a few rounds with Connie Garcia, and it does wonders
for the appetite.

I put on a pair of simple trunks (lavender with
iridescent silver stripes), sandals and a snow-white
terry robe. The Atlantic laps the shore just across
Ocean Boulevard from our house, making crossing
the A1A the most perilous part of my journey.
had my swim and returned to my rooms to shower
begin logging the rudiments of 'Serge the Seer' in

ny journal and dress in time for the family cock-
ail hour.

Thanks to the *seigneur* we are a family of tradition,
one of them being gathering for cocktails prior to
dinner where father mixes martinis that are not as
dry as I would like them but, like the rent on my
suite, they're free. When I appeared, father knitted
his brows, which is quite a skein of yarn, and uttered,
'When do we view the remains?'

In keeping with the theme of my date later in the
evening, I had elected to dress all in black. Jacket,
trousers, turtleneck, socks and loafers. Mother, bless
her, noted, 'You look just like Errol Flynn in *The Mark
of Zorro*.'

'That was Tyrone Power, mother, but I'd be happy
to be mistaken for either.'

Mother's given name is Madelaine and she is a
warm and loving person who, at near seventy, is as
radiant, if a little stouter, than the day she became
Mrs Prescott McNally. I know, because I have seen
her wedding photos and I am an expert on female
pulchritude, as witness the photo of Thelma Todd
I consider my prize possession. Her complexion is
florid, thanks to her high blood pressure, and I am
still her precious little Archy, thanks to her good
sense.

'How are you progressing on the Ouspenskaya
business?' father asked when he had served us his
idea of a martini (three parts gin to one of vermouth).

'In fact, sir, I am meeting him tonight, in situ as

it were. A séance at the home of Vance and Penny Tremaine.'

'Very good, Archy. I must say you've moved with remarkable speed on this one.' Coming from father, this was tantamount to being awarded the Nobel, Pulitzer and Oscar all rolled into one. Mother beamed her approval for Mrs McNally's favorite son.

'I will have more to report in the morning,' I said with a confidence I didn't feel, having no idea what the evening would bring. What it brought were enough surprises to keep my flabber gasted for a millennium of leap years. And *mon père*, not Ouspenskaya, began the beguine.

'Archy,' he said, 'your mother and I have decided on a second honeymoon.'

'I beg your pardon, sir.'

'Oh,' my mother cried, all in a dither, 'he means we're going on vacation.' But it was clear that she liked the idea of calling it a second honeymoon.

When I had recovered sufficiently to speak, I said, 'This is awesome, as the young say, and for good reason. Congratulations, sir, and it's long overdue. I'll miss you both but if you're not taking Ursi and Jamie, I'll survive. When are you going, and where?'

'We're going to cruise the Caribbean for two weeks. When depends on what ship we decide to cruise with. The *Pearl of the Antilles* or the *Atlantis*.'

Father was a crusty old thing who liked nothing better than to work and rule his domain, be it home or office, with an iron hand. But beneath the crust and pomposity was a genuine love for his wife and I suspected he was doing this with the hope that a carefree two weeks on the high seas would improve her hypertension, a condition that had us both more concerned than we cared to admit. From the look of pleasure on her lovely face, I would say he was getting off to a fine start.

I got up to kiss mother, drawing two red patches on her velvety cheeks.

Father produced a dozen colorful brochures detailing the amenities of the cruise ships he had mentioned and as we pored over them the McNally family enjoyed one of the happiest happy hours of our illustrious history.

Ursi, our cook-housekeeper, fed us scallops sautéed in a mixture of garlic-scented olive oil and clarified butter, accompanied by porcini risotto and steamed sugar snap peas with lemon zest. The lord of the manor uncorked a fine bottle of muscadet to go with the repast. Dessert was a ripened honeydew whose time had come, along with a plate of crisp cat's tongue wafers tipped with melted Valhrona chocolate. Surfeited, I was ready to face the unknown.

3

Roland welcomed me at the front door with a nod and a polite, 'Good evening, Mr McNally.'

'Good evening, Roland. Did Jamie tell you I was coming tonight?'

'No, sir. Mr Tremaine gave me the guest list.'

In the detective business, you win some and you lose some.

Roland had a British accent and a countenance that explained why it was always the butler who was suspected of having done it. In the Town of Palm Beach, authentic British butlers were at a premium and paid accordingly. If they had worked for a 'title,' they often received a bonus just for agreeing to leave foggy London for sunny Palm Beach. And, if they had so much as opened a door to a member of the royal family, their salary and perks began to take on the proportions of those enjoyed by the wunderkind of Silicon Valley.

Needles to say, authentic British nannies were also sought after on this side of the Atlantic, and were in

even scarcer supply. However, in Palm Beach, young
children were as scarce as authentic nannies, so the
situation was less desperate than the scramble for a
bona fide butler.

As I followed Roland through an entrance hall whose
furnishings would make Marie Antoinette Bourbon
look like a minimalist, I asked, 'Is everyone here?'

'All except Mr Ouspenskaya, sir.'

'Do you know Ouspenskaya, Roland?'

'No, sir. But I've heard of him.'

'From who?'

'Jamie Olson, sir.'

And the circle was complete.

While still digesting Ursi's dinner and father's news,
I was dealt the second surprise of an evening that
seemed to have an endless supply. Roland announced
me and upon entering the Tremaine drawing room the
first thing to meet my gaze was the gorgeous Fitz in
gold toreador pants and matching halter. *Olé*.

Besides the host and hostess, I was greeted by
Emily Fairhust and her secretary, Arnold Turnbolt.
The Fairhursts, John and Emily, were landed aristocracy of the Plymouth Rock variety who had never
employed a British butler or, when their children
were tots, a British nanny. Mr Fairhurst was not a
social animal, as they say, so in their senior years Mrs
Fairhurst had discovered the advantages of employing
a 'walker,' the name assigned, for obvious reasons, to
men who escort rich ladies of a certain age.

The fact that Turnbolt was also Mrs Fairhurst's

secretary made this extra duty less apparent, and the fact that Turnbolt was charming, witty and clever made him a natural for the job. Last, but most important, the fact that Turnbolt was gay made the arrangement above suspicion.

Roland took my drink order, a tall vodka and tonic, at which point everyone spoke at once, assuring each other that they did not believe in psychic phenomena, reincarnation, UFOs, witches, ghosts or the healing powers of crystals.

'We're here for a lark,' Penny said, holding fast to her husband's arm. Penelope Brightworth Tremaine was as plain as homemade soap. Vance, who had been on every deb's most-wanted list when he was an Eli, was blessed with the kind of good looks that improve with age. In the words of a Ziegfeld comedienne of yore, 'The groom was prettier than the bride.'

If money couldn't buy happiness, it could buy the most remarkable substitutes, and for a quarter of a century Penny had fought to protect hers. The strain was beginning to show. One wondered why she didn't dump the satyr for a more reliable shoulder to lean upon. Could it be that she loved the guy? Indeed, it could very well be.

Vance was eyeing Fitz in the manner of a dog on a short leash who had just spotted a fire hydrant.

Arnold Turnbolt was saying, 'A gypsy in West Palm read my tea leaves a few months back and told me a beautiful woman would soon end my bachelor days. I said, "Honey, if that's the best you can do you should seriously consider a career change."'

'Oh, Arnold,' Mrs Fairhurst chided. 'I'm going to ask Mr Ouspenskaya if my daughter, who's in the family way again, is going to have a boy or a girl.' Emily Fairhurst had not been a great beauty, but this was more than made up for by a charisma that was as enchanting as it was infectious. Like many great ladies, Emily was equally at home in the back seat of her Rolls or at the wheel of her station wagon.

'That would give him one chance in two of being right, Mrs Fairhurst,' I told her. 'We have to think of something more difficult for Ouspenskaya and something we can verify immediately, not nine months from now.'

'Six months, Archy. Sarah is three months along,' Mrs Fairhurst answered.

'I would ask her obstetrician,' Vance said, 'and I'm sure he'll charge less than Ouspenskaya. What do you think, Fitz?'

With a smile that had Vance blinking, Fitz answered, 'I'm going to ask him if I should accept an engagement ring from my Ensign suitor, just out of Annapolis, or a dreamboat just out of SMU who's been drafted by the Dallas Cowboys.'

'I'll take your discard,' Arnold called from the bar.

'Oh, Arnold,' Mrs Fairhurst scolded.

When my drink arrived, I managed to corner Fitz. Eyeing me, she said, 'You look like a shadow, Archy.'

'And you look like Fort Knox. So what's a nice girl like you doing in a place like this?'

Fitz is a blue-eyed brunette with a creamy complexion. This was affixed to the prototype female form from which the word 'nubile' derived its root and, when she looked into your eyes, she made you believe she was actually interested in what you had to say. From Fitz I learned that Mr Fitzwilliams had passed his flu on to his wife, rendering them both housebound. Fitz was sent to us as a stand-in for her mother.

'And I'm here as a stand-in for your father. Do you believe in kismet, Fitz?'

'I believe that Mr Tremaine is panting after me, Arnie is panting after Mr Tremaine and Mrs Tremaine is sorry she got herself into this mess.'

'Why did she get into this mess? Do you know?'

'My father – you know he's on Wall Street – says a European cartel is after the Brightworth chain and Daddy thinks Mrs Tremaine is trying to contact her father to ask him if she should hold on or let go.'

'Her father, I take it, has passed over.'

Fitz nodded. 'He's in hamburger heaven, Archy.'

You didn't have to be on Wall Street, or psychic, to know there were big bucks at stake here and I said as much to Fitz.

'The opening bid is ninety million,' Fitz informed me.

'Dollars?'

'We're not talking enchiladas.'

Penny was still holding firm to Vance as they chatted with Mrs Fairhurst and Arnold. Vance kept looking our way and nodding at Fitz each time he caught her eye. This guy did not believe in the inviolable sanctity of the home.

'This place gives me the creeps,' Fitz complained.

Looking around the Tremaine drawing room I thought, 'One man's creeps is another man's crepes.' If Ouspenskaya raised Louis Quatorze, Quinze and Seize, their majesties would think they were back at Versailles waiting for dinner to be announced.

What was announced was 'Mr Serge Ouspenskaya,' by our Roland with a supercilious air and a stiff upper lip.

Standing in the doorway was a vision best described as an extra from *Passage to India*. Shortish, plumpish, white turban, white Nehru jacket, white trousers and white shoes. If his namesake was the character actress Maria Ouspenskaya, his face bore a remarkable resemblance to the actor Turhan Bey who enjoyed a brief popularity in the forties, thanks to Uncle Sam, who had Hollywood's leading men otherwise engaged. The skin was darker than olive and the eyes peering out of a moon shaped face were a luminous black.

In short, it was all too corny not to be real. Serge Ouspenskaya was either the Prince of Fools or the Prince of Knaves.

He walked directly to his hostess with all the captivating pomp and swagger of a maharajah and bowed from the waist, keeping his hands firmly at his sides. As intended, this discouraged Penny from offering him her hand. Perhaps he thought it prudent not to appear overly anxious to grasp the hand that was about to grasp ninety million bucks. The night's pickin's could be very lucrative for this middle-aged Sabu and I couldn't wait to hear what the dearly departed Mr Brightworth had to say to his daughter. 'Don't sell short' came to mind.

To be sure that I have correctly described the magnetic powers of Mr Serge Ouspenskaya, I will say now that for the first time since I entered the room Vance Tremaine had taken his eyes off Fitz in favor of the psychic. And that, believe me, is saying a mouthful.

'Mrs Fairhurst, I know,' Ouspenskaya bowed to the lady as Penny led the introductions. 'A pleasure, once more, madame.'

His English was perfect. So perfect that I could not detect a trace of an accent that bespoke his origins either here in America or abroad. Like his appearance and carriage, was this yet another indication of theatrical training?

Even Arnold, who was never at a loss for an acrimonious retort, was awed into silence as he was presented. It was interesting to note that as Ouspenskaya acknowledged each of us he made no attempt to amaze his audience with individual comments such as guessing one's astrological sign, place of birth or the name of a pet cat or dog that had just passed over. If it were all an act, he wasn't playing to the balcony.

I got a curt nod. Was it my imagination or was Ouspenskaya giving me a wide berth, like a ship skirting an iceberg? Could it be my attire, which was the complete antithesis of his, that repelled rather than attracted and if so, was my choice of dress a harbinger?

When he came to Fitz he broke his silence and stated, 'Ah, a classical beauty.'

'Would you care for a drink, Mr Ouspenskaya?' Vance offered.

'Thank you, no,' he responded. 'I take nothing before a sitting. If we are successful, however, I might bother you for a glass of champagne when we're done.'

'And if we're not successful?' I asked.

'Then, Mr McNally, I will still insist on my glass of champagne.'

This, as intended, got a laugh, and Ouspenskaya pointed to the round table and seven chairs already in place at the far end of the room. 'Shall we proceed? As you may know I discourage socializing before a sitting and arrive late not to make a grand entrance but to avoid the necessity of engaging in banal conversations. This only hinders the purpose of our meeting.'

Arrogant? Maybe. But very clever. The less said, the less one could accuse him of picking our brains for helpful hints the spirits might find useful later in the evening.

As we took our places as described earlier – clockwise, with Ouspenskaya in the number twelve position, we had Arnold, Mrs Fairhurst, Vance, Penny, yrs. truly, and Fitz – Roland moved about the room turning off the ornate lamps. When we were settled, the butler left the room, dousing the ceiling light from a wall switch abutting the door. With the window curtains drawn, the room was now in total darkness.

'Let us all join hands,' Ouspenskaya instructed, 'and empty our minds of all worldly thoughts. I will not take questions, but wait to see what comes to me – or through me, if you will. Think of me as a radio. You are going to mentally switch me on and tune me in. I hope you like what comes out, but like a radio I am not responsible for the content of the broadcast. I do not create, I convey. Now, please, let us all imagine a taper – tall, slim, its wick aglow. Concentrate on the flame, please.'

His voice in the darkened room was so perfectly modulated it could have been coming from one of those recordings that people employ to achieve blissful tranquility via alpha rhythm, a pattern of slow brain waves that adherents of the therapy believe make one receptive to daydreaming while fully awake. However, it was tension, not relaxation, I felt in the hands holding mine and I suspected this was the psychic's intention in spite of what he was saying.

'The flame is the radio's dial. Look into it. See what you will. Don't go from station to station. Select one. The one you want to hear from. The one that has a message just for you – be it a person, place or thing. Let your imagination soar. On the other plane all things are possible. All things.'

Was Penny seeing her father's image in the flame? Fitz, her two current beaus? Arnold, Fitz's two current beaus? Vance, no doubt, was trying to tune in Fitz and

Mrs Fairhurst, the child her daughter was carrying. I kept seeing the *Atlantis*, or was it the *Pearl of the Antilles*, weaving in and out of the flame like the *Flying Dutchman* on a foggy sea.

There came a long pause. So long I thought Ouspenskaya had fallen asleep.

'Do the words "Top Banana" mean anything to anyone present?'

It was Ouspenskaya's voice, but its comforting vocal caress was now as cold and matter-of-fact as a train conductor announcing the next stop.

My hands, as well as my heart, did a quick squeeze. Fitz didn't respond but Penny returned the pressure. Good grief, what did that mean?

'I repeat, is anyone at the table familiar with the words . . .'

'A Top Banana is an archaic name for the lead comic in a burlesque show.' This from the smart-ass know-it-all, Arnold Turnbolt.

I had come to expose Serge Ouspenskaya but it looked as if Ouspenskaya was about to expose me. What I mean is, my grandfather, Freddy McNally, was a Top Banana on the Minsky circuit. The old pratfalling Freddy had sent his son to Yale and made him a lawyer while buying up Palm Beach real estate for a pittance. The latter made his lawyer son, my father, a rich man. In spite of all this, my father thought it best to pretend that Freddy McNally never existed and that he, son Prescott, arrived on our planet as a freshman at Yale with no past and only great expectations in his future.

How the hell did Ouspenskaya know this? Or, perish the thought, was Freddy actually with us? I stuck to the aphorism I have lived by all my life and one that has seen me through many a stormy sea and into a safe port. *When in doubt, keep your mouth shut.*

'Tell them to book the *Pearl*,' Ouspenskaya advised, 'the *Atlantis* sucks.' Pause. 'Does this mean anything to anyone present?'

For the sake of my psychic partners, I hoped the palms of my hands were not as wet as my forehead. This was too much and it was making a convert of this nonbeliever.

'No one seems to know this horrid person,' Penny Tremaine said. 'Can't you block him out so others can get through?'

'I don't think it works that way, dear,' Mrs Fairhurst told her hostess.

Seeing as Penny Tremaine was footing the bill tonight, I think she had a right to complain. And if Ouspenskaya wanted to feather his nest he would be better disposed to call up old man Brightworth and put a gag on Freddy. Why was Ouspenskaya doing this? *How* was Ouspenskaya doing this?

'I played the Lake Worth Playhouse in '24,' Ouspenskaya all but shouted. 'It was the Oakley Theater then. SRO three straight weeks. I was on the bill with Lolly Pops, who did amazing things with three strategically positioned balloons. The men in the audience were frisked for hat pins, darts and pencils with sharp points. You won't be the first

45

McNally on the bill there. You hear me, Archy? You hear me?'

'Archy!' Penny Tremaine harangued.

Fitz giggled.

'Lolly Pops?' Arnold Turnbolt screamed.

Unlike the last owners of Penny Tremaine's *ameublement* I got out of the palace with my head attached to my shoulders and, of all things, Fitz attached to my arm. If I had inadvertently rained on my hostess's parade, I had, with malicious aforethought, deluged the conflagration that raged within the savage breast of my host. Thanks to Serge Ouspenskaya, Archy McNally was now persona non grata at the Tremaine residence.

To wit: After fingering me as the person to whom the so-called Top Banana was shooting off his mouth, Ouspenskaya refused to continue with the séance, or sitting, because of the quote, disruptive personality, unquote, of said comic. Meaning that Freddy had clogged the airwaves with enough ham to thwart any other channels from coming through. This Ouspenskaya had the *cajones* of a brass monkey. Arnold's near hysterics over the name Lolly Pops did not help my cause.

I said earlier that I thought Ouspenskaya was skirting me when we were introduced. I now believed that he knew the reason I had attended the séance and had set out to goad me, embarrass me and warn me off. He had succeeded in two out of three. At the close of my first inning with the psychic the score was one to zilch, in favor of the spooks.

But how did he know? More important, if he was wise to me, he had to know who had hired me. And if he had put off catering to the ninety-million-dollar baby in order to get me off his back it meant that he had long-range plans for mining the rich turf of Palm Beach. He had also managed to K two B's with one stone this evening by demonstrating his powers to me and impressing the rich folk at the same time.

Naturally, I had to admit that family lore had it that my grandfather 'dabbled' in theatricals. Let's face it: How often do you get the spirit of a Top Banana and an ecdysiast called Lolly Pops at your neighborhood séance? Penny couldn't wait to set up a private sitting with Ouspenskaya and tune in to daddy dearest. Fitz, it seemed, had been dropped off at the Tremaines' abode by her brother and it had been decided that the Tremaine chauffeur would see her safely home. The Tremaine chauffeur had come down with a bellyache induced, no doubt, by the green-back Vance must have slipped him to play sick. The gallant Vance volunteered to see Fitz to her front door. Penny turned the color of Ouspenskaya's turban at the thought of her husband and Fitz zipping along the A1A under a starry sky and stopping God knows where for God knows what along the way.

Seeing the chance to redeem myself in the eyes and heart of Penny Tremaine for being the grandson of a Top Banana, I immediately said that I would drop Fitz wherever she wanted to be dropped. Both Penny and Fitz thought this a fine idea. Vance thought that a better idea would be to have me drawn and quartered.

Vance had invited me to partner him at his club in a tennis doubles match later in the week. As Fitz and I left, he suddenly remembered the match had been canceled and implied that I might never see the inside of the Bath and Tennis again in my lifetime. I didn't bother telling him I had been barred from far more prestigious institutions, i.e., Yale University.

So it was Archy who zipped along the A1A under a starry sky with the gold-clad Fitz by my side. A heady experience, indeed. 'Was your grandfather really a comic in a burlesque revue?' Fitz asked, seemingly fascinated with my lineage.

'The Minsky circuit,' I ceded.

'Neat,' came her reply. 'Maybe Lolly Pops is your grandmother.'

The young have rich imaginations. Should such a rumor make the rounds of Palm Beach, the sire's retribution would be heartless and Archy would be homeless. 'Grandmother,' I revealed to Fitz with great solemnity, 'was raised by the nuns and short-listed for sainthood upon her demise.'

'Oh,' said Fitz.

Not knowing where Fitz lived, I had to rely on her directions. This got us to the Ta-Boo' bar and restaurant. 'You live here?'

'Practically,' she said. 'It's just about midnight and the bar should be in full swing. I'll stand you a drink, Archy.'

For those not familiar with Palm Beach in season, midnight is when the social set starts socializing and the only difference between Tuesday night and Saturday night is seventy-two hours. The bar was in full swing with every stool taken and it was none other than Buzz Carr who abdicated his throne for Fitz.

'Hi, Archy. Hi, Fitz,' Buzz welcomed us.

'You two know each other?' I questioned.

'Not in the biblical sense,' Fitz said, 'but the night is young.'

I can forgive Buzz Carr his Adonis body, his perfectly layered head of dark hair, his gray eyes and his face that launched a thousand yachts. I cannot forgive him the way beautiful young women and rich old women, both of whom should know better, are all over him like a cheap suit, seemingly oblivious of his reputation as a gender swinger. Or was that part of his lure? Could no temptress resist the challenge of getting Buzz to mend his ways, courtesy of *her* irresistible charms?

I ordered a bourbon and branch water. Fitz asked for a tall scotch and soda. Buzz clung to his bottled beer – no glass. When we were served, Buzz couldn't wait to inform us, 'I'm going to be in a show.'

I closed my eyes, pressed thumb and forefinger against my forehead and proclaimed, 'The Palm Beach Community Theater proudly presents *Arsenic and Old Lace*.'

'How did you know?' Buzz was very impressed.

'We just came from a séance and the spirits are still with us.'

'The Ouspenskaya guy,' Buzz guessed correctly. 'Lady Cynthia is wild about him.'

'He contacted Archy's grandfather who was a Top Banana,' Fitz announced.

'What's a Top Banana?' Buzz wanted to know.

'Never mind,' I broke in. 'It's all nonsense.' I needn't have worried about discouraging talk of my ancestor as the very young don't stay focused on one topic for more than one sound bite, especially when an aspiring actor is on a roll.

'Bet you'll never guess who's gonna be my co-star,' Buzz bragged.

If Ouspenskaya knew I was working for Desdemona Darling's husband, that was already one person too many who knew. Prudence told me to repeat the act I had put on for Connie so I feigned surprise when Buzz said, 'Desdemona Darling.'

'Who's she?' Fitz asked, taking the wind out of Buzz's sails.

'One of the biggest Hollywood stars ever,' Buzz insisted.

'She was a wee bit before your time, Fitz, my dear.' To Buzz, I said, 'I take it she plays one of the old maid aunts.'

'Right, Archy. And we still haven't cast the other old maid aunt or any of the other roles, but there's a great part in it for you, Fitz. You can play my girl.'

Halfway through her tall scotch and soda, Fitz appeared unimpressed with being discovered at Ta-Boo'. 'I've never acted,' she told Buzz.

'Neither has he,' I said. 'You would be perfectly matched and pose no threat to the memory of Lunt and Fontanne.'

'Who are they?' Fitz asked.

Present company considered, I declared the question moot.

'We open at the Lake Worth Playhouse . . .' Buzz rambled on, but what else he had to say was lost on this listener.

'The Lake Worth Playhouse?' Fitz repeated. 'Didn't Ouspenskaya mention that place, Archy?'

I felt the fickle finger of fate's icy digit slither up my spine as I answered, 'Indeed he did. Indeed he did.'

4

Against my better judgment and feeling almost as wanted as lumps in a classic sauce béchamel, I left Fitz at Ta-Boo' with her future co-star. Yes, Buzz talked Fitz into becoming an active member of the PB Community Theater. What else he may have talked her into is not germane to this tale. I left the budding Tracy and Hepburn in the wee small hours of the morning and returned to my third floor nest where I undressed, washed, brushed, donned a silk robe and, taking my Mont Blanc in hand, added a few sentences to the saga of 'Serge the Seer' in my journal, most of them ending in question marks.

Late to bed and late to rise makes a man healthy, wealthy and – late for breakfast. An early-morning call from Arnold Turnbolt didn't help my cause. 'What do you think, Archy? I was très impressed.'

Figuring it didn't take much to impress Arnold, I answered, 'I'm reserving judgment.'

Not knowing restraint, Arnold went right on. 'I don't

know how you can say that when he called up your
grandfather and a stripper named Lolly Pops. It's too
much, Archy. What do you think Lolly was hiding
behind those three balloons?'

'What do you think Ouspenskaya was hiding under
that turban?' I really liked Arnold Turnbolt but I liked
breakfast better.

'I don't see why you're so chagrined, Archy. I would
be delighted to have a show business personality in
my family tree. Even Lolly Pops – or should that be,
especially Lolly Pops?'

'We're not ashamed of Freddy,' I lied, 'we just think
the dead should rest in peace and not be called upon
to amuse the rich at their parlor games.'

'So what were you doing there?' Arnold was no
fool.

'I was doing Vance a favor and filling in for
Fitzwilliams.'

'That's not the way Vance tells it.'

So Vance Tremaine must have started bad-mouthing
me as soon as I left his domain with the door prize
on my arm. And if Vance told the crew I had invited
myself to the séance, there was a good chance he had
told Ouspenskaya the same thing when he called the
psychic to report my substituting for Fitzwilliams.
Ergo, Ouspenskaya was aware I had muscled my
way in and after checking my credentials he didn't
have to wait for a news flash on his psychic radio to
guess I was there on business.

'If Ouspenskaya is not the real thing, how do you

think he did it? And do those two cruise liners mean anything to you, Archy? You never told us.'

'How do you know he was referring to cruise ships, Arnold?'

'*Atlantis* and *Pearl*. I remembered seeing an advert for a cruise ship out of Lauderdale called the *Atlantis*. I contacted a travel agent friend down there and he told me the two most popular ships out of Lauderdale are the *Atlantis* and the *Pearl of the Antilles*.'

'You just did it, Arnold.'

'I did? What?'

'Demonstrated how Ouspenskaya did it. You had a little knowledge, you built upon it with a little research, and you came up with the right answer. Now I must leave you as I have a date with a cup of coffee. It's been très nice, Arnold.' And I hung up.

Father, whose metabolic functions are in perfect sync with Greenwich Mean Time, had breakfasted and left for the office an hour before my arrival in the family kitchen. Mother was in the greenhouse tending to her begonias. The maid, mercifully, was not in the backyard hanging up the clothes, but in the kitchen, where she belonged. Jamie, engrossed in the morning paper over a cup of coffee, was also present.

'Good morning,' I began, cheerfully.

I think I caught Jamie nodding a response and I know I heard Ursi state, 'Your grandfather has a big mouth.'

'The news is already out?' I ventured.

'Jamie is tight with the Tremaine butler,' Jamie's

wife informed me. Jamie agreed with a sound that was either a grunt or a groan. Conversations between Jamie and Roland must be as exhilarating as watching paint dry.

'Was Roland listening at the door?' I foolishly asked.

'What do you think?' Ursi replied, placing a glass of freshly squeezed orange juice before me.

'Does father know?'

'If he does, he didn't hear it from me,' Ursi said.

'Nor me,' Jamie echoed to his newspaper.

It was merely a reprieve from the inevitable. If father had not heard the news at breakfast, he would surely hear about it at the office or, at the very latest, over lunch. Freddy's broadcast being a direct result of an investigation father had initiated was my consolation but not my salvation. The sire would demand an explanation and right now I had none to offer. But then I function poorly on an empty stomach.

'What would you like for breakfast, Archy, or do you want me to surprise you?' Ursi asked.

'Surprise me, Ursi, but don't shock me. I had my fill of that last night.'

I was served four slices of Ursi Olson's marvelous French toast (made with thick-cut challah) with honey-apricot preserve and a pot of black coffee. Happily sated, I expressed my gratitude by saying to our housekeeper, 'Will I ever find a wife who can cook like you?'

'There's a cover for every pot, Archy,' came her sage

reply. I wondered what Consuela Garcia would think of that.

As I prepared to take my leave, Jamie chastised his newspaper with, 'You forgot to mention Kate Mulligan.'

This stopped me cold. 'Who, or what, is Kate Mulligan?'

'Dear lord,' Ursi complained, 'what with the second honeymoon and the voodoo man it's a wonder I can remember my own name. Kate Mulligan, Archy, is the woman your father hired to tend to the garden while he and your mother are away. Praise be I don't have to do it as I don't have the green thumb, whatever that means.'

Disappointed that Kate Mulligan was not a new stew we might be having for dinner, I asked, 'When is she expected, Ursi?'

'Momentarily. I'm to send her directly to the greenhouse to meet with Mrs McNally.'

Which was just where I was headed. Outdoors my spirits were immediately lifted by a perfectly smashing day. Warm sun, cloudless blue sky and an exhilarating sea breeze that was as welcoming as a kiss. Mother smiled when she saw me approach. 'How splendid you look, Archy,' she exclaimed.

How nice that she should notice, as I was wearing one of my favorite outfits. Fawn silk slacks, a plum-colored Sea Island cotton knit shirt, a dark green linen sport coat and Cordovan loafers, sans socks. I kissed her rosy cheek in gratitude as she told me the plant she was administering to with TLC was called an Eyelash begonia. At last count, mother had six million varieties of begonias. Could this Eyelash be six million and one?

'Mother, do you remember the actor Turhan Bey?'

'Oh, yes, Archy. He was so good in *The Rains of Ranchipur.*'

'No, mother, that was Richard Burton beneath a thick layer of pancake makeup.'

'Are you sure, dear?'

'Yes, mother. Turhan Bey's big move was *Dragon Seed.*'

'It wasn't *Dragonwyck*?'

'No, mother, that was Vincent Price.'

'Oh, Archy, how do you keep all that straight in your head?'

'Perhaps because I have so little else in there.'

'Don't say that, Archy. You must never sell yourself short. Your father is very proud of you even though he may not always show it.'

I don't know how proud father would be when he learned I had tuned in to Freddy and an exotic called Lolly Pops for the likes of the Fairhursts and Tremaines to gloat over.

'I can remember the day you were born,' mother said, 'but I can't tell you what I had for breakfast an hour ago.'

'I imagine my arrival was more interesting than Ursi's French toast.'

'Yes, French toast. How did you guess?'

I refrained from pulling the psychic act but was spared the need to answer when mother cried, 'Here she is and I forgot her name.'

Turning, I saw a woman exiting our back door with Ursi behind her, pointing the way to our modest greenhouse. 'Her name, mother, is Kate Mulligan and aren't you the grand dame with your own gardener. What next? Your personal lady in waiting?'

'Oh, Archy, I certainly hope not. I would keep forgetting her name. And having someone come in to tend my garden was a condition of my going on this trip. I'm doing it to please your father and because I know he needs the rest.'

'That's very kind of you, mother. And here's Ms Mulligan.'

The woman entering the greenhouse was, I would guess, in her early forties, with auburn hair cut short, vivid blue eyes, a trim figure and a fine pair of legs her waterproof Top-Siders could not disguise. She did nothing to hide the freckles that dotted the bridge of her nose and most likely because she knew they were as fetching as her smile. 'Hello. I'm Kate Mulligan. You're Mrs McNally, I presume.'

'Yes, dear, I am. And this is my son, Archy.'

'Charmed, I'm sure,' Kate said, taking first my mother's hand and then mine. 'Your garden is lovely, Mrs McNally. Begonias are my favorite flower. That's an Eyelash, isn't it?'

'Why yes, it is.' Mother beamed with joy.

I didn't know how much Kate Mulligan knew about

horticulture but she sure knew how to please a prospective employer. She wasn't doing bad with the employer's son either.

'I will leave you ladies to your labors,' I said, giving mother a goodbye peck on her cheek. 'I'm sure I'll be seeing you again, Ms Mulligan.'

'Call me Kate, please, and I'll be bold enough to call you Archy if I may. Are you going on holiday with your parents?'

'Like you, Kate, duty prevents me from leaving the salt mines of Palm Beach in season. I'll be right here.'

'Then I know I'll be seeing you again, Archy.'

Hobo followed me to my Miata and I paused long enough to pat his head and whisper, 'She ain't a stew, Hobo, but man does not live by bread alone.' Hobo responded by putting his tail between his legs.

I ran into Joe Anderson outside my father's office. A retired postal worker well over seventy, Joe is the sole employee of our mailroom and, like me, the de facto reigning king of his turf. Need I add that Joe's office is larger than mine? – but then so is your handkerchief.

'How is Binky?' Joe asked, forcing me to procrastinate facing the guv'nor, which was fine with me.

'Binky is well, Joe. I saw him last week and he asked for you.'

Binky's interest in Joe's well-being is not strictly altruistic, something which pangs me, as I am the matchmaker who brought them together in what I had hoped would be a mutually beneficial relationship.

My young friend, Binky Watrous, has been in the job market for the past twelve of his almost thirty years. Ursi's comment notwithstanding, the pot has not been invented for the cover Binky Watrous has to offer.

'Twas a month before Christmas last when I secured Binky a temporary position at McNally & Son to assist Joe Anderson in coping with the holiday mail rush. Mrs Trelawney took an instant liking to my friend more because Binky actually blushed at her risqué humor than his expertise in handling the company mail. In appreciation, Mrs Trelawney promised Binky that when Joe retired for a second time, either by Joe's own volition or that of God's, Binky would be crowned king of the mailroom on Royal Palm Way.

Not since Pip has anyone anticipated their future with the wonder, joy and trepidation that Mrs Trelawney's offer aroused in the heart and mind of Binky Watrous. In preparation for his date with destiny, Binky has devoted himself to the study of tomes with such riveting titles as *The ABCs of Mail Room Procedure for Mini and Mega Corporations* – as well as a morbid interest in Joe Anderson's health which, bless him, is better than Binky's.

'Tell him I was asking for him,' Joe said, 'and I put your mail in your office.'

My mail consists of envelopes stuffed with dozens of tiny stick-on return address labels in return for which I am asked to make a generous donation to the unwed mothers of a variety of banana republic countries; catalogs offering everything the thinking detective needs, from bugging devices disguised as earrings to earrings capable of photographing unfaithful husbands being unfaithful; and for the junk-food addicted, the deplorable offerings of fast-food joints spanning the state from Miami to Jacksonville, inviting me to fax my order for prompt delivery.

'He's been asking for you,' Mrs Trelawney said, jerking a thumb at the don's office door. 'Herb rang me to tell me you had arrived. I wish you luck.'

'You've heard the news?'

'Binky called at nine this morning,' she informed me.

'Binky?' I cried. 'Was he hiding under Ouspenskaya's turban?'

Mrs Trelawney shook her head of gray Dynel. 'He wandered into Ta-Boo' for a nightcap and ran into . . .'

'Say no more, Mrs Trelawney.' By now my misadventure with Serge Ouspenskaya was probably being typeset at Lolly Spindrift's gossip sheet.

Father was seated at his desk wearing a vested blue suit and a Countess Mara tie that looked like an original de Kooning. 'Sorry I'm so late, sir, but it was a long night.'

'So I heard. Have a seat, Archy, and give me the postmortem. I've already heard the news.'

'From who, sir?'

'Richard Holmes, who else? He got it from his wife who got it directly from the horse's mouth first thing this morning.'

Horse's arse would be more apropos, but father

is a proper Victorian and I don't buck the trend. 'Ouspenskaya actually called Desdemona Darling and told her what happened at the séance?'

'Not exactly,' father said. 'Knowing that the Tremaines were entertaining Ouspenskaya last night, Desdemona called Penny to learn how it went.'

'I didn't know they knew each other. Desdemona and Penny, that is.'

'As you may know, Desdemona and Lady Cynthia are old friends and Lady C took it upon herself to introduce Desdemona and her husband to the people in Palm Beach who count. After that, Desdemona joined a small clique of Ouspenskaya followers led by Lady C and Penny Tremaine.' Father tugged at his mustache in a most disconcerting manner. 'After hearing what Penny had to say, Desdemona called Ouspenskaya to verify the facts.'

'Interesting,' was my contribution.

'More interesting than you know, Archy. It seems Ouspenskaya, or should I say *my father*?, said something that no mortal knew, except for Desdemona and Lady Cynthia. Desdemona is now more convinced than ever that Ouspenskaya has the gift.'

'If she means the mention of the Lake Worth Playhouse, I learned from a source before the séance that Lady C and Desdemona got themselves involved with the community theater. After the sitting I learned their venue would be the Lake Worth Playhouse. There are very few secrets in this town, sir. Aside from that I have no idea what it could be.'

Father said thoughtfully, 'I think there's more to it than that. Tell me everything that happened, Archy.'

I gave father a detailed description of my evening at the Tremaines', leaving out only Vance's lusting after Fitz and Arnold's hysterics over the name Lolly Pops. When I finished, father gave his mustache a tug that surely must have hurt his upper lip. 'He knew about my proposed cruise right down to the ships I'm considering?'

'It would appear so, sir.'

'How does he do it, Archy?'

'The mention of the cruise ships, sir, I don't know,' I admitted, 'but I intend to find out. Grandfather's profession is not exactly classified information and a visit to the Lake Worth Playhouse should help me ascertain if grandfather played there in '24.'

With a sigh, father rose and went to his antique desk. 'That won't be necessary, Archy.' Opening one of the secret compartments he removed a sheet of paper and handed it to me. It was a playbill for the Oakley Theater dated January 1924, announcing the appearance of Freddy 'always leave 'em laughing' McNally and the 'Balloon Dancer,' Lolly Pops. An artist's rendition of Lolly's generous attributes made me wonder if her balloons weren't the size of a Luftwaffe zeppelin.

'I still intend to visit the theater, sir, to learn if they maintain an archive where this information is readily available.'

'Good idea, Archy.' Father retrieved the playbill

and returned it to the secret compartment. What other treasures were resting within the belly of that masterpiece of eighteenth century American crafts-manship?

I told father that I had asked Vance Tremaine if Ouspenskaya knew who would be attending the séance. 'Tremaine told me the psychic insisted on a guest list before agreeing to a sitting. He knew I would be there and I have reason to believe he knew I invited myself. A check on my association with McNally and Son would be sufficient for him to figure out what I was up to.'

'I agree,' father said, 'but does he know who hired you?'

'I think he does, sir, and I believe his performance last night was an exhibition of his powers aimed directly at me.'

'A warning, Archy?'

'It couldn't be clearer, sir.'

'What worries me is that if he knows who hired you to snoop around his operation it makes us look negligent in our promise of confidentiality to Richard Holmes and less than diligent in carrying out our duties. I don't like it, Archy.'

'Nor I, sir.'

Before leaving I told father that the person he had hired to tend mother's garden had arrived that morn-ing.

'Yes,' he said, 'Kate Mulligan, I believe. Mother flatly refused to go on the cruise unless I hired someone to see that her garden and greenhouse didn't suffer for her absence. What's the woman like, Archy?'

'Very pleasant, I would say, sir. She told mother that begonias are her favorite flower and immediately won mother's approval.'

Father smiled sheepishly, which is a rare occurrence, and admitted, 'I informed the agency that mother raised begonias and to instruct whomever they sent to make a point of praising the begonia family.'

'Agency, sir?'

'Yes. An agency in West Palm that supplies all sorts of temporary help. Mrs Trelawney has used them for clerks when needed and she made the arrangements for mother's helper. The agency called me for personal details, which I thought very prudent, and from what you've told me it seems to have worked very well.'

And from what I had seen of Kate Mulligan, I would have to agree.

5

In my office I called my friend and compadre at the PBPD, Sergeant Al Rogoff. Al and I have worked together on several cases, usually to our mutual satisfaction.

'Sergeant Rogoff,' he answered.

'Archy McNally here,' I said. 'How was your week in New York?'

'Great. I rode the ferry to the Statue of Liberty, took the elevator to the top of the Empire State Building and hit all the topless bars the mayor hasn't pressured into closing.'

'Nice try, Al, but I'm not buying it. You were at the ballet every night. Right?'

'Can it, Archy,' he stage whispered into the phone. 'If that gets around the palace the Joe Sixpacks will be hanging tutus in my locker.'

The palace is Al's euphemism for the Palm Beach police station and Al is a closeted aficionado of the classical arts, from ballet to opera and all the stops along the way. One should not be misled by his passion for Mahler and Mendelssohn because Al Rogoff is as macho as they come and built like a bull. However, in a china shop he wouldn't upset a Limoges teacup.

'I'll not betray you, Al,' I assured him. 'Can I buy you lunch?'

'Sorry, pal, I'm spoken for.'

'If you're turning down a free meal it must be serious business. Who's the lucky lady, policewoman Tweeny Alvarez?'

'Jesus, Archy, I'd rather have lunch with you.'

'Then why don't you?'

'You pay the lunch bill, Archy, but I end up with more work, more stress and one large headache, so no thanks. Solve your own problems.'

'What makes you think I have a problem?'

'Because you don't invite me to lunch to gaze into my blood-shot eyes, but to pump me for information – or ask me for help.'

My word, have he and Connie Garcia been commiserating? 'May I ask one question which you can charge against our next lunch date?'

'One, and make it snappy, I work for the overburdened taxpayer.'

'Of which I am one, Al.'

'If we had to depend on your contribution I'd be out of business.'

'Be that as it may, Sergeant, have you ever heard of one Serge Ouspenskaya?'

'A foreigner?' Al asked.

'He pretends to be. More to the point, he's this season's most promising psychic.'

Al uttered a descriptive expletive before griping. 'Don't tell me you're involved with one of them again, Archy.'

'One of *those*, Al. Obviously you remember Hertha Gloriana.'

'How could I forget? That one ended in a shootout at a sleazy motel. Goodbye, Archy.'

'Not so fast, Al. I'm hoping this one doesn't come to that. The guy is not the shootout type. Would you let me know if any complaints come your way citing Ouspenskaya as the perp?'

'Okay, I'll nosy around, Archy. Can I know your involvement with this Ouspenskaya guy? Are you working on a case?'

'I'm on a case, but that's all I can tell you right now.'

'So what else is new?' he quipped, but his tone belied the words. I had piqued his interest and his cavalier attitude gave way to the business at hand. 'I'll check from my end and if you turn up anything on the guy let me in on it ASAP. I would hate to see you clobbered with a crystal ball.'

'Ouspenskaya transmits via shortwave radio, Al.'

'Is he selling air time?'

'I believe he is, Sergeant.'

'I'll be in touch.'

'Thanks, Al. I owe you.'

'We're here to serve, pal.'

One of the advantages of having a firm like McNally

& Son to lean on is their library which is supervised by our in-house paralegal, Sofia Richmond. Besides her legal expertise, Sofia is a qualified librarian, a computer whiz, and a researcher who doesn't have to ask a pol if he wears briefs or boxers because, so she claims, she has X-ray vision. Sofia's age I imagine to be somewhere between forty and terminal.

I have long believed that if Sofia let down her hair – worn pulled back from her face and knotted in a ridiculous bun at the rear of her head – removed the horn-rimmed glasses, sturdy oxfords and shapeless hopsack suits, there would emerge if not a butterfly, certainly a dragonfly. Archy, the optimist.

Sofia has never made a play for me, which means she has a lover who would make Charlie Atlas look like a sissy, or a girlfriend who looks like Charlie Atlas. Did I also mention that Sofia Richmond is the only one in the office who can read between the lines of Lolly Spindrift's blind items? In a word, Sofia not only knows all but, if pressured, will reveal what she knows.

'You look lovely, Archy,' Sofia welcomed me into her world of books, magazines, computers and yesterday's half-filled cardboard coffee container. Neatness is not Sofia's driving force, but then McNally & Son was not paying her to be a *hausfrau*.

'You don't look bad yourself, Sofia,' I said.

'You lie like a rug, love. I know I need work, but then who doesn't?'

She wouldn't get an argument with me on that score. 'What's the latest scuttlebutt, Sofia?'

She lit a cigarette and tossed the used match into an ashtray that held enough unfiltered butts to span the Golden Gate Bridge if placed end to end. 'Desdemona Darling is among us, love, fifty pounds overweight but as lovely as the days when she gave new meaning to the name *Homo erectus*.'

As you can see, Sofia knows how to turn a phrase.

'What was her husband doing locked up with you and the old man yesterday?'

Were the pater to hear *that* turn of phrase he would hit the ceiling but he wouldn't fire Sofia. Father knew the value of a good and dedicated employee. 'You are not supposed to know that Desdemona Darling's husband paid us a visit,' I cautioned our librarian.

Sofia took a deep drag on her cigarette, which had me clutching the English Ovals in my jacket pocket. I had smoked one at Ta-boo' with Fitz last night and a second while writing in my journal before bed. I refrained from lighting one now but found no solace in my restraint. Sofia expelled a long stream of smoke along with the words, 'I never saw him.'

I had no choice now but to ask her what I had come to learn. 'What do you know about the psychic Serge Ouspenskaya?' Sofia's eyeballs, huge behind the thick lenses of her glasses, widened wide enough to tell me she had immediately connected Richard Holmes's visit to the psychic. I knew she would, but I also knew she would heed my warning and forget my query as she had promised to forget Holmes's visit. Sofia knew when to ante up and when to fold her hand.

'I hear he's the current favorite of the ladies who lunch.'

'Anything else?'

'That's all I know,' she said. 'That kind of thing is not my cup of tea, love. I deal in the here and now.' With a wave of her cigarette she quoted, '"Yesterday is a memory, gone for good forever / while tomorrow is a guess / what is real is what is here and now / and here and now is all that we possess."'

'Nicely put,' I complimented, 'and here and now I would like you to put your bloodhound instincts on the trail of Serge Ouspenskaya and let me know what you come up with, like where he came from and, more important, *quo vadis*.'

Sofia shrugged. 'I would imagine he got his start as a traveling carny fortuneteller and he's not going anyplace as long as the ladies who lunch keep him on their menu.'

'Never underestimate a man with the conceit of a cat burglar who walked off with the jewel in the crown – and is ready to bargain for its return. I met him last night.'

'So I heard,' Sofia said. 'Lolly Pops? Good grief, Archy.'

'Who did you hear it from? Mrs. Trelawney?'

'No. From Binky. He called this morning.'

When I get my hands on Binky Watrous I am fairly

certain I will strangle him. 'Is there anyone Binky hasn't called?'

'I doubt it. He keeps in close touch with the staff. He begins by asking how I am and ends with wanting to know if Joe is showing any signs of shortness of breath when he brings in the mail.'

'If I have my way Joe Anderson, along with the rest of the world, will outlive Binky Watrous.'

Sofia smiled, recalling no doubt the days when Binky brought in her mail. 'He's a good boy, Archy.' Binky and his doe eyes inspire women to talk such gibberish. Older women, that is. Binky doesn't have much luck with his contemporaries of the opposite sex.

Relegating Binky to a list labeled *extermination*, I asked our librarian, 'Another favor, Sofia, if I may?'

'You may.'

'What do you know about a Mrs Ventura?'

'The lady who almost gave her diamond clip to the Goodwill people. Can you imagine the look on the face of the lucky recipient if she had been handed Mrs Ventura's slightly used frock?'

'I see that story has made the rounds of polite society.'

'It has made the newspapers, thanks to Lolly Spindrift,' Sofia announced.

'Lolly seems to have taken a shine to Ouspenskaya and I doubt if the psychic is Lolly's type.'

'Buzz Carr is more Lolly's type and I hear, by the by, that Phil Meecham is furious with Lady Cynthia . . .'

I held up my hand like a policeman at a school crossing. 'Enough, Sofia.' The fancies and foibles of the Palm Beach rich interest me only when they are relevant to one of my cases which, unfortunately, is almost always. 'What can you tell me about Mrs Ventura,' I asked the eyes and ears of McNally & Son.

'For the record, she's the second Mrs Ventura. The first died a few years back and Mr Ventura, James I believe is his name, married the current Mrs Ventura, Hanna, before a respectable period of mourning.'

'How long is respectable?'

'A year, usually, but six months is the absolute minimum.'

'And how long did James wait?' I asked.

'About six weeks.'

'It borders on the obscene,' I observed.

'Some say it crosses the line. The loudest objections came from the Ventura boy, William, and are still coming.'

'How old is William?'

'Twenty-one, give or take,' Sofia said, poking about for a space in her ashtray to put out her cigarette.

'What does Ventura's exchequer look like?'

'Loaded. New money via Wall Street. But you're supposed to ask the age of the new Mrs Ventura.'

'I'm asking.'

'Twenty-one, give or take.'

'Are you implying that she and young William were an item?' I inquired as Sofia's smoldering cigarette

74

exposed me to the dangers of secondhand smoke – which I greedily inhaled.

'It's said that William had some friends in for a party one night and Hanna was among them. For papa James, it was love at first sight. How close William and Hanna were before Daddy Dearest entered the picture is not known. What is known is that William now hates her and doesn't even try to hide his disdain. He was his mother's pet and poor William feels that he's been usurped as heir apparent.'

'Does the boy live at home?'

'Oh, yes,' Sofia nodded. 'In fact there were those who believed William had swiped Hanna's diamond clip for pin money. The boy is usually in debt and begrudges the money his father lavishes on her.'

'The *enfant terrible*,' I said.

'If you like the expression. I think *pain in the butt* is more descriptive.'

As I said, Sofia knows how to turn a phrase. She also knows more dish than anyone in Palm Beach. I refrained from asking her if the Ventura men wore briefs or boxers for fear that she would tell me. Instead I thanked her for her time, reminded her to forget everything we discussed, took a final grateful sniff of the polluted library air and fled.

Another resource of McNally & Son is Mrs Evelyn Sharif, the chief of our real estate department. Mrs Sharif is married to a Lebanese gentleman who operates a haberdashery on elegant Worth Avenue. To be sure, McNally & Son does not sell homes or condos but

represents our clients at closings, advises on leases and
also recommends investments in lots and commercial
property.

Without even consulting the Palm Beach telephone
directory I knew that the Venturas would be ex-
directory. The only people listed in the Palm Beach
directory are those who call people who are listed
in the Palm Beach directory. Mrs Sharif possessed a
big black book that not only identified the residents
of Palm Beach along with their addresses and phone
numbers, but also cited an estimate of the value of
their property and its potential rental income, in and
off season.

'Archy,' Mrs Sharif exclaimed as I entered, 'what a
surprise. You must want something from me.'

'A kiss,' I answered.

'I'm a married woman, Archy.'

'The British Princes of Wales only courted married
women,' I reminded her.

'You are not any of the Princes of Wales, Archy. So
what do you want to know that I probably shouldn'
tell you?'

'The address and phone number of James Ventura.

'Why?'

'Discreet Inquiries' business, Mrs Sharif. Very cloak
and-dagger. The less you know, the safer you'll be.'

Mrs Sharif mulled this over before stating, 'Isn't Mrs
Ventura the woman who located a lost piece of jewelry
with the help of a psychic?'

'One and the same.'

'One and the same psychic that raised your grand-father from the dead last night?'

I took a deep breath and counted to ten back-wards. 'You've been talking to Binky Watrous, Mrs Sharif.'

'In fact, I have.'

'Well, be assured that you will never hear from him again.'

'Why not, Archy?'

'Because I am going to kill him before the sun sets on this accursed day. Did he also inquire after the health of Joe Anderson?'

'It's the only reason he calls, Archy. But be kind. Binky is a good boy.'

I wondered if Binky shouldn't rent himself out as a pet to rich, middle-aged women and give up waiting for Joe Anderson to throw in the towel. 'If I were Joe Anderson,' I said, 'I wouldn't let Binky within gun range of my person.'

Mrs Sharif shook her head in dismay. 'Binky wouldn't hurt a fly, Archy.'

'I agree, Mrs Sharif, but I'm still going to throttle him. Now may I have the Ventura address and phone number, please.'

'Do you want to compare notes with Mrs Ventura on your mutual out-of-this-world experiences?'

'How did you guess?'

As surreptitiously as if she were purloining the Dead Sea Scrolls from an ancient crypt, Mrs Sharif removed the big black book from the bottom drawer of her desk,

put on her reading glasses and revealed the Venturas
address and phone number.

I made it back to my cubbyhole without encountering
another soul who had talked to Binky Watrous that
morning, passing only Joe Anderson pushing a shopping cart filled with mail and whistling merrily as he
rolled along.

I dialed the Ventura home and was greeted with a
melodious 'Hello' by a female I assumed to be the
housekeeper.

'Is Mrs Ventura in, please?'

'This is Mrs Ventura.' The melodious voice took on
a southern accent.

'I'm Archy McNally, Mrs Ventura, and I'm calling . . .

'Archy McNally! Why, what a coincidence. I mean
this is truly serendipity. I was just talking to Penny
Tremaine and she told me about your sitting with
Mr Ouspenskaya last night and I said – I said –
"Why, Penny, I just have to talk to Mr McNally
and compare notes." That's what I said and now –
just like that – here you are. We are experiencing
something remarkable, Mr McNally. Can't you just
feel it?'

What I felt was an assault on my eardrum but if
getting to meet with Hanna Ventura was this easy, I
would have to admit that, yes, it was very remarkable.

'Are you free this afternoon, Mrs Ventura?'

'No, sir. I am not. I have an appointment with M
Archy McNally. I'll expect you in one hour and – do
you have the address, Mr McNally?'

'South County Road,' I answered.
'Serendipity,' Hanna Ventura cried.
'Bingo,' I cried back.

6

The door was opened by a uniformed maid and only after I assured her that I wasn't a born-again zealot soliciting converts, or selling the Encyclopedia Britannica, did she lead the way to her mistress. I followed her down a long entrance hall decorated with land- and seascapes by the school of artists known as California Impressionists, mounted in ornate gilded frames. The hallway led to a screened patio and a rear patio door led to a backyard of green lawn, palms, royal poincianas and the swimming pool. It also contained Mrs Ventura.

The lady of the house was seated at an umbrella table and rose as I approached, quickly wrapping a sarong-like skirt around a pair of slim hips. I assumed she was covering a bikini bottom rather than bare flesh but I wouldn't swear to it. The hand, remember, is quicker than the eye. In this case a most regretable verity.

'Mr Archy McNally, I presume,' she said, offering her hand.

Hanna Ventura was a true blonde with big brown eyes, a bosom that taxed her white bikini top, a tiny waist and shapely tanned legs. It was easy to see how she had turned a grieving widower into an ardent suitor after one brief encounter.

'Mrs Ventura,' I said, taking her hand which was still cool from the chilled glass she had been clutching when I arrived. 'It's a pleasure.'

'Oh, let's not be formal. I'm just plain Hanna to my friends.'

'And what a lovely name is Hanna,' I answered. 'Did you know it's derived from the Greek? It translates, "God has favored me."'

With a wave of her lovely hand that seemed to indicate her two acres of South County Road real estate and everything on it, she beamed, 'He sure did. But how clever of you to know that. Won't you sit down? That big ol' pitcher of lemonade is really vodka and tonic so if you are not opposed to an alcohol libation before lunch just pour yourself a toot.'

As she spoke she removed the cover from an ice bucket and pulled out a glass, filling it with crescent-shaped cubes before passing it on to me. 'I told Margaret, she's the new girl, to bring us lunch after a while. Nothing formal. Just a shrimp salad and warm biscuits. You haven't eaten, have you?'

I poured my libation but before I could state that I had not had a bite since breakfast, Hanna went right on. 'Margaret is new. It's so hard to keep help, don't you think? Most of them are college girls who take jobs down here in season hoping to catch a rich husband. Ever since that Rockefeller boy married the au pair they all want a shot at the brass ring. Well, who am I to talk?'

Who, indeed? But talk she did. I wondered if I would ever be required to join in. Shaded by the umbrella and enjoying my drink – although I preferred my vodka and tonic with lime, not lemon, but I suspected the lemon wedges were to fool the likes of Margaret – I sipped and listened attentively. I had come to discuss other worlds and found myself in one – the land of Loony Tunes.

'Now tell me, was last night your first meeting with Mr Ouspenskaya?'

Hanna went from subject to subject without benefit of a connecting line or two. Just as well. What Hanna did not need was an extra line or two. I waited long enough to be sure she wanted an answer before answering. 'Yes, it was.'

'And he contacted your grandfather. Is that correct?'

'It is.'

'Now tell me, Archy – I may call you Archy? – did you ever meet Mr Ouspenskaya before last evening? Do you have any friends in common? Anything like that?'

'No,' I told her, 'but don't jump to conclusions. There are many tricks to the psychic trade. My grandfather, as I'm sure Mrs Tremaine told you, was on the stage. A public figure, easily traceable if one knows where to search for the facts.'

'But you said you never met Mr Ouspenskaya. You have no friends in common. Why would he look up your ancestor?'

I couldn't tell her what I suspected so I had to confess I didn't know, but it was becoming very clear that Hanna Ventura wanted to authenticate, not invalidate, Serge Ouspenskaya. 'He did know I would be at the séance. I'm told he requires a guest list before agreeing to a sitting, as he calls it.'

She jumped on this like a duck on a June bug, as they say where Hanna comes from, which my guess was Georgia via Arkansas. 'But he didn't know I would be at the Fairhurst party. He looked right at me and said, "Something is troubling you, young lady." And before I could answer he said, "You have lost something of great value – both financial and personal – is that not correct?" I said I had, but I never told him what it was. Never. He said I should go straight home and look carefully at a pile of clothing I had put together for the Goodwill people. He said my consideration for the less fortunate would be rewarded. I remember every word, Archy. It still gives me goose bumps.'

'And you came home and found the diamond clip?' I concluded for her.

'Not right away. You see, I was certain I had taken the clip off the dress the night I wore it for the last time.'

Finally, something interesting. 'Are you certain of that, Hanna?'

'I thought I was, but I was wrong, wasn't I?'

'Please, tell me what you thought you had done with the clip. It may be important.'

'You wouldn't have a cigarette on you, would you?'

Reaching for my English Ovals I proffered them to her. 'What are they?' Hanna asked, taking one.

'English Ovals. You'll like them. And I'll join you.' I struck a match, held it for her, and then lit my first cigarette of the day.

'James doesn't like me to smoke so I don't keep them around. James is my husband.'

'I'm trying to quit,' I confessed. 'I have it down to a couple a day.'

'I mooch whenever I get a chance so I think I smoke more than if James allowed me to keep them in the house.'

Margaret came through the patio door pushing a tea trolley that held our lunch. As Hanna had promised, the spread consisted of a fresh shrimp salad, warm biscuits in a wicker basket covered with a heated cloth, butter patties and a tray of shiny black olives and celery sticks. This picnic fare was served on fine bone china accompanied by the family silver. Hanna freshened our drinks before we dug in.

'*Bon appetit*,' she advised.

As we ate, I encouraged Hanna to tell me what she thought she had done with her diamond clip.

'Well, we had been out that night. James and I. Someone who shall be nameless remarked that I had worn the same dress to several parties this season – and wasn't it lovely. Meow, meow. I decided to get rid of it and a few others on the spot.' Hanna seemed to lose interest in her shrimp salad but not in her alcohol libation.

'When we got home I thought I took the clip off the dress and laid it on my dressing table. Then I thought that if James saw it, he would scold me and tell me to put it directly in my jewel case which is kept in a hidden safe in our bedroom. Truth is, I was a little tipsy and I didn't want to look up the combination to that damn safe, so I put the clip in my dressing-table drawer thinking I would put it in the safe in the morning.'

'And it wasn't in the drawer the next morning?'

'No, Archy, it wasn't.'

'What did you think happened to it?'

Hanna shook her blond curly head and exclaimed, 'I didn't know, Archy. I just didn't know. I was scared and afraid to tell James. Then I had to tell him. We searched all over the house and the car, too. We called the people whose house we were at that night and we even called all the other guests who had been there, and we came up empty-handed every time.' The agony she had gone through over the lost diamond clip was evident in her voice and eyes as she recalled the days following its disappearance.

'I was so sure I had put it in the drawer. That's why I didn't rush home when Mr Ouspenskaya told me where it was. I just didn't think it was possible. Then I figured that if he knew I had lost the clip just by looking at me . . .'

'Easy,' I broke in. 'According to your story a lot of people knew you lost that clip. Maybe Ouspenskaya was one of them. It's very possible.'

'James said the same thing, Archy. But I did come home and I did find the clip where he said it would be. Doesn't that prove he has the power? Doesn't it?'

What could I say? The clip was where Ouspenskaya said it would be and that was the bottom line. 'But what about the fact that you were certain you removed the clip from your dress? What's your take on that now?'

Hanna smiled brightly. 'Oh, don't you see? It was a dream.'

'A dream? You think it was a dream?'

'I'm sure it was a dream. Like I told you, I was in my dressing room and James kept calling me – I mean he was eager – I mean – are you married, Archy?'

'No, Hanna, I'm not.'

'Then you wouldn't understand.'

'Oh, but I do understand, Hanna. I'm not a monk. I have enough vices without adding chastity to the list.'

I was hoping she would spare me a giggle but, alas, she did not. 'Well, I must have undressed – I know I undressed,' another giggle, the result no doubt of a paucity of shrimp salad and a surplus of vodka tonics. 'I went to bed and I must have dreamed that I did what I would have done if James hadn't been in such a rush. That is remove the clip from my dress. When we make love my mind tends to wander, you see – but you don't want to know that.'

No, I didn't, nor did James Ventura.

The patio door opened once again but this time it was not Margaret come to clear away our lunch, but a young man wearing the briefest of brief swimming togs. He was as trim and sleek as a Speedo model, with a dark crew-cut head of hair and a masculine beauty more indigenous to the Bay of Naples than the Bay of Biscayne. If he was who I thought he was, his looks and deportment were a gift of his Italian Ventura ancestors.

He marched past us as if we were either invisible or too insignificant to warrant so much as a nod. Reaching the pool he paused for one moment before executing a perfect dive, causing hardly a ripple on the water's surface. The dark, wet head emerged on the opposite end of the Olympic-sized bathtub and he began to swim laps with the efficiency of a seal.

Hanna and I watched the performance like spectators at an aquacade before Hanna introduced the star attraction. 'That's William. He's my son who's nine months older than me. Ain't that a laugh and a half?' The drinks were beginning to slur Missy's southern drawl.

'He came to see who I was entertaining,' Hanna said loud enough to penetrate William's waterlogged ears, 'so he can report the boring details to his father. William has been trying to catch me in the act since the day I married his father but so far he hasn't had much luck. Have you, Billy boy?'

William paid as much attention to her words as he had to our presence. It was a *film noir* moment in an Esther Williams Technicolor extravaganza. When F.S. Fitzgerald said the rich are different than you and me, he knew of what he spoke.

'You have to excuse us, Archy,' Hanna begged my indulgence. 'I guess all families have their problems. Ours is William. Pay him no mind, when he gets tired he'll haul his half-naked behind out of the pool and go about his business, which is borrowing money from his friends.' Hanna took a deep breath, her first of the afternoon, and queried, 'Now where were we? Oh, yes, Mr Ouspenskaya. I take it you are not an adherent.'

'I am a seeker of the truth, Hanna.'

'Are you on a spiritual journey, Archy?' she asked in all seriousness.

I wanted to tell her I was on a case but feared she would have me thrown out of her home – or into the pool with son William. I was also wishing she would ask for another cigarette so I could succumb to temptation with a clear conscience but she refrained. I imagined she was loath to puff on the weed in front of William for fear he would report the fact to daddy. Did William know the lemonade was in fact vodka and tonic? I suspected he did, and if I were Hanna Ventura I would worry more about James learning how much I imbibed in the afternoon than how many cigarettes I had smoked that day.

'Do you know that Desdemona Darling is here for the season?' Hanna asked without a preamble.

'I've heard rumors to that effect.'

'She was a very famous film actress of the silent era,' Hanna misinformed me.

'Not the silent era,' I said. 'Desdemona's moment was fifty or so years ago when the talkies were at their zenith. The wheel, electricity and talking photoplays had all been invented, my dear Hanna.'

'My, aren't you the smart one. Anyway, Penny Tremaine told me that Desdemona Darling told her that Mr Ouspenskaya told you something that no one on this earth knew.'

'So I've heard, but I can't imagine what it could have been. However, if Desdemona Darling knows what it is then at least one person on this earth knew it before Ouspenskaya made it public. Correct?'

'You're always putting him down, Archy.'

'Not really. I'm just highlighting the facts that show his broadcasts could be more planned than spontaneous. As I told you, Hanna, there are many tricks to the psychic trade and Ouspenskaya appears to have mastered them all.'

'Then how do you explain my diamond clip?'

'I'm so glad you asked,' I said. Looking not at her but at the swimmer in her pool, I continued, 'Suppose there existed someone who would take great delight in seeing your husband furious with you. Losing that clip, I imagine, would do the trick. And suppose you didn't dream you removed the clip from your dress and put it in your dressing-table drawer, but in fact you did just that. Then this person, who has great animosity toward you, removed the pin from the drawer and put it back on the dress you had discarded.

'But before the dress goes off to Goodwill, this person learns that Ouspenskaya is going to perform at the Fairhurst charity ball and this person, who is always in need of ready cash, sees a way to make a fast buck on your embarrassing situation. Naturally, this person can't pawn the clip because that would be too risky for a novice. Your insurance company would scour the pawn shops and jewelers all over the state of Florida and no doubt find it and trace it back to said person.

'So said person goes to Serge Ouspenskaya and, in return for a generous gratuity, said person tells Ouspenskaya how he can be the hit of the Fairhurst ball and pick up an array of wealthy followers. As they say, Hanna, one hand washed the other.'

Hanna, staring at William as he cut through the cool water with the precision of Johnny Weissmuller in his prime, hung on to my every word. After giving my hypothesis considerable thought she expelled a most audible hiccup and said, 'William was in London with friends the week the clip went missing and returned after the Fairhurst ball.'

'Oh,' I said.

In the detective business, you win some and you lose some.

* * *

The Lake Worth Playhouse is located on Lake Avenue and, according to the PB Chamber of Commerce, is one of the most respected community theaters in America. A young woman in the box office told me I could find the general manager by going to the stage door and asking directions.

I walked into a scene that was reminiscent of a Warner Brothers backstage musical, circa 1939, with one glaring exception: The chorus girls and boys looked to be not more than ten years old. An adult in bell-bottom jeans and a St John's University sweatshirt directed me up a flight of stairs where I followed my nose to the office of the theater's manager.

The office door was open and the man seated behind the desk was on the phone but he waved me in when he spotted me outside his domain. The walls of the small room were covered with playbills and autographed photos of actors of both sexes, many of whom I recognized. I didn't notice if Freddy McNally and Lolly Pops were among them, but I did spot a playbill announcing *A Star Is Born*, featuring Janet Gaynor, Fredric March and Adolphe Menjou.

Gaynor was the recipient of the first Academy Award ever handed out for her role in *Seventh Heaven*. Garland should have gotten an Oscar for the musical remake of *A Star Is Born* but got a Joey, her son, instead. The theater must have functioned as a film palace at one time.

'I have to think about it,' the manager was saying

to his caller, 'and get back to you. Yeah, sure, before next week.' With that he rang off.

'Are you a father?' he asked.

'Not that I know of,' I responded.

This drew a smile if not a laugh. 'As you must have seen, our children's workshop is rehearsing a musical. I thought you might be a parent demanding a solo number for your budding Travolta or Streisand. What can I do for you?'

'The name is Archy McNally and I want to know how difficult it would be to learn the name of the acts that played here in 1924.'

'Not difficult at all. Our archives are complete and readily available. Are you writing a thesis? Most requests like yours are from students working on term papers or their Ph.D.s.'

'I'm afraid I'm not,' I said, without stating my true purpose for the inquiry.

'Funny you should mention 1924. It was the year we opened as the Oakley Theater, a combination movie and vaudeville house. As you can see we've come a long way since then.'

He was more eager to expound on the merits of the theater than to learn the purpose of my visit. I came away knowing that the theater had acquired its present name, Lake Worth Playhouse, in 1953 and was now a year-round operation presenting musicals, comedies and dramas in their three-hundred-seat main auditorium. It also contained a seventy-seat black box theater that regularly featured contemporary plays and cabarets.

It boasted a children's theater group, workshops and classes that encouraged student performances.

'I understand the Palm Beach Community Theater is going to put on *Arsenic and Old Lace* this season,' I told the gentleman whose name I never learned.

'Bet you'll never guess who the star will be.'

'Lolly Pops?' I offered.

That got a laugh. 'Say, how do you know Lolly?'

'I heard her on the radio.'

I went to the PB library and checked out a copy of *Arsenic and Old Lace*. Then I went to a video shop in West Palm and rented the screen version of the play. I had seen the Warner Bros. film at the MoMA cinema in New York, where I had spent more time than in any lecture hall at Yale, and wanted to refresh my memory. Neither was going to tell me much about Serge Ouspenskaya but all work and no play makes Archy a dull boy.

I learned that *Arsenic and Old Lace* was produced by Howard Lindsay and Russell Crouse and opened at the Fulton Theater in New York on January 10, 1941. The *dramatis personae* was as follows:

  Abby Brewster (The lead spinster)
  Martha Brewster (Abby's sister)
  Teddy Brewster (The insane nephew)
  Mortimer Brewster (The smart, urbane nephew)
  Jonathan Brewster (The evil nephew)
  Dr Einstein (Jonathan's lunatic friend)

Elaine Harper (Mortimer's future bride)
Rev Harper (Elaine's father)
Minor players:
Mr Gibbs
Officer Klein
Officer Brophy
Officer O'Hara
Lieutenant Rooney
Mr Witherspoon

Desdemona Darling would no doubt play Abby Brewster and Buzz and Fitz would portray Mortimer and Elaine. This left a number of roles still to be cast. Having given the plum assignments to Desdemona and Buzz, I wondered who the Creative Director had in mind for the also-rans – especially the role of Martha.

Historical note: The Fulton Theater was later renamed the Helen Hayes in honor of the beloved actress. A group of diehards protested, stating that the actress should have changed her name to Helen Fulton.

7

At breakfast the next morning I gave father a progress report on my investigation of Serge Ouspenskaya, detailing my interview with Hanna Ventura and my visit to the Lake Worth Playhouse. 'As I suspected, anyone could peruse the theater's archives and learn who had appeared there and when they did so,' I told him. 'I find Mrs Ventura's story interesting, however.'

With his usual sangfroid the don asked, 'What part of her story do you believe, Archy? That she actually removed the clip from her dress or that she dreamed she did?'

Over my eggs scrambled with caramelized onions and smoked salmon, I said I believed she had removed the clip in fact and not in fancy.

'Then who returned it to the dress?'

'When I learn that, sir, I will have solved the mystery of Serge Ouspenskaya.'

'The sooner the better,' he said. 'People like Ouspenskaya are more of a nuisance than a serious threat to the well-being of our community.'

Unless it's your money the nuisance is playing free and easy with, I thought but did not say. Archy, the pragmatist.

Father, as usual, was dressed in a three-piece business suit while I had elected to deck myself out in chinos, cord jacket and a lavender silk shirt that was a perfect match for my lavender suede loafers. Father might look at me askance but he seldom commented on my attire. I returned the favor.

Refusing Ursi's offer of a second cup of coffee and pressing his linen napkin to his lips, the master rose and asked if I wanted to drive to the office with him. 'Thank you, sir, but I'll take my car. I may need it this afternoon and it would expedite things to have it in the office garage.'

I accepted Ursi's offer along with a slab of freshly baked sourdough bread, toasted and spread with butter and her homemade beach plum jam. 'Is mother in the garden?' I asked Ursi.

'Oh, yes, Archy. She went out right after breakfast, like always.'

'Is Kate Mulligan due today?'

'She is,' Ursi told me. 'I understand she's to come in every morning for a few hours to work with Mrs McNally before she takes over when they leave for the cruise.'

Mother never looked lovelier than when she was puttering about her greenhouse. The morning sun, filtered through the structure's glass walls, gave the array of colorful blooms and the gentle woman tending them the surreal air of a watercolor.

'Oh, Archy,' she said as I entered. 'I was expecting Kate.'

'I just wanted to say goodbye before I left for the office, mother.'

'That's nice of you, dear. Your father did, too. How lucky I am with the men in my life.'

'That's because you deserve it, mother. How are you getting on with Kate Mulligan?'

'Very well, Archy. She's such a lovely woman and she seems to know her business. Of course, I instruct her on how I want things done and she jots it all down.'

'That's as it should be, mother. You're the boss.'

'I'm afraid I do ramble on a bit but she doesn't seem to mind.'

'You ramble all you want,' I said as I bent to kiss her cheek. Out of the corner of my eye I could just about make out the label, printed in mother's hand, on the earthenware pot holding the enormous begonia Kate had admired yesterday. It read, EYELASH.

Leaving mother to her labor of love, I headed for my Miata and met Kate Mulligan in our driveway just getting out of a new yellow Volkswagen Beetle. Mother's station wagon and Hobo were both missing so unless we had been carnapped and dog-napped, Jamie was out with both the Ford and the pooch.

'I've always wanted to ride in one of those,' Kate said, admiring my red Miata.

Now there was an invitation if ever I heard one. I

recalled an old college drinking toast that counseled, 'If you don't do it, when you come to it, may you never come to it, to do it again.' I took its sage advice and answered, 'Would you like to fulfill the longing this evening?'

I must say she looked fetching in a denim skirt and white blouse. Again, the sensible Top-Siders did not distract from a fine pair of gams, which were two good reasons why Kate Mulligan never seemed to wear pants. 'Will you take me for a ride?' she called, walking toward the house.

'Even better, I'll take you to dinner.'

'And if I refuse will I be fired?'

'Of course. I come with the job.'

She had stopped now and seemed to be considering my offer. 'The bane of the working woman,' she sighed, but retraced her steps back toward her car and me. 'Only on the condition that I pay my own way.'

'A liberated woman?'

'No, Archy, a smart woman. I don't like being beholden to anyone. Especially men. And what makes you so sure I'm not married, or don't you care?'

'Oh, I care, Kate. But I noticed yesterday that the third finger of your left hand holds not a ring but a band of white flesh the sun has not yet darkened. Newly divorced?'

'You're very observant, Archy. I'm impressed.'

I would have liked to tell her that I was even more observant than she realized. 'I take it I'm catching you on the rebound, Kate,' I said instead.

'I didn't know I had fallen.'

She was quick on the draw and feisty. A combination that went a long way in egging me on. Giving her my hundred-watt smile I told her, 'I invited you and I'm paying. Take it or leave it but remember, this is the only red Miata in Palm Beach.'

'What should I wear?' she asked by way of accepting my offer.

I repressed the reply that came immediately to mind and said, 'Something informal. I'm not as rich as my father. Do you like Tex-Mex?'

'I never met a man named Tex I didn't like. I'm not so sure about Mex.'

'Cute, but I'm supposed to make the not-so-witty puns. Shall we say seven?'

She gave me the address of her apartment in West Palm, near Currie Park. Not bad. Neither was the new VW. Kate Mulligan didn't do badly as a part-time gardener, or was it her alimony that kept the wolf away from her door? Well, one was going to come a-knocking this evening. I beeped twice as I pulled out of our turnaround and Kate Mulligan gave me a wave and a smile as I drove off. The lady was a flirt, but then, who's perfect?

In my office I found none other than Binky Watrous sitting in my visitor's chair. Two adults in my office at the same time gives the space all the comforts of a New York subway car at rush hour. I reminded myself to ask father to install hanging straps in the event I was ever blessed with two simultaneous visitors.

'Well, if it isn't the cellular Paul Revere. One if by the Top Banana and two if by Lolly Pops.'

'Hi, Archy.'

'Is that all you have to say? Hi, Archy? Well, hi, traitor.'

'What's the matter with you?'

'Nothing is the matter with me, except that my best friend called everyone in this office to repeat gossip he picked up in a bar. That's what's the matter with me.'

Binky remained unfazed which was his way of dealing with stress.

'You mean that business with the psychic, Ouspenskaya? Relax, Archy. It's all over town. And it's the truth, isn't it?'

'Yes, it's the truth but in this case, Binky, the truth will not set you free. It will only land you on the unemployment line.'

'Fitz thinks Lolly Pops is your grandmother,' Binky said with a grin intended to be lecherous but thanks to his doe eyes it came off as a plea for mercy.

'Fitz,' I accused, 'is a helium head.'

'But what a dish, eh, Archy?'

'Never mind that, buster. Tend to your own garden, as Mr Voltaire cautioned. Which reminds me, you must refrain from asking after the health of Joe Anderson every time you converse with the staff here, which I understand is every day.'

'I don't wish him ill. I like Joe. But let's face it,

he's a hundred years old. The old generation passes away and a new one takes its place, Archy. It's only natural.'

I sank back in my chair in unadulterated exasperation. Binky quoting the Bible has that effect on me. 'And the sun also rises, Binky, and sets, and Joe's will set when he's damn good and ready. We're all entitled to our four-score and ten.'

'I think Joe is over the limit, Archy.'

'Shame on you. I suggest you seek gainful employment while awaiting your place on the staff of McNally and Son.'

Binky looked as if he was about to burst into tears but I knew from experience that he was smiling at me. 'I've done just that, Archy. I signed up with Temporarily Yours yesterday.'

'And just what is Temporarily Yours, may I ask?'

'It's what it sounds like. A temp agency in West Palm. You register with them, tell them what you can do, and they place you when they get an assignment that fits your skills. The job can be for a day, a week, a month or a year. You never know. Mrs Trelawney put me on to them. Who knows, Archy, I might end up right back here before Joe retires.'

Mrs Trelawney? Didn't father tell me Mrs Trelawney recommended the agency that got us Kate Mulligan? If so, our Kate must be with Temporarily Yours. I thought it best not to tell Binky of this connection in the very likely event that Binky proved to be the most temporary component of Temporarily Yours.

The old aphorism cautions us never to ask a foolish question because it will only elicit a foolish reply. This said, I asked Binky, 'And what did you tell them your skills are, Binky?'

The boy almost leaped out of his chair. 'I'm a mail room pro, Archy. Four weeks in training with Joe Anderson. And I was a bank teller trainee, a cab driver trainee, a pet store clerk trainee, a supermarket clerk trainee and a stage manager trainee.'

Only the last entry caught me off guard and recalling who the boy had been chinning with the night before last, I thought I knew how it had become part of his curriculum vitae.

'Stage manager, Binky?'

'Oh, I guess you haven't heard.'

'No, Binky, I haven't. And I don't think I want to know.'

Not taking the hint, he told me. 'Buzz Carr, it rhymes with star, is going to be in a play. *Arsenic and Old Lace*. Fitz is his leading lady and they asked me to stage manage. Isn't that a gas, Archy?'

Archy wanted to take gas. 'Do you know what being a stage manager entails, Binky?' I asked the foolish boy.

'Sure, Archy. He's the director's right hand. He sees that everything and everyone is where they should be when they should be.'

'And who told you that? Buzz Carr?'

'Yeah, Archy.'

'*Arsenic and Old Lace* is being presented by the

community theater of Palm Beach and Lady Cynthia Horowitz is the Creative Director of the group. She, and she alone, will select the stage manager. Buzz had no right to offer you the job.'

Sitting high in his chair Binky informed me, 'Buzz called me this morning to say that he talked to Lady Cynthia about me for the stage manager job and she told him it was okay with her. What's the matter, Archy, did you want the job?'

The Palm Beach Community Theater presents *Arsenic and Old Lace*, starring Desdemona Darling, with Buzz Carr and Fitz Fitzwilliams, and Binky Watrous as stage manager. What I wanted was a window to jump out of. As I appraised the incipient stage manager something that had been knocking around my unconscious since I saw him sitting in my office suddenly burst into my cerebrum and caused me to proclaim, 'You've shaved your mustache.'

'Yeah. How do you like it?'

The fact that I had not immediately noticed the clean-shaven upper lip of Binky Watrous is proof that when it was there it was as imposing as peach fuzz on a twelve-year-old. Binky's former pale blond mustache was a sparse and limp attempt at attracting a mate. It turned out to be more of a detriment, perhaps because females viewed it as a harbinger of things to come. 'Why did you shave it?' I inquired.

'Mrs Trelawney suggested it,' Binky answered.

'And if Mrs Trelawney suggested you shave your head, would you do that, too?'

'I don't know what you're getting so sore about, Archy. You've been telling me to get rid of it for years.'

Nihil est dictum, quod non est dictum prius. ('There is nothing one can say, that has not been said before.')

My ringing telephone distracted me from this apotheosis of absurdity. Picking up the dastardly instrument I was greeted by the one voice I did not want to hear today, tonight and, most probably, tomorrow – Connie Garcia.

'You are being summoned, sweetheart,' Connie informed me.

Knowing for whom Connie toiled, I knew who had issued the summons. 'What does she want from me?'

'Ask me no questions and I'll tell you no lies.'

'Which means you don't know.'

'You got it, Archy. She'll expect you this afternoon. After lunch. She was very specific about after lunch.'

'I'm with a client, Connie.' Here, Binky looked over his shoulder to ascertain if we were no longer alone. 'And I'm busy this afternoon.'

'As you wish, Archy. Only I thought you would be dying to meet Desdemona Darling. Bye, bye.'

'Hold on,' I shouted. 'Is Desdemona Darling going to be with Lady C this afternoon? On the level, Connie? Don't toy with me, I'm having a hard day.'

'We expect La Darling at three. Do you want to change your mind?'

Indeed I did. I could get to meet the leading lady in my case without blowing my cover and perhaps learn a little more about Serge Ouspenskaya from his most ardent follower. 'I'll be there,' I told Connie. 'After lunch.'

'What are you doing tonight, Archy?'

'I'm taking Binky Watrous for Tex-Mex. It's his birthday.'

'How sweet of you,' Connie said. 'Give Binky a birthday kiss for me. See you at three.'

'Thanks, Archy,' Binky said when I rang off. 'But it's not my birthday.'

'Then I'm not taking you to dinner. But don't tell Connie.'

'I think you're up to no good tonight, Archy.'

'Much foofaraw about nothing, Binky my boy. Can I buy you lunch?'

'The Pelican?'

'I fear not. The longer I get in the tooth, the shorter I get in reasons for taking friends to business lunches. But I know a little joint you will like. It's a show-biz hangout.'

'Really, Archy?'

'Trust me, kid.' And, alas, he did.

We drove to a pizzeria on Federal Highway, south of the Port of Palm Beach, where we indulged in a pie adorned with broccoli, slivers of artichoke hearts, sun-dried tomatoes and Gorgonzola cheese, atop a thin crust. Two nuns, wearing particularly ornate white wimples, came in for a slice and I immediately pointed them out to Binky.

'You know them?' he asked.

'Chorus girls from *The Sound of Music*,' I told him.

'Wow!' Binky said.

There are those who say I am devious. I prefer adroit. The difference is subtle but, for the likes of me, momentous.

Back on Royal Palm Way I consulted the yellow pages in search of psychics and found several listed as Psychic Advisers – all licensed, bonded and not averse to credit cards. I couldn't imagine what the criteria was for licensing a psychic. Serge Ouspenskaya was not among them but one, Madame Hildegarde Berlin, advertised that she would answer one question, free, by telephone. I was tempted to call and ask Hildegarde if she could name the composer of *God Bless America*, but stifled the urge.

I called information and from them learned the telephone number of Mr Serge Ouspenskaya with an address on Clematis Street in West Palm. Tired of being the ugly stepsister of the Town of Palm Beach, West Palm has been going through a period of gentrification, a word coined by real estate brokers, and Clematis Street was as gentry as West Palm will ever be.

A young man answered the phone and I asked him if I could speak to Mr Ouspenskaya.

'May I ask who's calling?'

'Archy McNally,' I informed him.

'One moment, please, Mr McNally.'

Several moments later the perfectly modulated voice

of Serge Ouspenskaya came over the wire. 'Mr McNally. I thought I would be hearing from you.'

Would it be considered redundant to tell a psychic he thought correctly? 'I was very impressed with your sitting, Mr Ouspenskaya,' I began.

'You are a charming liar, Mr McNally. No offense, please. I meant it as a compliment. Far from being impressed I imagine you paid a visit to the Lake Worth Playhouse the very next day and asked if anyone had been to see them lately regarding the appearance of Freddy McNally some seventy years ago.'

It was close enough to the truth but, as Nathan Detroit of *Guys and Dolls* would say, the odds were better than twelve to seven that any nonbeliever out to prove their point would have done just that. 'In fact I did, sir.'

Without a smug 'I told you so' retort, he asked me if I was familiar with Greek mythology. 'Specifically the story of Narcissus and the poor Echo.'

'The youth Narcissus, who was the beloved of Echo, saw his reflection in the water of a pond and fell in love with himself. For this, the gods turned him into a flower and Echo, heart-broken, languished until all that was left of her was her voice.'

'Very good, Mr McNally. I ask because last night I had a dream that was similar to the myth but in reverse. That is, I dreamed that a lovely narcissus flower turned into a beautiful youth. The youth dove into the pond and swam rapidly away from the shore. I heard the echo of a laugh and turning I saw you, Mr

McNally, watching the swimmer while nibbling on a shrimp.'

I felt those icy fingers tap-tap-tapping on my spine again. 'Have you been speaking to Mrs Ventura?'

'No, I have not. Why? Do you find my dream pertinent? Is the lovely Mrs Ventura involved?'

He was too clever to be lying. But how did he do it? And had I given away my hand by immediately bringing Hanna Ventura into the picture? Most likely. Serge Ouspenskaya was proving himself more adroit than Archy. 'I was merely curious,' I said, 'because I paid a call on Mrs Ventura yesterday.' That was as much as he was going to get out of me.

'You questioned her about her diamond clip, I presume.'

'We spoke of many things, sir. One of them being a rumor that Desdemona Darling has put it out that you told me something no one could possibly know – with the exception of Desdemona Darling, to be sure.'

'Yes. Mrs Holmes spoke to me about it the very next day.'

Mrs Holmes? How formal. 'I would like to know what it was that you said, sir.'

After a long pause he replied, 'I would rather she told you, Mr McNally.'

'Why, sir?'

Another pause. 'Y is a crooked letter, Mr McNally.'

'A child's response,' I accused.

'Out of the mouths of babes, Mr McNally. Out of

the mouths of babes. Ask Mrs Holmes when you see her this afternoon. Three is it? She'll tell you.'

The guy was either tapping my phone or camping out in my back pocket. Or was he for real?

8

An unfamiliar face opened the door to me at the Horowitz mansion. 'Mr McNally?'

'That's me.'

'You're expected, sir. This way, please.'

'Where's Mrs Marsden?' I asked, following her across an entrance hall whose square footage was on par with the dimensions of a cozy starter house in Suburbia, USA. Mrs Marsden was Lady C's regular housekeeper of long standing.

'Visiting her daughter, sir. I will be attending Lady Cynthia until Mrs Marsden's return.'

I thought of Hanna Ventura's lament on the transient aspect of help in Palm Beach and concluded that no one was above its bitter sting. My hostess and her friend were in the drawing room seated in brocade wing chairs and looking for all the world like dowager empresses awaiting a gallant knight to deliver them from ennui. Guess who answered the call?

'You're late,' Lady C scolded as I entered the presence.

Lady Cynthia Horowitz is rude to me only when she is enjoying the company of a live-in protégé. The degree of her rudeness depends on the virility of her mate. Judging from her tone this afternoon, I would rate Buzz a seven out of ten. When the lady is footloose and on the make, I am the object of her affection.

'It's just three,' I countered.

'I was early,' Desdemona Darling intervened. 'You are Archy McNally. I like a man who's not timid about wearing lavender shoes. It says he's all male. The gay men in Hollywood wear army boots. I'm Desdemona Darling.'

The Golden Girl had retained her beautiful face, if not her figure. Her hair was as white as snow, her eyes a vivid blue, her complexion a flawless pink and, thanks to the excess weight, as smooth as fine porcelain. She wore a black muumuu which covered her from neck to ankle and no doubt concealed a multitude of sins. I don't like to admit it but, as a perennial fan of the silver screen, I was awed just being in the same room with her.

Lady C, on the other hand, had retained her perfect figure as well as her ugly face. Her droopy nose and the upward tilt of her chin always seemed in danger of meeting to render her speechless. Both women, I recalled, had had six husbands each, turning marriage into a cottage industry from which they were both still drawing handsome dividends.

As I compared these septuagenarians of fame and fortune, and for reasons best known to Herr Freud,

I could not help thinking of an obscure Tennessee Williams short story entitled *The Resemblance Between a Violin Case and a Coffin*.

'Pull up a chair, lad,' Lady C ordered, rather than invited. 'I'm not offering drinks. It's too early. And I assume by this time you've already had lunch.'

'I don't want a drink and I've already had lunch because I was told you wouldn't be serving.'

'Ha,' Desdemona said with great delight. 'That's telling her. You were right, Cynthia, he's just what we need.'

Need? What did that mean? To nip any bit of nonsense in the bud I declared, 'I'm not for hire, Ms Darling.'

'Please, call me DeeDee.'

'We don't want to hire you, lad. We expect you to volunteer,' Lady C said.

'In this world, Lady Cynthia, there are no victims, there are only volunteers.'

'Ha,' Desdemona Darling let one out again. 'I like this guy. And the fact that his grandfather agrees with our choice makes it clear that we picked a winner.'

What goes around, comes around, and what was coming around was Serge Ouspenskaya. I could feel it up and down my spine. 'My grandfather is dead,' I told DeeDee.

'I know he's dead,' DeeDee said. 'If he was alive I wouldn't trust him as far as I could throw him. I never worked burlesque but I dated a few of the comics in my day and you're safer feasting with panthers, Archy, believe me.'

The expression was not original, but having been fed lines by scriptwriters and press agents all her adult life, it was only natural that a few should creep into her conversation from time to time. 'Has this got something to do with what the psychic, Serge Ouspenskaya, said to me at the Tremaines' Monday night?' I asked. When dealing with Lady C, I have learned to go for the jugular. It saves a lot of time.

'It has everything to do with that,' Lady C answered. 'Do you remember what he said to you?'

'Your grandfather, that is, not Mr Ouspenskaya,' DeeDee interpolated.

DeeDee's comment left no room for doubt that she and Lady C firmly believed Freddy spoke through Ouspenskaya and not, as I believed, that Ouspenskaya spoke for himself regardless of who he claimed was doing the talking. I had no choice but to go along with the charade – for now. 'He said my parents were in the process of choosing a cruise ship for a proposed vacation. He also said he had played the Oakley Theater, now called the Lake Worth Playhouse, in 1924.'

'That's it,' Lady C cried. 'The Lake Worth Playhouse.'

'If you're referring to the community theater's production of *Arsenic and Old Lace*, I knew about it before the night of the sitting.'

Lady C jumped on that. 'Who told you?' she demanded, no doubt hoping to catch Connie Garcia at betraying a confidence.

'A contact,' I said, 'who told me on the promise of anonymity.' I delivered the line in the manner of a Hollywood lawyer which seemed to please DeeDee. To take the heat off Connie I added, 'And your protégé, Buzz Carr, told me you had engaged the Lake Worth Playhouse for the run of the play. It was the night he took on Fitz as his leading lady and Binky Watrous as stage manager. Buzz has a big mouth, in case you don't know it.'

'I hear he's got a big everything,' DeeDee bellowed with glee. Strange. On the screen she had a voice that could lull a babe in arms to sleep. One never knows, does one?

'Shut up, DeeDee,' Lady C snapped at her buddy.

My, my. It appeared these two old-timers gossiped about more than just old times.

'Mr Ouspenskaya said something else to you, Archy. Think. What was it?' DeeDee prompted.

I had been thinking ever since both father and Hanna Ventura told me Ouspenskaya had said something no one could possibly know, with the exception of Desdemona Darling and her pal, Lady Cynthia. I presumed I was about to find out what that was. 'Sorry, but I don't recall what else he said.'

DeeDee dug into the pocket of her muumuu and came up with a piece of notepaper. Holding it at arm's length, she read, '"You won't be the first McNally on the bill there." That's what he said, Archy. "You won't be the first McNally on the bill there." Now do you recall it?'

In fact I did. However, it was so inane a statement I had simply passed it off as an extra added attraction of Ouspenskaya's act. Why it had Desdemona Darling so riled up, I had no idea. 'It means nothing to me,' I told her.

'On the contrary, lad. It means everything. You see . . .' This was as far as Lady C got before DeeDee cut her off.

'Let me tell him, Cynthia.'

Lady C shot DeeDee a menacing look but clammed up. DeeDee was too excited to notice, not that she would care if she had, and continued, 'What she means is, we have decided to ask you to direct *Arsenic and Old Lace* at the Lake Worth Playhouse.'

Of all the *meshuga* ideas I have ever heard this one took the prize. 'You've got to be kidding?' The banality of that retort is an indication of my dismay.

'A little birdie told me you were involved with the drama society at Yale University,' DeeDee cajoled.

The little birdie in the other chair must have gotten that piece of information from Connie. I was, briefly, a member of Yale's drama society. Everything I did at Yale was brief due to the brevity of my stay in New Haven. What I did while a member of that group was recite Cole Porter's 'Miss Otis Regrets' to loud applause and fair notices. But direct? This was madness.

'Now do you understand why we're so excited?' DeeDee exclaimed.

'I hate to be a party pooper, but I have no idea why

you're excited nor do I have any intention of directing anything more than a stiff bourbon and branch water to my parched lips. Good day, ladies.'

'Oh, cool your heels and get back in your seat,' Lady C commanded. 'I'll ring for what's-her-name and get you something to drink.' She yanked on a bellpull hanging from the wall near her chair and I imagined what's-her-name in the kitchen, enjoying a cup of coffee and a smoke, leaping to her feet.

'I don't think you get the full significance of all this, Archy,' DeeDee told me.

'No, ma'am, I don't.'

What's-her-name appeared and Lady C ordered her to bring us a pitcher of papaya juice, ice and glasses. I wasn't going to get an eye-opener from the old shrew and she wasn't going to make a director out of me. I loathe papaya juice.

'What time was your sitting with Mr Ouspenskaya?' DeeDee asked me.

'I believe he arrived at ten.'

'That's what Penny told us,' Lady C commented.

'Why would I lie?' I questioned.

'Quiet, lad, and listen,' Lady C cautioned.

'Ten,' DeeDee repeated. 'So you sat at ten-fifteen, ten-twenty?'

'Correct.'

DeeDee looked as if she were about to explode which, given her size, could start World War Three. On Monday night I had dinner with Cynthia, right here. We discussed the play and Cynthia said she wasn't happy with the man who had been directing at the community theater. As you might know, Cynthia is the new Creative Director and there are those who resent her intrusion into what they consider their personal company. Nonsense. It's a community theater, not an Actor's Equity ensemble. But you know how people are?'

I sure do. Especially when they've been invaded by the likes of Lady Cynthia Horowitz.

'Cynthia thought, and I agreed, that it would be best to bring in all new blood to revitalize the group. You know, out with the old, in with the new.'

Conquer and divide was a decree of Lady C as well as that of the early Romans. After conquering her six husbands she separated them from their money.

'People like Buzz Carr and Fitz Fitzwilliams,' DeeDee continued. 'Isn't Fitz a beauty? You know I almost got the ingenue role opposite Cary Grant in the film version but it went to what's-her-name?'

'Priscilla Lane,' I informed her as our what's-her-name arrived with the papaya.

'Yes,' DeeDee said, 'Prissy Lane of the Lane sisters. There were hordes of them.'

'Five, I believe,' I told her.

'And five too many,' DeeDee proclaimed, unkindly.

'You are straying, DeeDee,' Lady C said, pouring out the juice.

'Where was I?'

'Out with the old, in with the new,' I reminded her.

'Yes. After dinner – that would be about nine, right, Cynthia? – we came in here and . . .'

'And decided to ask you to direct,' Lady C finished. 'An hour later Mr Ouspenskaya told you, via your grandfather, that you would be appearing on the bill at the Lake Worth Playhouse.'

'We did not leave this room until midnight and we did not discuss our choice of you for director with anyone,' DeeDee exploded, vocally. 'He's for real. Mr Ouspenskaya is for real. Cynthia and I are proof of that.'

'Can you doubt it, Archy?' Lady C asked.

What could I say? Hanna Ventura's diamond clip was on the dress and Archy was destined to be on the playbill.

'You are being summoned from the grave,' DeeDee reminded me.

I summed up the situation in less time than it took what's-her-name to pass around the papaya. Richard Holmes had hired me to discredit Serge Ouspenskaya because Holmes believed the psychic was bamboozling Holmes's wife, Desdemona Darling.

Now, Desdemona Darling was asking me to direct her in a show and she believed her choice of director was sanctioned by Ouspenskaya's prophecy. If I accepted the job I would be fulfilling the prophecy, validating Ouspenskaya and betraying my client. If I declined, I would be banished by Desdemona and Lady Cynthia who, along with the ladies who lunch, were my most viable links to the psychic. And, more important, I would lose the opportunity of getting to know Desdemona and perhaps learn more about the infamous one-reeler and the man who shot it.

To be their director or not to be their director: that was the question. To suffer the slings and arrows of the husband or the wife: that was the choice. It was pure folly but – to direct the legendary Desdemona Darling in what might very well be her last public appearance – what a way to go!

'I'll do it,' I heard myself say.

'Of course you will, lad,' Lady C said.

'Cynthia, this juice will give me a sour stomach. It needs a good shot of rum to cut the acid,' DeeDee complained.

Rum and papaya juice? I knew immediately I had made the wrong choice.

Reluctantly Lady C had the girl fetch a bottle of rum and DeeDee introduced a dollop to each of our glasses. 'To you, Archy,' she said, raising her drink.

I took the requisite sip and to DeeDee's credit must say it improved the taste of the papaya. 'We should be doing this with elderberry wine,' I noted.

DeeDee beamed. 'You see. He knows everything.'

'What she means,' Lady C said, 'is that as soon as the cast is set I'm giving a reception for the whole company and the press and serving elderberry wine. I'm going to put the Palm Beach Community Theater on the map, lad.'

I had taken it for granted that Desdemona Darling, the star, would portray the lead spinster, Abby Brewster, played by the grand character actress Josephine Hull in the original Broadway production as well as on the screen. Buzz would play their good nephew, Mortimer, and Fitz his fiancée, Elaine Harper. The only other major parts were the second spinster sister, Martha, and the evil nephew, Jonathan.

Playing the director, I asked, 'What roles are still open?'

'The other spinster,' DeeDee answered, 'but we have a few potentials in the wings.'

'And the evil nephew, Jonathan?' I pressed on.

'You're familiar with the play.' DeeDee was impressed. 'You're going to do just fine, Archy.'

'Phil Meecham has applied for the role of Jonathan,' Lady C said with little enthusiasm for Phil's community spirit.

'You know, the guy Buzz used to live with,' DeeDee exclaimed.

'Shut up, DeeDee,' Lady C again castigated her friend.

Let me see. Desdemona Darling had agreed to take part in amateur night after meeting Buzz. I was certain Meecham had applied for the role to be near Buzz and talk him into coming back aboard the yacht. The way Fitz had eyed Buzz at Ta-Boo' made it clear she had joined the caravan because she wanted to be Buzz's leading lady on and off the stage. What a merry little company this was going to be. No wonder Lady C was nervous.

'The other minor roles are all cast except for the old

man the sisters almost murder. Any ideas, Archy?
DeeDee asked her director.

'I'll think about it,' I said, fretting that I had mor
to think about than I cared to think about.

9

arrived back at our castle in time for my swim, a quick shower and to dress for my date with Kate Mulligan. The events of the day were so portentous and the amount of information being processed through my brain so momentous I feared I would short-circuit before my debut at the Lake Worth Playhouse.

Therefore, in the interest of self-preservation, I pulled the plug that connected me with the sublime and hooked myself up to the ridiculous. In the words of the tune-smith Johnny Mercer, I was determined to accentuate the positive and eliminate the negative. To this end I decided to impress Kate with my sartorial splendor. I selected a dove-gray suit of summer flannel, a blue-and-white french-cuffed shirt and a silk cravat in matching navy entwined in a Windsor knot. I shod myself in a pair of black wingtips and was ready to step out with my baby when the phone rang.

'Archy here.'

'Lolly here.'

I almost dropped the instrument. 'Lolly Pops?'

'No, Archy, Lolly Spindrift, but thanks to you there'
a rumor going around that I was named after you
grandmother.'

'The lady is not my grandmother and anything
appearing in print to the contrary will be dealt with
legally.'

'Touchy, touchy. I'm calling to say congrats on you
appointment as director of our community theater.
couldn't wish it on a nicer guy.'

Did I detect a tad of malice in the seemingly friendly
gesture? I did, and it meant Lolly wanted the job fo
himself. 'So the news is already out.'

'Lady Cynthia called me the minute you left her and
told me everything, including the delicious fact tha
Desdemona Darling herself will be the show's sta
Of course I knew it ages ago, thanks to Buzz Carr'
nonstop babbling about his debut, but I refrained
from using it until Lady Cynthia made the forma
announcement. She doesn't like to be upstaged.
pass this on as a cautionary measure to the nev
director.'

'Tell it to Buzz,' I said, wondering what a deliciou
fact tasted like. 'I intend to keep a low profile. Yo
know your pal Phil Meecham is going to read for th
role of the evil nephew.'

'Typecasting, Archy, believe me.'

This meant Lol was not speaking to Phil, a cir
cumstance that occurred with the regularity of ou
ocean's tides.

'Desdemona Darling lending her name and talent t

126

he community theater makes this year's production
ront page news. Sorry I can't say the same for your
ddition to the crew, old boy.'

'Fools' names like fools' faces often appear in public
places – like gossip columns.'

'Can I quote you, Archy?'

'Only if you attribute it to Mr Anonymous.'

'Do you know Desdemona Darling married at least
hree of her directors? Careful, Archy, this gig might
ost you your independence, if not your virginity.'

'Desdemona is now a married woman,' I said.

'That never stopped her before, Archy. Ta, ta.'

'Before you ring off can you tell me in twenty-five
words or less what you know about Serge Ouspenskaya?'

'I could write volumes on the man. I met him at
Lady Cynthia's "who-done-it," where he selected me
s the victim.'

I wonder why? I pondered.

'He also named the murderer and was right on
oth counts. Have you heard about Hanna Ventura's
liamond clip?'

'I have.'

'There have been rumors of other amazing incidents
ttributed to Ouspenskaya but nothing as exciting
s Hanna's clip until he called up your grandfather
nd predicted your involvement with the community
heater, which has come to pass.'

'Lady C is already spreading the word,' I said.

'Is she ever. And can you blame her? Between
Ouspenskaya's prediction and Desdemona Darling's

appearance, she's going to have the SRO notice posted for the run of the show.'

'What do you think of Ouspenskaya, Lol?'

'I think he makes good copy and that's what pays the rent and gets me invited to dinner parties six nights out of seven. What's your interest, Archy?'

'Nothing special. He seemed to focus right in on me at the Tremaines' and I'm curious to know why. I also hear he's very thick with Desdemona Darling and Lady C.'

'You suspect collusion between your creative director your star and the psychic?'

'Drop your pen, Lol. Like I said, I'm only curious.'

'But you'll keep me posted?'

'Only if you promise to do the same, Lol.'

'Oh, I will. Ta, ta, Archy.'

A hint of scandal dropped into Lolly Spindrift's ear was like depositing money in an interest-bearing account and with a nemesis like Ouspenskaya I needed all the help I could get.

Rather than face father with the complicated news of my involvement in the community theater, I popped into the kitchen and told Ursi to inform the pater and mother that I had a date and would see them anon. The stars were just about to show themselves when I hopped into my Miata and the moon was rising over the ocean. I took this to mean the gods were smiling down on my evening with Kate Mulligan.

Her pad was in a condo complex of two-story garden

apartments, with mini-balconies in the rear overlooking a pool and tennis courts. A cookie-cutter Florida establishment.

Having not been told what to wear, she opted for a knee-length black slip-style skirt, a satiny white blouse with a V-neck of just the right depth and strappy black sandals with a wedge heel. All in all, not bad.

'Don't you look spiffy,' she welcomed me.

'Not as spiffy as you.'

'I couldn't decide between chaps or a serape so I settled for the basics,' she said.

'Good choice. I like your place,' I lied. It had all the charm of a Holiday Inn.

'It needs work to make it a home. I haven't had a chance to put my stamp on it. It came furnished with the basics and cries out for tchotchkes.'

The 'basics' were items of furniture once referred to as 'Danish Modern,' which I doubt any thinking Dane ever bought into. 'A few tchotchkes are fine. More than that and it becomes a secondhand emporium,' I advised. 'How long have you been here? Palm Beach, that is, not the apartment.'

'A few months in both places.'

She didn't offer to say where she had come from and I thought it rude to ask too many questions too soon. 'Do you feel like taking a bit of a ride? The restaurant I have in mind is in Fort Lauderdale.'

'If you promise to put the top down on the Miata.'

'Oh, it is, and I intend to keep it that way.'

'I'm sorry I can't offer you a drink other than a glass of the designer water I have in the fridge. I haven't had a chance to stock the place for entertaining.'

'I'm doing the entertaining tonight, Kate. Grab a shawl, it'll be breezy driving down the coast.' She added a head scarf to keep her hair in place – very Grace Kelly – and we were off on our first date.

One of the perks of a long drive before dining with a stranger is that by the time you arrive, you're old friends. Without asking, I learned that Kate Mulligan was born in New York, New York, did time, as she called it, in Las Vegas working as a show-girl (with those legs I could believe it) and 'ended up a magician's assistant in a lounge act when they kicked me out of the chorus for the heinous crime of growing old.'

'That was their loss.' In the early evening light, with the scarf framing her oval face and a complexion that needed nothing more than a touch of lipstick, she was the embodiment of a sexy lady in her prime.

'Why thank you, kind sir. How gallant.'

'Did the magician saw you in half?'

'No, he married me. Then he sawed me in half.'

That needed no response so for the next few miles we drove in silence. I was basking in the pleasure of speeding along the A1A with the top down on the kind of night featured in *Moon over Miami*, and if the lady next to me wasn't Betty Grable, you couldn't prove it by her legs.

When the silence became more intrusive than serene, I asked, 'When did you get interested in gardening?'

She laughed and turned to me. 'Cat and mouse, Archy?'

It was the response I was hoping for. Kate Mulligan did not disappoint. 'You don't know a damn thing about gardening,' I amended my question.

'I know any respectable garden needs a little sun and a little water to survive.'

'And with that Temporarily Yours took you on?'

'Give me a break, Archy. I knew you were on to me when you told me how you noticed my missing wedding ring. I figured you must have seen the label on that big plant as clearly as I had.'

'Not that day. I knew my mother usually labeled her plants so I went back to the greenhouse the next morning to have a peek. But still, you couldn't have known it was an Eyelash if it wasn't labeled.'

'Now what makes you so sure I couldn't?'

'Las Vegas chorus lines and lounge acts. They don't add up to Mary, Mary, quite contrary, how does your garden grow.'

'I needed the job,' she stated. 'Temporarily Yours advertised and I applied, but there didn't seem to be any openings for middle-aged chorines or magician's assistants. I can type with two fingers but I discovered that the typewriter is hardly a high-tech piece of office equipment these days. I don't know a word processor from a toaster oven and the only computer I'm familiar with is an adding machine.

In their listing of job titles I spotted Gardeners and
Gardener Helpers . . .'

'And you told them that gardens need sun and water
and they took you on. Remarkable.'

'Okay, I lied a little.'

'How little?'

'I told them I worked for the botanical gardens in
Las Vegas.'

'Las Vegas doesn't have botanical gardens.'

'I know that and you know that, but Temporarily
Yours doesn't know that.'

She started to laugh and it proved infectious. I went
along with the joke, if you could call it that. 'Are you
going to report me?' she said, placing her hand gently
on my thigh.

'No. My mother likes you.' Not to mention my
thigh.

'She's lovely, Archy. And she's so particular about
her begonias she won't let me do anything but watch
her work. All I do is make notes to follow when she's
gone. But trust me, I'm a quick study.'

'I'll bet you are.'

Of course there was a lot still unexplained. For
instance, the new VW and the condo. She might have
gotten a cash settlement from the magician but her
pay at Temporarily Yours wouldn't cover the upkeep
of either the pad or the car. I didn't press the issue
because I liked the lady and didn't want to give
the impression I was moonlighting for the Interna
Revenue Service. She had guts. She wasn't afraid to

dirty her hands, literally, to make an honest living and if she had to tell a few lies along the way, well, that's sometimes what makes the world go 'round. And, mother liked her. So did Archy.

The restaurant wasn't the Waldorf but neither was it a Taco Bell. The hostess seated us at a corner table and presented us with menus before taking our drink order. Kate went for a margarita and I went along to keep her company. They arrived in stem glasses large enough to hold a mama goldfish.

'Your health,' Kate toasted.

'Skoal,' I responded.

'Perfect,' she said, after taking a dainty sip. 'And what a lovely place. Do you come here often?'

'Only when I crave heartburn.'

'Are you ever serious, Archy?'

'Only when I crave heartburn.'

Our waiter was more Tex than Mex and he told us the evening's special was a vodka-basted loin of pork in an ancho-lime crust, accompanied by a black bean tortilla topped with a pineapple salsa. 'Hot?' I asked.

'Is the Pope Catholic?' he answered. Kate liked that one.

She turned down the vodka-basted pork on the grounds that it might clash with the margarita. I approved of her reasoning. She went for a shrimp and crab fajita in a creole sauce that came with sautéed onions and peppers.

I ordered the jambalaya along with black beans in

aninflammatorysauce. For starterswesampledthebasic chili pot, which rendered our stomachs impervious to what followed.

'What would you like with your entrées?' our waiter asked as we sampled the chili.

'How about a fire extinguisher?'

Ignoring my wit, he proffered a wine list. As I perused it Kate said, 'Let's go all the way and have the sangria.'

I winced. Jug wine loaded with fruit and ice cubes. I would lose my sommelier palate but the thought of munching on an ice cube between the chili and the jambalaya made me throw caution to the wind and I went along with the sangria. Besides, I like a lady who suggests going all the way.

We ate *con gusto* and somewhere along the way Kate asked me what I did for a living. 'A little bit of this and a little bit of that,' I told her.

'You're not a lawyer?'

'No. Father is the lawyer at McNally and Son. Archy gathers information and assists in cases where the law needs a helping hand.'

'You're a shamus,' she exclaimed.

'My dear girl, you've tarried too long in the desert sun.'

But Kate was all smiles and fluttering eyelashes. 'I think it's thrilling. Do you carry a gun?'

I could have answered that one with a famous, or infamous depending on your scruples, Mae West line but thought it best to leave the *caliente* in the sauce and

134

out of the conversation. 'If I did I would probably end up shooting myself in the foot.'

Looking at me with a mixture of awe and fascination, Kate said, 'I still think it's exciting. I've never dated a detective before tonight. Are you working on a case now?'

'Of course. The case of the Gardener's Assistant. Very potent stuff. Missing wedding bands, magicians, begonias and botanical gardens flourishing in the desert.'

'Oh, be serious. Are you?'

'Nothing I can talk about, I'm afraid.' So why didn't I practice what I preached? Because – a loaf of bread, a jug of wine, a beautiful woman and – Archy, the fool. Tell me, Kate, in the realm of show biz do psychics fall into the same category as magicians?'

With her fork in midair she gave this a moment's thought.

'Not really. You see, magicians amaze their audience while defying them to guess how they pulled the rabbit out of the hat. What I mean is, magicians don't pretend to be miracle workers, including the famous Houdini.'

'And psychics do,' I put in.

Kate nodded. 'Right. They want you to believe they have the gift, as some of them refer to their psychic powers. If they don't have the gift, they're labeled fakes. Magicians don't have that problem. Everyone knows they're tricksters.'

As the bus person cleared the table our waiter

recited the dessert list. Stomach pumps not being among the offerings, we settled for coffee.

'Did you know any psychics in Las Vegas, Kate?'

'When you work a lounge act in Vegas, you meet all kinds. Yes, I knew several.'

'Any you believed were the genuine article?'

Kate put a drop of cream into the coffee our waiter had placed in front of us – no sugar – and as she stirred the brew she said, 'I'll put it this way, Archy. In Las Vegas, the seer's stock in trade is promising to make you rich. You know, the winning lottery numbers, blackjack, roulette, the sports pools and even faro, which, as I'm sure you know, requires as much skill as learning to chew gum. If these guys know all the answers, why are they hitting on the rubes for peanuts when they could be cashing in their own chips?'

Smart lady, Kate Mulligan.

The ride up the coast was as enchanting as the ride down. Kate turned on the radio and my easy listening station delivered Nat King Cole crooning 'It's Only a Paper Moon.' Kate and I joined the King and when done I exclaimed, 'You knew all the words.'

'It's my kind of music,' Kate informed me. And I was beginning to believe Kate was my kind of girl.

'If I had the necessary components I would invite you in for a drink,' she said, as we entered West Palm.

'I could pick up a bottle of brandy if you could supply the snifters.'

'I think brandy snifters are some of the few items I

salvaged from my trousseau. But I never heard of a P.I.
who drank brandy. Isn't two fingers of bourbon their
drink of choice?'

'You're thinking of Sam Spade. I'm Archy McNally.'

'I know. And isn't that nice.'

The snifters were real crystal and I lit my first
English Oval of the day to celebrate the fact. 'You
don't mind?' I asked Kate.

'No, go right ahead. I gave them up years ago.'

'So did I.'

She put Frank Sinatra on the CD player and we
danced cheek to cheek until Kate kicked off her pumps
and rested her head against my chest. I removed my
jacket – Frank's lyrics encourage this sort of behavior
– and when we had removed all our inhibitions Frank
told us that music leads the way to romance. And he
was right.

10

I tore myself away from Kate after midnight but before dawn. Hobo elected not to leave his canine abode when I pulled into our driveway. Our sentry was a heavy sleeper. All was dark in the Olsons' apartment over the garage and ditto our house. Archy had to find his way to his third-floor aerie by touch, a feat I had performed too many times to count.

Mark Twain wrote of man's inhumanity to man. As I lay sleepless in the eerie predawn light, guilt had me contemplating man's inhumanity to women. Namely, Consuela Garcia. To soothe my febrile brow I fingered my worry beads to the mantra that I had made no promises to Connie and was true to her in my fashion. Unfortunately, it was not a fashion that suited Connie. This seemed to prove, to me at least, that open relationships work only when the liberated couples are endowed with an abundance of forgiveness and a paucity of guilt.

Connie, I fear, had exhausted her supply of forgiveness, while the older I got the less I dallied. This should have fostered a period of détente between us but all it had me doing was counting the years instead of sheep. Number forty was on the horizon along with the new day and I still subscribed to Cole Porter's certainty that 'raising an heir could never compare with raising a little cain.'

I gather my rosebuds while I may and when I feel the sting of a thorn I remind myself that the trick of life is learning to live with our ills, not trying to cure them. (Thank you, A. Gide.) And if I'm a bit of a fop, well – Archy, the Scarlet Pimpernel of Palm Beach. With that I fell into a dreamless sleep and awoke bright-eyed and bushy-tailed about the time the nine-to-fivers were taking their first coffee break.

Ursi asked me if I would be agreeable to a scrambled omelette and I told her there was very little in the way of food to which I was not agreeable and especially so to a *l'omelette brouillée*, as the French call this manner of preparing eggs. I inquired as to whether a Brie filling was possible. It was, praise be.

My father had left for the office and as Ursi broke eggs into a bowl she told me Jamie was off with mother and Kate Mulligan in search of the perfect begonia. In lieu of orange juice I was presented with half a grapefruit which I literally dug into, feeling a bit of relief at not having to face Kate in the bright light of day. I knew there had to be a morning after, but it didn't have to be the very next morning.

'Late night,' Ursi stated rather than asked.

'Sometime after midnight,' I said. 'Rye toast please,

Ursi. I feel a health binge coming on.'

'Three hours after midnight,' she proclaimed, scrambling the eggs to a perfect consistency before folding them over the Brie.

'How do you know?'

'I heard you.'

'Not even Hobo heard me,' I said.

'I think Hobo is deaf,' Ursi proclaimed, moving the omelette from pan to plate.

Great. We now had a former chorus girl and magician's assistant tending our garden and a deaf watchdog guarding our home. I would speak to father about increasing our insurance coverage. As Ursi poured my coffee I sampled the omelette. The dear woman had added bits of diced ham to the Brie. Superb.

When I arrived at the garage beneath the McNally Building, Herb returned my wave with his forefinger pointing at the ceiling. This did not mean that he was mimicking the Statue of Liberty but that he had been alerted by Mrs Trelawney to tell me to report directly to our president and CEO upon my arrival. In Monopoly-speak it meant go directly to jail, do not pass Go, do not collect two hundred dollars.

Before ascending I asked Herb if he had ever done any acting.

'You mean like Marlon Brando, Archy?'

'Yes. Or even Ramón Novarro.'

'As a matter of fact, I did, once.'

Well. This was interesting. I may have found our

Mr Gibbs, as I believe the old potential victim of the Brewster sisters is called. 'When was that?'

'In the sixth grade, I think it was. I had one line to recite in the class play.'

'And how did you do, Herb?'

'I was so scared, I upchucked all over the stage. Why do you want to know?'

'No particular reason, Herb. No particular reason.'

Upstairs, Mrs Trelawney warned me that Mr Richard Holmes was with father and had been with him since nine o'clock – waiting for me. This did not bode well. When I entered father's office I found Mr Holmes pacing the floor and father tugging at his mustache.

'Finally!' Mr Holmes exploded. 'Where the hell have you been?'

Where I had been was none of his business, so I had no qualms in answering, 'Keeping Ouspenskaya's office under surveillance. I want to know what time he arrives, when he leaves and where he goes when he leaves. Also, I'm interested in learning if any familiar faces visit him on a regular basis. Informants, if you know what I mean.'

This stopped Holmes's pacing and father's tugging. Did I even detect a trace of a smile on the master's lips?

'It's worse than ever, Archy,' Holmes complained. 'DeeDee is convinced that Ouspenskaya is for real, thanks to you.'

'I can hardly be held accountable for one of Ouspenskaya's predictions, sir. In fact I attended the séance on your behalf. The man said some remarkable things, all directed at me, which makes me believe he knows you put me on his tail.'

'How is that possible?' Holmes demanded.

'That's what I'm trying to learn, sir.'

'And now you've got yourself involved in this damn show. I hope you're not doing it on my time, young man.'

I glanced at father. The smile had been replaced by a frown. Thanks to his roots and his pomposity father had an aversion to show business as either a career or avocation. As much for him as for my client, I carefully explained why I had accepted the position of director for the community theater, fulfilling Ouspenskaya's prophecy. 'I will be working with your wife, sir, and in a position to gain her confidence without showing our hand. Through her I can become a member of Ouspenskaya's inner circle and what better place to learn where the guy is coming from?'

'But you think he's on to you,' Holmes insisted.

'I know he is.'

'He'll be on his guard.'

'I'm sure he will be. But his ego is the size of an elephant's behind and he won't be able to resist dazzling me with his cleverness. The more risks he takes, the greater the chance of his tripping over himself. When he does, I'll be there to watch him fall.'

Holmes's jowls quivered like jelly on a plate but I was sure he was starting to see the wisdom of my maneuver. 'You've seen the guy in action. What's your take on him, Archy?'

'I was impressed. Did father tell you about the cruise ships?'

'I did,' father said.

'How does he do it, Archy?' Holmes asked again.

'There are tricks to every trade, sir. But tell me, if Mrs Holmes is convinced of Ouspenskaya's powers, how does she explain the fact that he has not located that can of film and the guy who owns it?'

With a gesture of despair Holmes began, 'He claims to be the radio, not the broadcaster, so he has no control over what comes through.'

I was familiar with the routine, which seemed to be Ouspenskaya's standard megillah.

'But get this, Archy,' Holmes continued, 'like the con artist Ouspenskaya is, he has the brass to blame his failure on DeeDee.'

The radio blaming the listener for what was being broadcast? Here was a turn of the screw worthy of a plot by Henry James. 'What's his rationale, sir?'

'Ouspenskaya says that DeeDee is so fearful of the film being made public and so intimidated by the guy who sends the letters that she is subconsciously denying their existence. Meaning, during the sittings she's tuning them out instead of in.'

'So he dabbles in psychoanalysis on the side,' I concluded.

'Archy,' Holmes said, 'when DeeDee tells me what some of the ladies discuss with Ouspenskaya, I blush. It's embarrassing.'

Being familiar with the distaff half of Palm Beach's

upper crust, I could believe this. 'Due to Mrs Holmes's subconscious reluctance to tune in to her blackmailer,' I observed, 'I guess Ouspenskaya has to try and try again. Correct?'

'Right,' Holmes concurred. 'At five hundred bucks a pop. Now do you see why I want this guy stopped?' As if overburdened by this financial loss, Holmes sank into father's visitor's chair.

'Mr Holmes, you told us that Ouspenskaya knew what your wife was seeking before she told him. Does he know the nature of that short film?'

'I may have misled you on that one, Archy,' the man confessed. 'What he said was, "You are seeking something related to your career in Hollywood." I think that's how it went.'

How ingenuous people are, and especially actors. Ouspenskaya may have heard rumors of Darling's one-reeler and had come up with a sentence that said nothing and everything at the same time. 'Have you ever attended a séance, or sitting, as Ouspenskaya calls his radio show?' I asked Holmes.

'Me?' Holmes shouted. 'Never. I ain't that balmy.' Giving this some thought, he recanted, 'Not yet, anyway.'

'Have you ever met him?' father asked, no doubt anticipating where this was leading.

'Several times,' Holmes told us, 'and I wasn't shy about expressing my views on psychic phenomena.'

And people wonder how practicing psychics know

what they do. We tell them, that's how. When I turned up at the Tremaines, Ouspenskaya didn't have to consult his tarot cards to tell him who had sent me. Holmes was the psychic's number-one critic, but Holmes's wife was Ouspenskaya's number-one promoter. The self-styled seer had to sustain a very delicate balance to keep one at bay and the other happy, and it was my guess that Serge Ouspenskaya welcomed the challenge.

Looking at his watch, Holmes said, 'I have to go. I'm picking up DeeDee at Cynthia's – say, is that Cynthia really a lady?'

'With a capital L,' I told him. 'Her last husband was knighted for devoting his life to watching beetles mate.'

Holmes's jowls did a freeze. 'You've got to be kidding.'

'Afraid not, sir.'

'And I thought all the kooks were in southern California.' Dressed in yellow linen slacks and a lime-green blazer, Richard Holmes had brought a touch of southern California to Florida's east coast. 'Well, keep me posted, Archy, and I didn't mean to hassle you. In my business we go for the kill and tie up the loose ends before the five o'clock whistle blows. Thanks for your time, Prescott.'

If Holmes was referring to pork bellies, I refused to even imagine the killing and tying out of respect for my *l'omelette brouillée*.

Opening the door, the man stopped and turned, saying, 'I almost forgot. There's a cocktail party at my place tonight for everyone involved with that theatrical production. You'll get a call from Cynthia's secretary. Pretty gal, she is.'

'Consuela Garcia,' I informed him.

'Latin! Nothing like a little cha-cha-cha to keep the blood flowing. About seven, Archy. See you.'

When the door finally closed, father breathed a sigh of relief. 'Insipid man,' father said. 'I've had him in here since nine this morning.'

This was the sire's way of telling me I was late but that wasn't the true purpose of his ire. 'Must you get involved with that damn theater group?' he protested. *That* was the true purpose of his ire.

'I'm afraid so, sir. As I explained, I didn't want to make an enemy of both Desdemona Darling and Lady Cynthia by refusing. I want to gain Darling's confidence and, if I may remind you, sir, Lady Cynthia is a very valued client of this firm.'

Father opened his arms and shrugged his shoulders. 'If it has to be, it has to be.' His ceding to the inevitable was based more on Lady Cynthia's lucrative business than on my need to cultivate Desdemona Darling. But I must say, Archy, the more I learn about this Ouspenskaya, the less I like him.'

'Having met him, sir, I agree with you.'

'Richard Holmes is very angry and will do everything in his power to thwart his wife from continuing to consult with the psychic. If one can believe Holmes, it's his money that pays for Desdemona's indulgences. Holmes could cut off the flow, which would result in a great financial loss for Ouspenskaya.'

'Do you think Ouspenskaya will do everything in his power to stop this from happening?'

'What do you think, Archy?'

'I think, sir, that Serge Ouspenskaya is too smart to commit murder, if that's what we're talking about, to retain a client. My hunch is that he'll string Desdemona Darling along as far as he can, for as long as he can. I intend to shorten the distance, the time and his profit by half.'

'I hope you're right, Archy. And may I ask a favor?'

'Of course, sir.'

'Be a competent enough director to appear bright, but inept enough so that you don't get invited back next year.'

'I'll try my best, sir.' I wondered what our lives would be like if Alfred Hitchcock's father had requested a similar favor from his son. For a change of pace, I asked, 'Have you decided what ship you and mother will cruise with?'

'I think we'll go with the *Pearl of the Antilles*,' father announced.

'That was grandfather's recommendation, sir.'

'I'll pretend I didn't hear that, Archy.'

'And I'll pretend I didn't say it, sir. When does she sail?'

'Two weeks. Your mother is very excited and, I admit, so am I. Mother is pleased with the woman the agency sent to oversee her garden. I trust you'll keep an eye on her while we're gone.'

'You have my word, sir.'

'Good. Now I have work to do. We missed you at dinner last night and I assume you'll be out again tonight.'

'Duty calls, but I'll give Desdemona Darling your regards.'

'Please do. By the way, what does she look like these days? Have the years been kind?'

'They've been generous, sir. Let's say that even off the screen Desdemona Darling is still larger than life.'

Joe Anderson was just putting my mail on the desk when I got to my office. 'Hello, Joe. How's it going?'

'It's going and at my age that's all that matters.'

'Have you heard Binky has signed with a temp agency in West Palm?'

'So he told me. And he called this morning to say he got his first assignment at an animal hospital in Delray Beach.'

I could only be thankful that it wasn't a people hospital. Binky would add veterinarian trainee to his long and weary list.

'I expect to see Binky tonight . . .' And a light bulb went off in my head. 'Say, Joe, have you ever acted?'

'Why do you ask?'

'I'm directing at the community theater this season and I need a man your age to . . .'

'*Arsenic and Old Lace*,' Joe said.

'How do you know?'

'It was in Lolly Spindrift's column today. Starring Desdemona Darling. Binky tells me he's the stage manager. I take it you want me for the lonely old codger the spinster sisters try to do in.'

'You know the play?'

'I know the movie. I'm a genuine old codger, Archy. You won't believe this, but I was a child actor in the early days of talkies. I even did a few turns with Mickey McGuire before he made it big as Mickey Rooney.'

I had struck gold. 'How did you end up in this line of work?'

'You know the old show business saw, Archy. One child actor in a thousand makes the transition to adult roles. I was number nine-nine-nine.'

'If you take the role, Joe, you can claim to have done a turn with Desdemona Darling.'

'If I say yes, when do I get to meet her?'

'This evening, at her home for cocktails.'

'You serious?'

I grabbed a pencil and tore a sheet off a note pad and scribbled on it. 'Here's her address on Via Del Lago. Seven this evening. Binky will be there, too. Is that serious enough?'

Joe is tall, painfully thin and a casting director's dream for the role of Mr Gibbs. Score one for Archy. Joe leaned against his mail cart for support. 'I'm going to meet Desdemona Darling,' he chanted.

'In person, Joe.'

'Will she be wearing that pink bathing suit?'

'That would be *stretching* a point, Joe, believe me.'

11

The guests are met, the feast is set: May'st hear the merry din.

But it wasn't the Ancient Mariner who broke up the shindig. It was Archy, resplendent in jodhpurs, riding boots and Stetson and brandishing a megaphone.

Desdemona Darling announced my entrance with a scream that would have knocked Fay Wray off her pins and sent King Kong running for cover. 'Blessed Mother of Maude Adams,' Desdemona cried, 'I thought it was my old buddy, Mr DeMille. You know he wanted me for *Samson and Delilah* but he had to settle for Hedy Lamarr.'

In this evening's formal muumuu – white, appliquéd with iridescent silver and gold spangles – Desdemona could have played the Mount of Olives as well. 'Everyone, everyone,' she went on, waving a martini glass in the air, 'this is our director, Archibald McNally.'

As I took a bow to thunderous applause someone in the sea of faces before me shouted, 'Speech, speech.'

It sounded very much like Connie but before I could digest that startling fact others took up the cry. Could I deny my adoring public? Never.

I raised the megaphone and spoke into it. 'Ladies and gentlemen, tonight marks the first step on our journey to theatrical history.' Applause. 'I will work you harder than you've ever been worked before.' Groans and boos. 'But when you need a shoulder, I'll be there.' Applause. 'I expect you to be on time for rehearsal and to know your lines.' Groans and boos. 'With Desdemona's star to guide us, we ain't got nothing to hit but the heights, so let's all go out there and break a leg.' Great applause and a kiss from the hostess.

'Archy, you're a ham,' DeeDee said. 'Where did you get the outfit?'

'From his closet. It isn't a masquerade, he always dresses this way.' It was indeed Connie, elbowing her way into the conversation.

'Oh, you two know each other,' DeeDee said. 'I'm so glad. Connie is going to be our prompter. I insisted. My memory isn't what it used to be.'

'This is news,' I said to Connie.

'I called you last night to tell you but you weren't home.'

'I was out with Binky, remember?'

'Of course, I forgot. How was the Tex-Mex?'

'Hot.' Now I had to get to Binky before Connie did. I spotted him across the room in deep conversation with Joe Anderson.

I turned to DeeDee. 'Did you meet Joe Anderson, the man I took on for the role of Mr Gibbs?'

DeeDee's still-beautiful face smiled up at me. 'I did and he's a peach. He came with the boy, Binky, who's going to be our stage manager. Joe told me he worked bit parts in films when he was a kid. But that was before my time.'

About five minutes before, I judged. Glancing around the crowded room I saw Fitz talking to Buzz and – was I seeing things? – William Ventura. 'Is that the Ventura boy?' I said, rudely pointing.

'It is,' Connie answered. 'He's playing one of the policemen. Isn't he cute?'

'You should really meet all the cast, Archy,' DeeDee said, 'or as many of them as we have to date, but first I want you to meet my husband. Excuse us, Connie.' DeeDee took my arm.

'I'll amble over and talk to Binky,' Connie said. It sounded dangerously like a threat to me.

'Before you do, Connie, would you check my megaphone. I think I've made my point.'

'And your entrance.' Connie took the cumbersome thing from me.

'Give it to Jorge or put it in one of the bedrooms if you can't find him. Lord knows, I never can,' DeeDee advised her.

The Holmeses' winter rental on Via Del Lago was a generous ranch on a good acre, comfortably if not elaborately furnished. The great room where we were gathered lived up to its name. I could see a portable bar set up at the far end with a bartender officiating and there was a girl in uniform passing around pigs in a blanket and mustard dip.

Jorge must be the houseboy who had let me in and whom I surmised to be of Philippine extraction. Most folks in Palm Beach employed a housekeeper but leave it to the visiting firemen from Hollywood to set up shop with a houseboy in black trousers and a starched white shirt.

'There he is. Richard. Richard,' DeeDee called. 'Come and meet our director, Archy McNally. He's dressed just like Mr DeMille who wanted me for *Samson and Delilah*.' What I had suspected was now evident. Our hostess and star attraction was tipsy.

'Nice to know you, Archy,' Holmes said, extending his hand.

As I reached to take the offered hand a white blob appeared in the corner of my vision and when it came into focus it took the unmistakable form of a turban. Ouspenskaya was standing next to none other than Vance Tremaine and Arnold Turnbolt. Blessed Mother of Maude Adams, indeed. All the usual suspects were gathered in the same place at the same time. This wasn't supposed to happen until the finale and we hadn't even brought up the curtain on Act One. Had DeeDee cast the psychic as the play's lunatic Dr Einstein? That would be too good to be true.

'How do you do, sir,' I said to Holmes, playing my part.

With a sly grin on his moon face, Ouspenskaya was

telling me from across the room that he wasn't fooled
for a moment.

'Grab yourself a drink, Archy,' Holmes invited. 'The
bar is that way.'

'Thank you. It's just what I need.'

'No, DeeDee,' Holmes said, hanging on to his wife's
elbow. 'Archy can find his way and you should circulate.
They've all come to see you, dear.'

'They can hardly miss me,' DeeDee sighed.

On my way to the bar I steered a clear path around
Ouspenskaya, Vance and Arnold; got a peck on the
cheek from Fitz, a slap on the back from Buzz and a
nasty look from William Ventura. I saw Connie, minus
the megaphone, heading for Binky and I beat her to
him by half a minute. 'We had Tex-Mex last night,
Binky. Hello, Joe.'

'We did, Archy? Where?'

Good question. 'That dreadful place near Deerfield
Beach, south of Boca.'

'How was it?' Binky asked.

'I thought it was lousy, but you loved it.'

'What did I have, Archy?'

Connie was upon us. 'Improvise,' I told him.

'What the devil is going on?' Joe pleaded.

'Hello, Binky. How was the Tex-Mex last night?'
Connie plunged right in.

'Archy hated it, but I loved it.'

'It's like a Marx Brothers routine,' Joe observed, but
he seemed to be enjoying the show.

I left Binky to introduce Joe to Connie and continued

my trek to the oasis. The bartender was young and good-looking, so guess who was hanging all over the portable bar. 'Hello, Phil,' I greeted Meecham. 'Lolly says the part of the evil brother was made for you.' I like to play the devil's advocate with Phil and Lolly; it keeps them out of more serious trouble.

'Lolly is fuming because he wanted to direct, so watch your back, Archy. *Et tu Brute*, if you get my meaning. Now what's your poison? This charming young man makes a mean martini. His name is Victor.'

I asked Victor if he stocked Sterling vodka and got a negative response. It was a foolish question seeing as the pâté de maison was mini-franks. I ordered a double bourbon on the rocks with a splash. 'Cheers,' I said, turning to Phil, only Phil was gone and Serge Ouspenskaya had taken his place.

'Cheers, Mr McNally.'

He was holding a champagne flute filled with the bubbly. Now where did he get that? Certainly not from Victor. Did Holmes know the guy was imbibing carbonated wine with the hot dogs, or was Ouspenskaya being fed, as well as watered, differently?

'I see you have taken your grandfather's advice and joined Lady Cynthia's charming group.'

'Let's say I was drafted as opposed to enlisting.'

'How we fulfill our destiny, Mr McNally, is of no consequence. That we do so is all that matters.'

Ouspenskaya talked like the Dalai Lama, looked like Turhan Bey and drank like Diamond Jim Brady. If he wasn't a man for all seasons, who was? I took a good swig of my bourbon, I needed it, before saying, 'And have you joined Lady Cynthia's charming group?'

'Me?'

'Forgive me,' I said. 'I thought this gathering was for active members of our community theater.'

'But it is, and I am here at the request of Mrs Holmes. As an observer, as it were.'

Checking our vibes, no doubt, to determine who stays and who goes. This had to be an all-time first. A clairvoyant as casting director. 'And are you going to predict what the critics will say about us before we take our final bows?'

'Never, Mr McNally. If I predicted success, no one would work very hard. If I forecast failure, no one would work at all. You wouldn't want that, would you?'

I might be the director but Ouspenskaya was making it clear, once again, that he was the puppeteer pulling the strings. I motioned to Victor to freshen my drink. 'I saw you talking to Vance Tremaine and Arnold Turnbolt. Have they joined the community theater this season or are they, too, observing?'

'I think they are part of the group, Mr McNally, but you should know that better than I.'

If Vance and Arnie had volunteered it had more to do with the presence of Fitz and Buzz, respectively, than with a burning passion to serve the community of Palm Beach. Add in DeeDee, Lady C and Phil Meecham and I would have to quell raging hormones as well as stage fright to put this show on the road. I didn't need Ouspenskaya to tell me I should collect my megaphone and go home. Not heeding my own advice, I said, 'I'm the new kid on the block so I think I had better make the rounds and meet my cast and crew.'

Ouspenskaya smiled his best condescending smile and said, 'And I noticed you have already met Mr Richard Holmes.'

The guy was playing me like a trout at the business end of a slippery hook and I decided to end the charade. 'Mr Ouspenskaya, you know damn well Richard Holmes and I met before this evening.'

'Bravo!' He raised his champagne flute just enough to spill a few drops. The sloppy gesture took a little of the bite out of his retort. Maybe the tide was turning in my favor. 'So, we are through with this tiresome artifice and I am pleased. We lay our cards on the table, like the dummy in bridge, and play out our hands. You agree, Mr McNally?'

'And which of us is the dummy, Mr Ouspenskaya?'

'That, my friend, remains to be seen, but the fact that Mr Holmes has hired you to expose me as a charlatan gives you a cutting edge to the title.'

In the interest of propriety I refrained from telling him to go suck a lemon. 'I didn't say Mr Holmes had hired me to do anything.'

'No. I did.'

No one had come up to the bar for a refill and I found this disquieting. There was the steady hum of chatter and the occasional peal of laughter all around us but this didn't stop me from thinking every eye in the room was on us. 'How are you privy to Mr Holmes's private affairs?'

'That's for me to know and you to find out, Mr McNally.'

And Y is a crooked letter. Another childish response. The guy had a turban full of them and they were beginning to wear thin. 'I've taken up too much of your precious time, sir, so if you'll excuse me I'll let you get back to observing. I'm sorry I can't say it's been a pleasure.'

As I moved away from him, Ouspenskaya called, 'Remember my dream of Narcissus, Mr McNally?'

I nodded my response.

'I believe the youth of my vision is with us tonight.'

Another turn of the screw. With a quick glance to the left and right, I whispered, 'In a town like Palm Beach, Mr Ouspenskaya, I wouldn't tell too many people you dream about pretty boys.' It took him a beat to catch my meaning and I moved off just as his tan cheeks began to take on a tinge of crimson.

From this point on DeeDee's cocktail party took on the aspect of a human kaleidoscope as the guests met, mingled, parted and regrouped to the disco beat of a hidden sound system. Fitz, looking like a goddess in a long gauzy white skirt and coordinating tank, told me that she and Buzz had already started rehearsing their lines. I told Fitz to lighten up.

I introduced myself to William Ventura, who wanted

to know if Hanna had told me how the 'guru guy' found her diamond clip. When I told him she had, he said, 'Don't believe a word of it. They had it planned to help his career. She's getting it on with the guy.'

Nice kid.

I moved around the room, shaking hands, getting kissed and avoiding Connie, who had the undivided attention of Richard Holmes. Cha-cha-cha.

'What do you think of Desdemona?' I asked Joe Anderson.

'There's more to her than I remember,' he said with a sly wink, 'but she's still a beauty, Archy.'

At the moment DeeDee was literally hanging on to Buzz as Phil Meecham looked on with a smile on his face that didn't hide the malice in his heart.

'I thought our Creative Director would be here tonight,' Joe was saying.

'Our premier hostess, Lady Cynthia Horowitz, has several aversions, most notably cigar smoke, men who wear pinkie rings and other people's parties. She demands attendance but will not reciprocate, if you see what I mean. But knowing her as I do, I can assure you that she will not be outdone by Desdemona Darling and will give her own gala for the community theater participants in a matter of days.'

'According to Lolly Spindrift, she's an old friend of Desdemona's.'

'Friendly enemies, I would say. You see the hunk DeeDee is charming as we speak? Well, he belongs to Lady Cynthia and she got him from the guy who is shooting daggers at DeeDee.'

Before Joe could reply, Arnie Turnbolt, a little flushed from the green concoction in his glass, joined us and announced, 'I'm playing Dr Einstein, Archy. The role that gets all the laughs. Have you ever heard my imitation of Peter Lorre?'

'No, and I don't want to, Arnie. Let's try to be creative, not imitative.'

'Oh, dear, listen to our director. I think our hostess is in her cups and do you know Fitz and Buzz are rehearsing their love scenes nightly?'

'And no gossip,' I warned him. 'What's Vance doing here?'

'For the record, he's going to take the role of Teddy, the demented nephew. Off the record, he's doing it to keep in close proximity to the gorgeous Fitz. Penny is furious because she wanted the role of the other spinster sister so she could keep an eye on Vance, but Lady C told her the part was spoken for.'

'Really? Who's getting it?'

'You tell me, you're the director.'

Lady Cynthia and Desdemona Darling were running the community theater like two steamrollers on a rampage. The sooner I asserted my authority as director, the better the chances of my surviving this ordeal. Just as I was about to put this to DeeDee the unbelievable sight of Binky Watrous, on his hands and knees, crawling around and between people's legs, caught my eye. 'What in the name . . .' I shouted.

'Oh,' Joe said. 'I forgot to tell you. A young lady lost an earring and Binky is helping her look for it.' As if the sight of Binky on all fours was a precursor of things to come, Joe bid me goodnight with a wave of his hand. 'I'm history, Archy. See you at the office.'

It was now near nine o'clock and the rest of the partygoers looked like they were about to join Binky on the floor. Suddenly, everything seemed to be happening at once and a few days hence, when the laughter had turned to tears, I would try to recall all the little dramas taking place around me, never suspecting at the time that one of them was a prelude to murder.

Joe was saying his goodnight to DeeDee when she suddenly began to list, like the *Titanic* in its final hour. Ouspenskaya rushed to her side but Richard Holmes got there a moment later and confronted the psychic, roughly pushing Ouspenskaya aside and taking charge of his wife. The Ventura boy, watching the episode, was clearly laughing at Ouspenskaya's plight.

Penny Tremaine chose this moment to crash the party and, followed by an angry Jorge, pushed her way through the crowd to get at Vance, who had cornered Fitz.

Phil Meecham was arguing with Buzz Carr and when Arnie stepped in to arbitrate, Meecham shouted something that sounded like, 'Get out of my face, Arnie.'

Connie, with my megaphone, and Binky, without

the girl who had lost an earring, were at my side. 'Are you kids ready to leave?'

'I think that would be wise,' Connie answered. 'I've had my taste of show business for one evening.'

'It's called "tripping the light fantastic,"' I informed Connie.

'Well, before we start tripping over the bodies fantastic, I suggest we get something to eat. If you're not afraid of going to the Pelican in those bloomers and boots, I'll buy you dinner.'

'And I'll tag along, if you don't mind,' Binky said. 'I came with Joe but he left without me.'

'He thought you were going with the girl who lost her earring,' I said.

Digging into his jacket pocket Binky came up with one pearl earring. 'I found it, Archy, but I lost the girl.' It was the story of Binky Watrous's life. Before he got back on his hands and knees to look for the girl, I led them out of the house on Via Del Lago.

It was decided that Binky would go in Connie's car, leaving me alone in my Miata where I lit an English Oval without having to hear one of them say, 'I thought you gave up smoking.' I knew I gave up smoking and didn't have to be reminded of the depressing fact on the rare occasions when I fell off the wagon.

Speaking of wagons, I wondered if my leading lady had a drinking problem or if tonight was the exception to the rule. I didn't want her getting into the elderberry wine during rehearsal so I made a mental note to tell our stage manager to fill the prop decanter with grape juice instead of the real thing.

By Palm Beach standards, DeeDee's party had offered all the components of a rousing success. The hostess got smashed. Her husband fought off a competitor. An irate wife came searching for her wayward husband. The gay boys got into a scrap and a rich kid poked fun at the season's celebrity psychic. As Noël Coward had put it, 'I've been to a marvelous party, and I couldn't have liked it better.'

Ouspenskaya and I had given up the cat-and-mouse routine, which suited me fine but didn't make a hoot of difference in aiding or frustrating my investigation. After my second encounter with the man I still had no idea how he was working his scam – unless he was the real thing, which I doubted. I would have to list in my journal everything Ouspenskaya had told me that he couldn't possibly know and begin in earnest to discover how he knew them. Right now I was anxious to discover what Chef Leroy Pettibone had brewing in his kitchen.

I had no reservations about appearing at the Pelican in my jodhpurs because the club was founded by a group of congenial men, like myself, who believe that there is a little bit of treachery in some of us and a little bit of lechery in the rest of us. Therefore the rules of the house are there are no rules and let he among us who is without sin cast the first stone. The cognoscenti would think I had just come from a polo match and forgot to change, while all others would assume I was a fugitive from the Royal Canadian Mounted Police. Just to play it safe, I left my megaphone in the Miata.

Simon Pettibone was behind the bar, Jasmine was greeting guests, son Leroy was in the kitchen, daughter Priscilla was taking orders, God was in his heaven and all was right with the world. The dining room was hopping and with the exception of a roll of her eyes, Priscilla had no time to comment on my attire as she sat us and handed out the menus.

I stuck to bourbon, Connie stuck to her favorite gimlets and Binky stuck to his beer. We rehashed the party as we drank and when there was nary a person or an occurrence left to rake over the coals, I said to Connie, 'I suppose you will give your lady boss a full account of the evening.'

'Not necessary,' Connie answered. 'By now she's getting a blow-by-blow report of the evening's proceedings.'

'From who, may I ask?'

'From whom,' Connie corrected me. 'Any one of her network of spies. They dish the dirt with Lady C and she keeps them on the A list. It's the supply and demand theory of Palm Beach society.'

I banged the table with my fist, startling Connie and Binky, before exclaiming, 'That's how Ouspenskaya does it. A network of spies. How else?'

'Are you still smarting from that séance, Archy?' Connie goaded me. 'Lolly Pops! It's all over town.'

'I hear everyone is calling Lolly Spindrift, Lolly Pops,' Binky joined in.

'A professional gossip by any other name is still a professional gossip,' I responded.

But I was certain that I had hit upon the answer to the mystery of Serge Ouspenskaya, or rather Connie had, inadvertently to be sure. Out of the mouths of babes, Ouspenskaya had said and how apropos to the moment. A network of spies. That had to be it. The FBI, the CIA, the KGB, big business espionage – it was the key to survival in the modern world and it had to be the key to Ouspenskaya's operation. But how many did he have? Where were they and who where they?

'Binky was telling me about his job on the way over,' Connie said, changing the subject, for which I was grateful. If there were spies about, the less said the soonest mended.

'Tell me, Binky,' I said, 'what are you doing at the animal hospital?'

'I walk the ambulatory patients three times a day.'

'Ambulatory patients?' I couldn't believe my ears. 'You mean the mutts who still have the use of their four legs?'

'They're called patients, Archy, and they have a patients' bill of rights.'

Priscilla rescued us from the depths of fatuous chit-chat with the news that *Caneton à l'Orange* (roast duck with orange sauce to the common folk) was the evening's special and we all went for it. Served alongside were garlic mashed potatoes and buttered asparagus tips. For starters we also agreed on a salad of roast peppers and anchovies with a vinaigrette embellished with herbs, capers and onions.

'You always look so lovely, Pris,' Connie complimented our waitress.

'Why thank you, Connie. So do you.'

Priscilla was an African-American of great beauty with a figure to match. If she spent the majority of her leisure time enhancing her natural attributes it was time well spent, as Connie had just observed. 'I love the way you use makeup, Pris,' Connie went on. 'It doesn't cover, it enhances as it should. What's your secret?'

'I learned how to do it at school,' Priscilla told us. 'The Venus de Milo School of Beauty in Lauderdale. They teach makeup, hair – the works.'

'Oh, we need you,' Connie cried, clapping her hands.

'You do? What for?'

'The community theater, Pris. We're putting on a show and we need a makeup consultant to help the cast look their best on the stage. Please say you'll do it.'

'Well . . .' Priscilla began.

'And you'll get to rouge the cheeks of Desdemona Darling. She's going to be our star,' Connie crowed.

Priscilla responded to this with a blank stare. 'Who's she?'

'She was a big star,' Connie said, 'before your time – and mine, of course.'

'I'm the stage manager,' Binky said. I didn't know if this was meant as an inducement or a deterrent.

'And what are you?' Priscilla asked me.

'Only the director,' I told her.

'So you don't get made up?'

'No, I don't.'

'Then I'll take the job, Connie,' Priscilla agreed.

'Wonderful,' Connie applauded.

'I'll see you at rehearsal, Pris,' Binky promised.

Having been auditioned and hired, our company's Perc Westmore reverted to the role of waitress. 'Would you like to see the wine list?'

'Just bring me a carafe of elderberry wine laced with arsenic,' I moaned.

12

Connie volunteered to drive Binky home but I insisted on that honor. I didn't want them comparing Leroy's repast with last night's Tex-Mex. But the two were going to see a lot of each other in the days and weeks to come. Connie had *muchos* orders for the stage manager, compliments of Lady C, the first of which was to pick up the show's scripts, being prepared by a service in Miami. Binky would also be supplied with the names and phone numbers of everyone connected with getting *Arsenic and Old Lace* before a live audience, as he would be liaison between them, Lady C and myself. And that was just the beginning.

'Don't worry, Archy. I can handle it,' he insisted when I expressed my doubts. 'The Duchess has promised to help me.'

The Duchess, a sobriquet to be sure, was the aunt who had raised Binky and was now looking for a return on her largesse. She would help him walk the ambulatory patients if she thought it would get him off the dole. 'Do me a favor, Binky, and keep the Duchess out of this. If you run into any problems, come to me, that's what directors are for.'

'Thanks, Archy.' When I pulled over to let him out he reflected sadly, 'No one mentioned my clean upper lip.'

'Tell me, Binky. Did anyone ever mention your mustache?'

'No, Archy. They didn't.'

'Good night, Binky.'

I was home before midnight where I prepared for bed, poured myself a diminutive marc, which is brandy made from wine sludge, and lit my second English Oval of the day. I deserved both.

I recorded the evening's events in my journal and then made a list of Ouspenskaya's revelations regarding yrs. truly. He knew the names of the two ships my father was considering for his proposed trip. He knew I had been hired by Holmes to investigate him. He knew I would be asked to join the community theater. And he knew every detail of my lunch with Hanna Ventura. If I were to accept my spy theory as fact, it meant the psychic had an informer in the homes of Lady Cynthia Horowitz, Richard Holmes, Hanna Ventura and our castle on Ocean Boulevard. Impossible. But once you rule out the impossible, you have to consider the improbable.

Did the spy have to be in these places to learn the facts? The way Lady C and Desdemona gossiped, they could have told almost anyone that they intended to ask me to direct this year's showcase and the someone could have passed it on to Ouspenskaya. Ditto my lunch with Hanna. Had she discussed our meeting with a friend over a pitcher of 'lemonade,' complaining bitterly of her stepson's behavior?

That left Holmes. He had been recommended to Discreet Inquiries by Bob Simmons. How much had Holmes confided in Simmons? And Simmons's son, Kenneth, was just about William Ventura's age. Could they be chums? They could. If Simmons blabbed to his son and wife, they may have passed the word along to a number of people in what I believe is called arithmetic progression, the final number being the entire population of Palm Beach. On this tight little island everyone's paths crossed sooner or later.

What proof was there, other than his word, that William Ventura was in England when the diamond clip went missing? And could the boy's animosity toward Ouspenskaya be a ruse? William Ventura might just be the most talented actor in our company.

The possibilities were endless and my efforts fruitless. It was time to check once more with Al Rogoff and see if the long arm of the law had managed to penetrate the hereafter.

I put out the light and went to bed thinking of Kate Mulligan. I shouldn't see her again but I knew I would. Or, I should at least wait until the mater and pater were on the high seas before doing so – but I knew I wouldn't. I doubted that our love was here to stay, as the Messrs Gershwins proclaimed in song, but I wasn't ready to write us off as a one-night stand. In spite of Kate's protestations that she was not on the rebound from her failed marriage, I felt our passion was an effort on her part to banish sad memories. I hoped I had not disappointed.

From a more practical point of view, I rationalized that Kate could teach me a few tricks of the magician's trade, thereby facilitating my dealings with Serge Ouspenskaya. In conclusion, my motives in courting the lady were not purely prurient – which is even harder to pronounce than believe. I have often promised myself to one day draw up a blueprint of my moral code; then, perhaps, I might know why I do what I do. Until then, I will just have to keep on doing whatever it is I do.

Sleep came so quickly I didn't even have time to stroke my cheek.

I breakfasted with my parents, like a good boy should. Father departed for the office in his Lexus and mother hurried off to the greenhouse to greet her begonias and await Kate Mulligan. I drove my Miata to the McNally Building, parked in our underground garage and used the phone in Herb's security booth to call a cab. I had the driver take me to a car rental agency in West Palm and drove out in a black Ford Escort GT, my usual choice for covert trailing or, in this case, surveillance.

I had told Richard Holmes that I was keeping an eye on Ouspenskaya's headquarters and now, after the fact, I was going to do just that – for whatever it was worth. The Clematis Street building was a four-story affair, white brick, glass entrance door and windows displaying identical white, horizontal blinds, all of them tightly closed to Florida's warm winter sun. I found a convenient parking space almost directly across the street from the building, pulled into it and waited. Then I noticed the yellow VW parked not fifty feet from the building.

If a red Miata was akin to a flashing neon sign, so was a yellow VW. While I was certain mine was the only red Miata in the Palm Beach area, I couldn't say the same for Kate's wheels. The new edition of VW Bug was proving to be as popular as its predecessor. I was so mesmerized by the possibility of its being Kate's car I almost missed seeing the creamy cocoa-colored Rolls that came to a halt directly in front of the glass entrance. A uniformed chauffeur jumped out and opened the rear door for Penny Tremaine. Looking very smart in a white suit with matching shoes and a wide-brimmed bonnet, she spoke a few words to her driver before entering the building. He got back into the Rolls and drove off. It was going to be a long session. Was she still trying to contact her father or was she putting out a contract for poor Fitz?

A few minutes later a cab deposited two women on Ouspenskaya's doorstep. One of them was Hanna Ventura and the other a woman I had seen last night at Desdemona Darling's cocktail party, but whose name escaped me, if I ever knew it. The cab drove off minutes before another chauffeur-driven Lincoln arrived, bearing two Palm Beach society matrons. The ladies who lunch were hell-bent on making Serge Ouspenskaya a rich man.

I waited another five minutes and decided no one else was expected to attend today's broadcast. I was curious to see who owned the VW but not curious enough to set up housekeeping in a rented Ford Escort. Like the rest of my investigation to date, my surveillance proved a flop. But in the detective business persistence is the name of the game. I turned the key in the Ford's ignition and just as I did so the glass door across the street opened and Kate Mulligan emerged. She was dressed in her gardening clothes, denim skirt and Top-siders, so I knew where she was headed once she got into the VW and drove off. This was an interesting turn of events, to say the least.

I slumped down in my seat as Kate drove past me and then got out of the Ford and marched up to the glass door. Entering, I was in an air-conditioned lobby of imitation marble and confronted with another glass door. An ebony plastic placard mounted on a chrome stand displayed the names of the building's occupants and their location in shiny white letters.

1. Interior Designs by Beaumont
2. Xavier Santiago, Accountant
3. Temporarily Yours
4. Serge Ouspenskaya

Coincidence? What else? Unable to resist, I entered

through the second door, pressed for the elevator and rode up to the third floor. The elevator door opened directly onto the reception area of Temporarily Yours. A woman who looked the prototype for a caricature of a schoolteacher, circa 1932, was seated behind a desk flanking the elevator. She had gray hair with a no-nonsense cut, wore rimless glasses, and sported a white blouse under a cardigan sweater. I couldn't see her feet but I imagined she was shod in brown lace-ups with a college heel. The sweater told me she was the office grouch who went around turning down the air conditioner when no one was looking.

'May I help you?'

'Please,' I responded. 'A friend recommended you and I was in the neighborhood and thought I would stop in. Is that all right?'

'Of course, sir. How can we be of assistance?'

'My wife took a fall the other day and broke her leg.'

'Oh, I'm so sorry to hear that, Mr . . .'

'Mark, ma'am. Tobias Mark.'

'I'm so sorry to hear that, Mr Mark. I'm Sally Duhane.'

'Thank you, Ms Duhane. She'll need some help in running the house for the next four weeks. That's how long it will be before the cast comes off.'

'I understand,' the woman replied.

'Nothing very special,' I said. 'Just someone to help with housework and shopping. I can handle the rest.'

'I'm sure we can help, Mr Mark.' Her tone and manner

were as reassuring as a school nurse administering TLC to a first grader with a scraped knee. She selected an application from a twin pile on her neat desk and offered it to me. 'If you'll just have a seat and fill this out for us, one of our placement people will be with you as soon as you're done.'

There were a half dozen student chairs in the room, each with a ballpoint pen resting on its broad arm.

'How long have you been here?' I asked her, taking the application.

'The agency has been in West Palm for a dozen years or more. We took it over last fall, moving to this more modern location and changing the name to Temporarily Yours. Catchy, isn't it? We've also managed to recruit some very skilled personnel.

'You see, Mr Mark, we advertise in newspapers as far north as New York and as far west as California, attracting people who want to relocate to the Palm Beach area, even if it's just for the season when we're busiest.' Her smile displayed a set of teeth that were as perfect, and perhaps as phony, as her demeanor. Did Kate Mulligan spot their ad in Las Vegas and head east in search of a new life – and a new husband?

Her editorial 'we' could mean she was the establishment's owner, a partner or just a gung-ho employee.

I took a chair and pretended to examine the sheet of paper she had handed me. Minutes later the door leading to what must be the interview rooms opened and a young man entered and exchanged a few words with the receptionist before retreating. This was obviously a perfectly legitimate business operation and I was beginning to feel a little foolish for having snooped.

Getting up, I asked Ms Duhane if I could take the application home. 'My wife is better qualified to describe exactly what we need.'

'Certainly, Mr Mark. You can return it yourself or put it in the mail.' She gave me a business card along with an envelope for the application.

I returned the Ford and took a cab back to the McNally Building. I called Al Rogoff but he wasn't at the station house. I left word for him to call me, giving my office number.

Then I called Connie to see if there was any fallout from last night's party.

'I was just going to call you,' Connie said. 'Madame is giving a reception for the community theater tomorrow night at eight. Come as you are, buffet dinner.'

I knew it wouldn't take Lady C long to go DeeDee one better. 'What did she have to say about last night's imbroglio?'

'She's furious at Desdemona for getting drunk but from what's being said I think our leading lady has been on a twelve-step program for years but can't seem to get past the first rise.'

Just as I had feared. 'Anything else, Connie?'

'Yes, as a matter of fact. Lady Cynthia is also furious with Richard Holmes for punching out Ouspenskaya.'

'He didn't punch him out,' I countered, 'he gave him a little shove.'

'A little shove goes a long way in this town,

Archy. Madame wanted Mr Holmes to apologize to Ouspenskaya. Mr Holmes told Madame what she could go do to herself and Madame said she would if she could. Then Desdemona threatened to quit the show unless Madame apologized to Mr Holmes.'

'And on top of all this Lady C is organizing a reception for tomorrow night? It's madness,' I told Connie.

'Lady Cynthia thrives on it, Archy. It's the quiet days that wear her out.'

'So what was the end result of all the verbal abuse?'

'The Holmeses came here, Madame mixed a batch of the hair-of-the-dog and the ladies fell into each other's arms and cried. Then they began planning the party.'

'You work in an asylum, Connie, and the inmates are calling the shots.'

'I know, but it pays well and until Prince Charming comes along and takes me away from all this, I have no choice. Which reminds me. I can't see you tonight, Archy. I'll be working late, preparing for the party.'

This was fortunate because I had no intention of seeing Connie that night. But, cad that I am, I immediately took advantage of her candor. 'Oh,' I sighed, 'the weather has been so nice I was going to suggest a picnic on the beach and a midnight plunge, in our birthday suits.'

'The last time we did that, Archy, a crab nipped you right on your . . .'

'I know where the crab nipped me,' I cut in before we were given an X rating by our local telephone exchange. Needless to say that cheeky crustacean also nipped any impure thoughts I may have harbored that moonlit night and for weeks thereafter I gorged myself on crab cocktails, crab cakes and linguine with red crab sauce, hoping to even the score.

'I thought it was Binky's job to alert the company as to where to be and when.'

'He's incommunicado at the pound, or whatever it is, and I figured I may as well make a start and give Binky any leftovers this evening if he gets home in time. He's picking up the scripts in Miami. By the way, Archy, the press was invited, too, and Lady C will formally announce the show and its cast and crew. I'll get my name in the paper and so will Pris.'

'Did you mention Priscilla Pettibone to Lady C?'

'But of course. She loves the idea of having a resident makeup artist. It makes us look very professional.'

With that, Connie rang off, only to have Al Rogoff take up the slack.

'Hi, Al. Where have you been?'

'Out protecting your butt from the slings and arrows of outrageous fortune. What's up?'

'You've been reading *Hamlet*. How quaint.'

'I think he should have abdicated and married the woman he loved.'

'That would make it soap opera, Al.'

'So what's wrong with the soaps? You're a snob, Archy.'

'And you're an intellectual posing as a policeman. What's the word on my friend, Serge Ouspenskaya?'

'Neat as a pin an' clean as a whistle.'

'That's not what I want to hear, Al.'

'I don't make up stories, pal. The guy blew into town last November and rented space on Clematis Street. It ain't cheap. He's licensed and bonded like the law requires and we ain't had no complaints about him.'

Al's intellectual pursuits did not include a crash course in remedial grammar. If slaughtering the King's English were a crime, Al Rogoff would draw fifty to life with Johnnie Cochran defending him. 'Do you know where he came from, Al?'

'Last known address, the City of Angels. Ain't that a misnomer? He put down two months' security on the office space and furnished references.'

'Who supplied them?'

'Archy, the guy is legit. We got no cause to probe more than I already have.'

'Sorry, Al. Did you happen to get his home address?'

'He has a rental in Lantana. Nothing too impressive. He lives with a woman and a young man.'

'Wife and son?'

'Who knows? Who cares? I didn't see a marriage license or a birth certificate. Ask him.'

'Thanks, Al. I'll send you a recording of *Swan Lake* by the New York Philharmonic.'

'No, Archy. It's by Tchaikovsky.'

'Now you're a comedian. See you when I see you, Al.'

'One more thing, Archy.'

'What's that?'

'Your friend charges five hundred bucks for a séance and he's averaging about ten a week. I make that out to be five G's every seven days.'

'That's more than you pull in, even with the graft.'

'I'll remember that the next time you want a favor.'

'Good night, sweet prince; And flights of angels sing thee to thy rest.'

'He should have married the girl, Archy.'

I rang off knowing I had reached the nadir of my case. That moment when you've hit an impasse in the shape of a brick wall and all you want to do is bang your head against it. I had exhausted all my leads, which weren't many to begin with, and had hoped that Al Rogoff would supply a few I could follow up on. All he had to tell me was that Hamlet never married and Ouspenskaya was on a roll – neither of which was exactly an epiphany.

I went home, changed into my swimming togs and threw myself into the Atlantic, contemplating playing Norman Maine and never returning to shore. But I did return after my two-mile workout. I showered, donned heather-gray briefs with matching T-shirt and slipped on a pair of jeans that would do a Gap ad proud. I accessorized with a classic Brooks Brothers button-down, loafers, no socks, and my original NY Yankees baseball cap.

Then I phoned Kate Mulligan and invited myself to dinner.

'I have nothing in the house,' she whined, 'and it's past four. Besides, I'm a lousy cook.'

'I'll stop by a little place I know and treat you to the best takeout in Palm Beach.'

'Not Tex-Mex, please.'

'Cross my heart.'

The little place I knew was our kitchen, which wasn't very little, and said to Ursi, 'Once, in the not too distant past, you put together a picnic lunch for me and I'm imploring you to do it again.'

'When, Archy?'

'Right now.'

'The best I can do is fill you a basket with what I'm preparing for tonight.'

'And what might that be, Ursi?'

'Fried chicken, cooled. German potato salad. A green salad of arugula and radicchio, raspberry vinaigrette and for dessert a blueberry tart with vanilla ice cream.'

'You're making me hungry, Ursi love. I'll get the picnic hamper. It's in the utility room, I think.'

'It is,' she called as I hurried out of the kitchen.

I also managed to snare a bottle of zinfandel from father's wine cellar before returning to help Ursi. In a little over an hour we had gotten it all together. I turned down linen napkins in favor of paper – after all, it was a picnic – and was off to Currie Park with my little yellow basket. I even remembered to bring a corkscrew.

13

Palm Beach lore has it that if you're planning a day at the beach, or an evening barbecue, do it on a day Lady Cynthia Horowitz is giving a pool party or a sit-down dinner al fresco, sans tent. It does not rain on Lady C's parades and her outdoor buffet for the community theater corroborated the maxim. Does God favor the rich? If he didn't they would be poor.

It was a sterling evening. No full moon, but there were a jillion stars lighting up the sky. I had attended several of Lady C's outdoor bashes and the decor and ambiance seldom varied. But if it ain't broke, why fix it? The patio surrounding the pool was aglow with Chinese lanterns and there were scented candles within the hurricane lamps on every table. The tables also held pots of narcissi growing straight out of their bulbs. Narcissi? A cryptic message for Archy? And would young William give us a demo of his swimming prowess wearing his naughty bathing trunks?

A portable bar was being manned by one of the caterer's staff and several young men and women were passing around the finger food – pigs in a blanket were not among the pickin's. The chef, wearing a *toque blanche*, was roasting perfectly trussed beef tenderloins (not chestnuts) on the open fire. Finally, as Cole Porter had put it, 'down by the shore an orchestra playing and even the palms seemed to be swaying.' The orchestra was a six-piece combo playing – who else? – Cole Porter, and the palms were truly swaying in a cool ocean breeze.

A class act? And why not when the hostess was said to be worth a hundred million, give or take ten mill? Tonight she wore a white sheath that I suspected served a dual purpose. It did justice to her still bewitching figure and made her chum, Desdemona Darling, pea green with envy. Bitchiness was one of Lady C's more noticeable traits. The rest of the gang, who hadn't seen each other since *L'Affair de Desdemona Darling*, as Lolly Spindrift had dubbed it, tonight cavorted in everything from jeans to cocktail dresses. I wore an Ultrasuede jacket in sand and navy pants.

Lady C, with Buzz at her side, was greeting her guests. He looked every bit the movie star in a yachting cap, double-breasted blazer and white flannels. Fitz was at a safe distance charming William Ventura and Arnold Turnbolt. I would notice, as the evening progressed, that Fitz and Buzz kept a wide berth in the presence of Buzz's patroness. But then illicit sex is always so much more exciting. I should know.

'Nice party,' I said to our hostess.

'Nice of you to notice, lad. You didn't happen to come in with your friend Binky, did you?'

'No, I didn't. Why?'

'He hasn't shown up with the scripts.'

'Lost between Miami and Palm Beach. It's happened before, Lady Cynthia.'

'Not to me, it hasn't.'

'I know all my lines, Archy,' Buzz said, pumping my hand. He had the grip of a vise.

'Knowing them is half the battle, Buzz. It's how you deliver them that gets the applause.'

'And we're counting on you to see that he delivers them to a standing ovation,' Lady C reminded me.

'I'll do my best, ma'am.'

'You'd better, lad.'

'There's Binky,' Buzz called. 'The scripts have arrived.'

I could see that Binky had arrived, but I wouldn't be too sanguine about the scripts. With nary a curtsey to our Lady of the Performing Arts I headed for the bar like a horse wearing blinders. I asked for a Sterling vodka on the rocks and got it. A minute later I was two sips closer to a party mood and began surveying the crowd when Richard Holmes approached. 'What's happening, Archy?'

'I could lie and say I'm working on a few leads, but that would be crap of the purest nature. Zilch, Mr Holmes. What's new with you?'

He was wearing his Lilly Pulitzer and drinking something the color of dirty water. A bullshot, I believe: a concoction of vodka and beef bouillon. I would rather drink castor oil while sticking pins in my eyes.

'DeeDee was a mess the other night, as I guess you noticed. She does that when her nerves get the best of her, otherwise she can hold her booze pretty good. Since the party she's been in constant touch with that effing con artist and I don't know what she's been telling him but I know what I told him.'

'And what's that, Mr Holmes?'

'I told him that I wasn't writing any more checks to Serge Ouspenskaya, that's what I told him. If DeeDee wants to continue seeing him the tab comes out of her own pockets, which ain't very deep, believe me.'

'And what did he say, sir?'

'He told me to have a nice day and hung up.'

A burst of raucous laughter drew our attention, and everyone else's. It was DeeDee, regaling a group of young people with stories of old Hollywood, Ouspenskaya by her side. 'He's here?' I bellowed.

'Cynthia insisted,' Holmes told me. 'She says he brings luck with him.'

'Well, he can take his luck someplace else. As director I'm going to insist on a closed rehearsal hall. Company members only.'

'Good for you, Archy.'

Another burst of laughter from DeeDee's admirers, which seemed to consist of half the guests.

'I hope she's not telling them who the most "endowed" actor in Hollywood was fifty years ago? It always gets that response. Christ, the guy was five foot two in his elevator shoes. I better go see no one is fetching her drinks.'

Five foot two in his elevators? Hmmm. A hundred-watter lit up in my head. Of course. But I'll never tell.

I got a refill before moving off into the crowd; waving, blowing kisses and trying to look like a director. I would have to pay my respects to my star but first I would indulge myself by ogling my starlet. Tonight Fitz was in a knee-skimming navy sheath with a matching navy topcoat, a single strand of pearls around her graceful neck. Her dark hair cascaded to her shoulders and her blue eyes sparkled like the stars winking down at us. But before I got to Fitz, Lolly Spindrift got to me.

'If you can keep your leading lady off the demon rum you might get a performance out of her.' Lolly wore a white suit with dress shirt and tie, and his trademark Panama hat, a look best described as *Saturday Night Fever* meets *Scarface*.

'And if you can keep your friend Meecham away from Buzz, I might get a performance out of both of them,' I rejoined.

'Then you had better keep Fitz away from Buzz before Lady C throttles your ingenue, and Vance Tremaine away from Fitz before his wife throttles him.'

'Am I directing a play or a sex circus?'

'Not to mention,' Lolly went on, 'that Arnie is in hot pursuit of William Ventura.'

'Really? What does William Ventura have to say about that?'

'He's too busy chasing after Fitz to notice.'

'I might kill myself, Lol.'

'If you do, give me an exclusive. I get extra bread for doing society obits. What's new with Ouspenskaya?'

'What have you heard?'

'That he's Mr Amazing. You lose it, he finds it. You want to speak to the dead, he connects you, but the rates don't go down after six. Did you hear about Liz Haberstraw?'

'No. Do I want to?'

For an answer, Lolly told me. 'At a sitting, her late mother told Liz to have a look in the bottom left hand drawer of the desk in her husband's study.'

'Okay. What did she find?'

'A first-rate porn collection. I'll be announcing the divorce in tomorrow's column. Remember, you heard it here first. Now I must fly. Arnie is chatting with William at poolside and Vance has managed to slip away from Penny and is heading for Fitz. Ta, ta, Archy.'

Penny Tremaine? Was she also here to bring us luck? If so, it wasn't Vance the gods were smiling upon. I spotted Priscilla Pettibone with a young black man who was as handsome as she was beautiful. I went to greet them, hoping for a respite from those with an axe to grind.

'So this is how the other half lives,' Priscilla said with a toss of her head.

'What do you think of it?'

'I could take it for a few hundred years. But no more than that. This is Henry Lee Wilson. He's playing one of the policemen. This is Archy McNally, our director.'

I shook Henry Lee's hand. 'You're with the company, Henry?'

'Call me Hank, please. Yes, sir. My second year.'

Lady C had managed to salvage some of the old members of the group in minor roles and as gofers. Conquer, divide and keep what you can use. One day she would get her comeuppance but I doubted I would live long enough to see it.

'Glad to have you aboard, Hank. I still haven't met all the members of the cast.'

'You will tonight,' Priscilla said. 'Connie told me Lady Cynthia is going to make a formal announcement later. Like a press release. Isn't it exciting?'

The director gets the news from the makeup artist. Give me a break. If I didn't start pushing my weight around, the Creative Director was going to walk all over me. Let her have her evening. When the real work starts, Archy is going to hand everyone a surprise, especially our Creative Director and the unrequited lovers of all three genders.

'What's with the six flags flying around the pool, Archy?' Priscilla asked me.

'They represent the ethnic backgrounds of each of Lady Cynthia's husbands.'

'She had six?' Priscilla was greatly impressed. 'I'll settle for one and the sooner the better.'

Henry Lee Wilson looked a bit uncomfortable with that one and I saved the moment by asking, 'Where's Connie?'

'In her office labeling the scripts for distribution later tonight,' Priscilla informed me.

The good news was that Binky had delivered the scripts. The bad news was that Lady C, as usual, was making Connie work when, as a member of the group, she should be enjoying the party. If she didn't appear soon, I'd go and rescue her. 'Nice meeting you, Hank. See you later, Pris. I'm off to pay my respects to our star.'

As the crowd surrounding her began to disperse, Desdemona Darling came clearly into our line of vision. 'I checked her out at the library,' Priscilla said. 'She really was a star and some looker. Wha' happen, baby?'

'She's still a looker,' Hank said, 'only now there's more to look at.'

'Her dress is not original,' Priscilla noted as if saddened by the former actress's choice of apparel.

'Where have you seen it before?' I asked her.

'Sheltering two cub scouts on a field trip.'

Hank liked that one and so did I, but I didn't let Priscilla know it. As I moved toward DeeDee I saw Hanna Ventura chatting with the woman I had seen her with on Clematis Street. The woman had been at DeeDee's party, too, so she must be one of the old members of the theater group. But what was Hanna doing here? Ouspenskaya seemed to draw them like flies. I also noticed that Hanna was as far removed from her stepson as the length of Lady C's patio allowed, while William had jettisoned Arnie and joined Vance, Penny and Fitz. I wondered what they were discussing – method acting or the price of alligator handbags on Worth Street?

'Archy, love.' Before I had a chance to respond I was on the receiving end of a wet kiss on the cheek from DeeDee; my nose told me it was one hundred proof. 'You know Mr Ouspenskaya? But of course you do. He's the reason you're here.'

Richard Holmes was nowhere in the vicinity and Ouspenskaya didn't seem the least bit perturbed at having been financially cut off by the pork bellies mogul. For that matter, neither did DeeDee.

'I'm here because you and Lady Cynthia asked me to direct our showcase,' I said, with a nod at Ouspenskaya.

'We meet again, Mr McNally,' Ouspenskaya acknowledged me with that patronizing grin I would have liked to wipe off his face, but under the circumstances had to settle for ignoring him. Facing Ouspenskaya and DeeDee, it occurred to me to wonder if I still had a client now that Holmes had given my mark the heave-ho. In retrospect, a most prophetic thought.

A passing waiter stopped to offer us caviar snuggled into new potatoes and dolloped with crème fraîche with minced onions. We all accepted as DeeDee proclaimed, 'Some spread, eh? Cynthia really knows how to do it, but then she's got the loot to do it with.

My husbands always managed to spend it faster than
I made it.'

Here, everyone's attention was drawn to a portable
table being erected under the watchful eyes of Lady
C and Buzz. Connie, Binky and Joe Anderson began
setting it with wine glasses as waiters carried over
decanters brimming with a dark liquid that could only
be wine. 'Now what?' I questioned.

'Just you wait and see. Cynthia has the whole thing
planned.' A roll of the drums drew everyone's attention and DeeDee took hold of my arm. 'Come on,
Archy, that's our cue.'

As the revelers gathered around Lady Cynthia and
her wine bar, DeeDee led me to stand beside our
hostess as Binky, Connie and Joe joined the onlookers.
Another roll of the drums silenced the crowd and Lady
C began her spiel. 'We all know why we're here, at
least I hope we do.' This got a sputtering of guffaws
because with Lady C no one could be sure if she
meant it as a joke or a reprimand. 'For the benefit of
the press I am, this evening, formally announcing that
the Palm Beach Community Theater, of which I am
Creative Director, will put on a production of *Arsenic
and Old Lace* at the Lake Worth Playhouse on a date
to be announced.' This got polite applause.

'Our own Archy McNally has agreed to direct.'
More applause. 'A written press release will detail
his credentials.' I couldn't wait to see them. 'A lady
whose credentials can be summed up in two words
– Desdemona Darling – will appear in the star role

of Abby Brewster.' This got an ovation, including whistles, cat calls and cries of 'Bravo.' DeeDee, beaming, opened her arms, embracing the crowd's adoration.

'I would like to quickly acknowledge the cast credits, which will also appear on our written release.

'Abby Brewster, Desdemona Darling;

'Mortimer Brewster, Buzz Carr;

'Teddy Brewster, Vance Tremaine;

'Jonathan Brewster, Phil Meecham;

'Dr Einstein, Arnold Turnbolt;

'Elaine Harper, Elizabeth Fitzwilliams;

'The Reverend Harper, Edward Rogers;

'Mr Gibbs, Joseph Anderson;

'Mr Witherspoon, Ronald Seymour;

'Lieutenant Rooney, William Ventura;

'Officer Klein, Penny Tremaine;

'Officer Brophy, Henry Lee Wilson;

'Officer O'Hara, Hanna Ventura.

'Our stage manager will be Binky Watrous, my own lovely Consuela Garcia will act as prompter and the beautiful Priscilla Pettibone will be in charge of makeup.'

Our Creative Director had turned two policemen into policewomen, satisfying the theatrical urges of Hanna Ventura and the bloodhound instincts of Penny Tremaine. Clever. Penny would keep Fitz away from Buzz and Hanna would keep her stepson's hands out of the till. Our Creative Director was more creative than I had given her credit for. The ladies who lunch were closing ranks. I wondered if our seer had managed to stir the pot.

'Did I miss anyone?' Lady C called out, playing to the crowd.

'Martha Brewster,' they shouted like a Greek chorus.

'Oh, dear, I almost forgot,' Lady Cynthia emoted. 'After careful consideration – and on the advice of someone whose instincts are legendary – I have decided to take on the role of Martha Brewster.'

There was a split second of thunderous silence before the audience broke into thunderous applause. In the din that followed the orchestra struck up Berlin's 'There's No Business Like Show Business' as Lady C and DeeDee hugged each other. Damned if they didn't look more like Laurel and Hardy than Abby and Martha.

'Desdemona and I have always wanted to work together but, until now, never had the opportunity,' Lady C announced.

'And it's about damn time,' DeeDee joined in.

Oy vey! I felt a headache the size of a football coming on. But, like they say in showbiz, you ain't seen nothing yet.

'And now,' Lady Cynthia proclaimed, 'we'll all drink a toast to our success with elderberry wine – served to you by the Brewster sisters.'

This got a laugh, as well as a few howls and shrieks as the two ladies began pouring the wine. They placed four glasses at a time on their trays and began distributing them to the crowd. Flash bulbs were popping all over the place at the sight of Lady Cynthia Horowitz and Desdemona Darling jockeying wine to lesser mortals. Our community theater would get space in newspapers from Miami to Hollywood, proving Lady Cynthia a public relations maven of awesome expertise.

When we had all been served, Lady C raised her glass, the drummer rolled, the trumpeter blared, DeeDee shouted, 'To us' and the elderberry wine made its way down many a hatch. Richard Holmes stepped out of the crowd to embrace his wife and fell to the ground at her feet, his glass rolling from his hand, the dark liquid staining the flagstones. DeeDee stared down at him before letting out a scream that could wake Ouspenskaya's departed cohorts.

Oy vey! – again.

14

In the days that followed I often thought about those perfectly trussed beef tenderloins we never got to eat. I supposed the catering staff took away one hell of a doggie bag that night and had themselves a beach party. The good Lord giveth and the good Lord taketh away. The caterer got the viands and Desdemona Darling lost her husband.

DeeDee's scream and the sight of Holmes falling caused half the crowd to back away in panic and the rest to advance for a closer look at the spectacle. The end result was a lot of people bumping into each other. I was on my knees a few seconds after it happened, holding Richard Holmes's wrist in search of a pulse in the time-honored tradition of film doctors. I am neither brave nor skilled in the medical sciences. I just happened to be the closest person to the stricken man and it seemed the thing to do.

'Give him air, give him air,' someone was shouting, but unless I had my fingers on the wrong spot all the air in the universe wouldn't help Richard Holmes draw another breath.

'His heart,' DeeDee was crying. 'It's his heart. They told him at L.A. General that his cholesterol count was higher than his bank balance.'

Ouspenskaya was comforting the new widow, telling someone to bring her a glass of cold water. Lady Cynthia was looking down at the dead man as if she'd like to kill him for stealing her show but a higher power had beaten her to the draw. Joe Anderson got a cushion from one of the patio chairs and, kneeling next to me, raised Holmes's head, slipping the cushion beneath it.

'Thanks, Joe, but I don't think he'll notice the difference.'

'He's gone?' Joe questioned.

'I'm no doc, but I can't feel a pulse and he's not breathing. What's your prognosis?'

'I don't like this, Archy,' Joe murmured.

'Neither does Richard Holmes, Joe.'

DeeDee was simultaneously sobbing and providing an account of her husband's medical history. 'He had the angina and they gave him pills for the attacks. They told him to live on fish and vegetables but he said that was for cats and rabbits.'

'Please take her inside,' I heard Lady Cynthia saying and a few moments later DeeDee's sobs retreated. In the dim light of the lanterns the crowd broke into small groups and began describing to each other the scene they had all just witnessed. There would be as many versions of what happened as there were people present.

The photographer with Lolly's rag was snapping away at the grieving actress and the recently departed Richard Holmes. Two other press photographers were doing the same thing. Lolly Spindrift would indeed get extra bread for this one and the community theater would get more press than Lady C had bargained for.

'What do we do now?' Joe asked just as we heard the siren of an approaching police car speeding up the A1A. Someone, practical Connie I guessed, had the good sense to dial 911. Another siren told us an ambulance was a few minutes behind the patrol car.

'We step back and let the people who know what they're doing take over,' I said, standing. Before I had a chance to consult with Lady Cynthia, Al Rogoff and his partner had arrived on the scene.

'I need a light,' Al ordered. The younger officer ran back to the squad car just as the paramedics came bounding onto the patio toting a stretcher, oxygen mask and what looked like a stomach pump. All they would need was one out of the three.

'Good evening, Sergeant,' Lady Cynthia addressed Al.

'Ma'am.' Al remembered to tip his cap. 'Who's the victim?'

The word *victim* sounded ominous but one could be the victim of a heart attack as well as a crime. I should say here that Sergeant Al Rogoff and I have what I like to call a closeted relationship, a term he abhors for obvious reasons. We have worked together on several cases, chat often and I believe I am one of the few people privy to his devotion to the ballet, opera, and classical music, and his middle name, Irving. However, when he's on the job and I happen to be present, we keep our distance and play it as it lays.

As Al gathered information from Lady Cynthia and jotted it down in his pad, the paramedics put Richard Holmes on the stretcher, covered him with a blanket and began to carry him to the waiting ambulance. Only Holmes's size-twelve black loafers were visible. The partygoers watched in stunned silence as the man they had been drinking and chatting with not twenty minutes earlier made his final exit – a reminder that we were all destined to one day follow in his size-twelve footsteps.

'I got what I need so we won't bother Mrs Holmes now,' Rogoff was saying to Lady Cynthia, 'but for the record you should prepare a list of everyone present tonight, including the help, and have it at the ready.'

'Why?' Lady Cynthia demanded.

'Until the medical examiner files his report we have to consider any sudden death, like this one, a suspicious occurrence, ma'am.'

'Suspicious?' Lady Cynthia repeated, taking exception to Rogoff's explanation. 'He had a bad heart. His wife will tell you that.'

'Is his wife a qualified medical doctor, ma'am?'

'Don't be ridiculous, officer. She's Desdemona Darling, the world-renowned actress.'

'Then we'll have to wait for the medical examiner to tell us how her husband died, ma'am.'

Good for you, Al, I thought. Then Al pocketed his pad and tipped his hat to Lady Cynthia, saying, 'They'll take Mr Holmes directly to the county morgue, ma'am. I suggest his wife come to the police station tomorrow, first thing, and we'll walk her through it from there. She'll have to identify the body.'

'We all know who he is, officer,' Lady Cynthia snapped back.

'Who he *was*, ma'am. Good night.'

Al's partner had retreated with the high-powered flashlight he had played on the supine body to assist Al and the medics. The sight appeared more gruesome in its harsh glare than it had in the flickering glow of the Chinese lanterns. As Al took his leave the onlookers broke their silence as they sheepishly returned their wine glasses to the table and surrounded Lady C with words of consolation. A few, including Joe Anderson and Binky Watrous, headed for the bar where I would have liked to join them but took the opportunity to chase, unnoticed, after Al Rogoff.

The ambulance had gone and the young officer with Al was sitting in the squad car. 'As soon as I got the nine-one-one call to this fancy address I knew I would find Archy McNally here rubbing shoulders,' Al said as he saw me approaching. 'What can you tell me?'

'Nothing more than Lady Cynthia told you. I'm sure it was his heart. But for the record, and now that it doesn't matter, Richard Holmes was my client. He's the guy who hired me to investigate the seer, Serge Ouspenskaya.'

'Was he here tonight? The Ouspenskaya guy, that is.'

'He was and still is. He took the new widow into the house to calm her.'

'Why did the deceased want this Ouspenskaya investigated?'

'He thought the guy was bamboozling his wife but it doesn't make any difference now. She can lean on Ouspenskaya all she wants with her husband's checkbook and without his interference.'

'Some dames have all the luck,' Al speculated. 'You have any idea why she consults this Ouspenskaya?'

'Can I speak in confidence, Al?'

'Like always, Archy, I won't repeat it unless it becomes police business and is pertinent to the case.'

'Fair enough. Desdemona Darling made a naughty one-reeler in her prime and the lucky cinematographer has been blackmailing her ever since. She wants Ouspenskaya to find the guy and the can of film.'

'Blackmail? She should have reported it to the police years ago. It's a felony.'

'In this case the felon doesn't ask for money, Al. He just threatens to release the film to your friendly neighborhood video shop and the thought drives the lady bananas.'

'With what you can rent today at any video store it wouldn't make a ripple,' Al noted.

'True. But the lady is adamant about preserving her image.'

'The camera guy might be dead after all these years,' Al said.

'It would be easier for Ouspenskaya to contact him if he were dead than if he were alive.'

Al shook his head. 'They're all nuts, Archy.'

'You'll get no argument out of me on that score, Sergeant.'

'What was the party for tonight? I saw a few beauties in the dim light of those paper lamps.'

You had to admire Al's professionalism. He had taken in the entire scene as he gathered information from Lady Cynthia and no doubt he was referring to Fitz, and perhaps Hanna Ventura. Al, and the rest of Palm Beach would read all about it tomorrow morning, so I gave him a quick briefing on the community theater and my involvement in it.

Al pulled a half-smoked cigar butt out of his breast pocket and began to chew on it. 'You're the director? What have you ever directed?'

'You can peruse my credentials in the early editions.'

'I never believe anything I read in the newspapers.'

Al Rogoff was many things, from intellectual to uncouth, but a fool he was not. Many a nefarious punk who judged him solely by his mannerisms and grammar had lived to regret it.

'So you're going to direct Desdemona Darling. Tell me, Archy, is she still a stunner?'

That was an interesting supposition. Was I going to direct Desdemona Darling? Would the show go on? Perhaps the show would, but would the widow Holmes? 'She's aged well, except for a few extra pounds,' I conceded to Al.

'How many is a few?'

'If you're thinking of carrying her over the threshold, Al, you might want to get fitted for a truss first.'

'I get the picture, Archy. See you around, and try to stay clear of falling bodies.'

'Let me know what the medical examiner has to say, Al, please.'

'It'll be in all the papers, pal.'

'I like to hear it from the horse's mouth.'

'Screw you, Archy.'

I could hear the party breaking up as I talked to Al under the porte cochere. I ducked into the house just as they began making their way to the parking area. The housekeeper who was filling in for Mrs Marsden told me Mrs Holmes was resting in one of the bedrooms and being attended to by Mr Ouspenskaya. I made my way to Connie's office where I found her, Binky and Joe Anderson.

'*Quel* mess,' Connie said as I entered.

'What's happening?' I asked the trio.

'Madame is upstairs with Desdemona and Ouspenskaya,' Connie answered. 'I hope they're not talking to Mr Holmes.' She gave a noticeable shiver as she verbalized the thought.

'That's macabre, Connie.'

'So is what happened tonight.'

'Binky told me the cop is a friend of yours, Archy. What did he tell you?' Joe asked me.

'Nothing. It was me who did the talking. Once the medical examiner gives his report the police will be done with the whole business.'

'You think it was a natural death?' Joe went on.

Interesting question. Why would anyone think otherwise? 'What's your take on it, Joe?' I asked.

'I guess it's the damn play,' Joe said. 'We get served elderberry wine and life imitates art. It gives me the creeps.'

'Do you think the play will go on?' Binky wanted to know.

I noticed the scripts, in blue plastic folders, piled all over Connie's desk and work space. Having performed his first chore successfully, Binky appeared reluctant to take early retirement from the stage-managing profession. 'I wouldn't give up walking your ambulatory patients just yet, Binky,' I counseled.

'The play will go on,' Connie said with certainty. 'There is nothing Lady Cynthia likes better than a challenge and that's just what getting this show on the road is proving to be. And it's not just for her boy, Buzz. From the beginning I suspected she wanted to get into the act herself and that's why she chose a play with two pivotal roles for older women. Vanity, thy name is Lady Cynthia Horowitz. If Desdemona Darling hadn't come out of the woodwork this season, Madame would have given herself the bigger role, believe me.'

It was true. If Lady Cynthia was thinking only of advancing the career of Buzz Carr I could think of a dozen plays with roles more suitable to showing off the charisma of a handsome young man. *Cat on a Hot Tin Roof* came immediately to mind. With Fitz as Maggie in that white satin slip we would go down in the *Guinness Book of Records* as the longest-running show in community theater history.

The thought of Fitz in her frilly lingerie prompted me to light an English Oval. The fact that none of my cohorts commented on the gesture was an indication of how preoccupied they were with the evening's unexpected finale. 'I see you didn't give out the scripts as planned,' I said to Connie.

'Under the circumstances I thought it wise to hold off. If I know my boss, and I do, there will be another formal announcement, most likely naming a replacement for Desdemona Darling, and then we can hand out the scripts.'

'Do you think Madame will step into the starring role now that Desdemona is prostrate with grief?' I speculated.

'That might be a little too ghoulish even for Lady Cynthia, but you can be sure Serge Ouspenskaya will be consulted every step of the way. Did you all hear about Liz Haberstraw?'

As Connie let Binky and Joe in on the intimate details of the pending Haberstraw divorce, I was thinking that my friend Ouspenskaya had insinuated himself into the lives of our matrons as had no other Palm Beach passing fancy. Now, without Richard Holmes to run interference, the seer was free to run amok. Was it Archy to the rescue, or should I consider the case and my stint with the community theater finis?

The new housekeeper stuck her head in the office door. 'The caterers are just finishing up,' she told us, 'and I'm going to bed.'

'Fine, Annie,' Connie said. 'What's happening upstairs?'

'Lady Cynthia has retired and Mr Ouspenskaya and Mrs Holmes have left.'

'We'll be history in a few minutes, too, Annie. Goodnight,' Connie said.

When the door closed behind Annie I asked Connie, 'Where did Annie come from?'

'I have no idea,' Connie told me. 'Mrs Marsden is in charge of the domestics and she arranged for her own replacement. She seems nice enough and Madame has no complaints.'

When Binky and Joe departed I said to Connie, 'If you didn't have your car I'd drive you home, Connie.'

'Thanks anyway, Archy. We'll talk in the morning. I imagine Madame will have a lot to say.'

We folded our tents as the curtain came down on Lady Cynthia's event – as well as the life of Richard Holmes.

I could see a light under the oak door of father's study so I knocked gently and got a 'Come' for my troubles.

Was Prescott McNally the last man alive to lounge before bed wearing a proper two-piece pajama set, with drawstring trousers and buttoned top, under a vermilion silk robe (from Sulka, if you please) and velour bedroom slippers? I believed he was.

Father was seated behind his big leather-topped desk reading one of the volumes from his set of Dickens, a glass of port in front of him. I think Dickens is all he reads for pleasure and I must say I admire his perseverance. He even remembers all the plots, a feat I doubt even Charlie could have performed. 'You're home, Archy.'

'Yes, sir. And I fear I've lost a client.'

'Richard Holmes has withdrawn from the case?'

'Richard Holmes has withdrawn from life, sir. He's dead.'

One of father's eyebrows ascended. He removed his reading glasses and placed them on his desk. 'When? How?'

'This evening, sir, at Lady Cynthia's party for the community theater. A heart attack is the consensus of opinion, thanks to Mrs Holmes, who told one and all that his cholesterol count was higher than his bank balance.'

'You've had a night, Archy. Would you like a glass of port?'

'Thank you, sir, I would.' I went to the liquor cabinet and helped myself to a generous measure before collapsing into one of the leather club chairs. 'Would you like a full account now, sir?'

'Please, Archy,' he said, reaching for one of the expensive cigars he kept in the top drawer of his desk. As he performed the ritual of snipping and lighting, I helped myself to my second English Oval of the day and then gave him a précis of my late client's final hours in this vale of tears. When I mentioned Joe Anderson's presence at the gathering father's eyebrows remained still. This told me that he was aware his mail person had been bitten by the acting bug. No happening at McNally & Son escaped the master's notice, thanks to Mrs Trelawney. No doubt I had been fingered as the heavy who led Joe astray.

'Will this put a stop to the play being performed?' father asked, hopefully.

'Knowing Lady Cynthia, I doubt it, sir. But Desdemona Darling is likely to drop out.'

'And this business will put an end to your investigation of the psychic?'

'With your permission, sir, I would like to continue with the case, pro bono I'm afraid.'

'Why, Archy?'

'Because Ouspenskaya used my grandfather's name and occupation to ridicule the McNally family, sir.'

Father sipped his port, stroked his mustache thoughtfully, and when a smile appeared on his lips he uttered, 'Permission granted, Archy.'

15

I dreamed that one of my silk berets, the puce actually, turned into a turban, which I donned, and then I began sawing Connie in half – lengthwise. I awoke in a cold sweat, attributing the nightmare to retiring on an empty stomach. I doubt if Palm Beach's resident psychiatrist, Dr Gussie Pearlberg, would agree but I had no intention of asking her.

I slept late, yet again, showered and shaved. I once bought one of those mirrors that are coated so as not to fog in steamy atmospheres and, imitating the smiling guy in the advert, I attached it to my shower wall with waterproof cement so I could shave while sluicing and save all of ten minutes every morning. On my first attempt I noticed a red hue in the water swirling about my feet and aborted the procedure before drawing the razor across my throat. The experiment having failed, I removed the mirror, plucking out a tile along with it. If there is a lesson to be learned in all of this, it escapes me.

I rinsed with witch hazel, the best aftershave known

to man, brushed my pearly whites and dabbed a bit of the smelly onto the nape of my neck. I tell all who ask that my scent is Royal Copenhagen, but it's a lie. Actually, it is a very expensive blend whose name I refuse to divulge because I don't want every man in Palm Beach who can afford it – which is every man, believe me – dousing themselves with my trademark.

I pulled on a pair of red briefs (the Chinese color of mourning) and a white T-shirt. This was as far as I got before my phone told me I was being hailed by someone fooling around with a similar instrument.

'Archy here.'

'What do you know, Archy?' It was Lolly Spindrift, already out gathering grist for his gossip mill.

'I know my stomach is gurgling. I haven't had a proper meal in twenty-four hours.' People who call before breakfast should be hanged by the thumbs.

'I'm on my cell phone, outside the police station.'

People who call before breakfast from a cell phone should be hanged by the *cojones*. However, in Lolly Spindrift's case, he might enjoy it. 'Why are you calling me from outside the police station on your cell phone, Lol?'

'Because something *el weirdo* is going on inside the station house, that's why.'

This conjured up all sorts of images, like our men in blue dancing cheek-to-cheek as the felons looked on approvingly. 'You have ten seconds to tell me what

this is all about, Lol, and then I'm hanging up. One –
two – three . . .'

'Desdemona Darling and Lady Cynthia Horowitz
arrived here at nine this morning and were met by the
paparazzi who had been camping outside the station
house since dawn.' Lolly spoke as if trying to get it all
in before I reached ten. 'Desdemona gave the boys a
statement prepared by her flack in Hollywood.

'They went into the station house and have not been
seen or heard from since.'

'What's that supposed to mean?' The truth of the
matter was, I had forgotten all about Al Rogoff telling
Lady C to have Desdemona report to the police first
thing this morning to ID her husband's body.

'It means they're being detained and haven't, as yet,
left for the morgue to ID Richard's body.'

'Detained?' I shouted. 'Lolly, you don't mean
they've arrested Desdemona Darling and Lady Cynthia
Horowitz?' That was more *el weirdo* than if he had told
me Tweeny Alvarez and Al Rogoff were doing a pas
de deux in tutu and leotard.

'They've been in there for over an hour. The police
spokesperson refuses to make a statement and just
when the press was getting bored a lawyer arrived
and was hustled into the station house, pronto. Now,
only an earthquake will oust the press from the station
house steps.'

'Who's the lawyer, Lol? Do you know?'

'That's why I'm calling, Archy my love. The solicitor
is from McNally and Son. Give Lol the scoop, Archy,

and I'll tell you about the most indecent romance going on in Palm Beach right under everyone's unsuspecting nose.'

Fearing he was talking about me, I swore to him that all I knew was what he had just told me. 'I'm standing here in my B.V.D.'s, Lol, and haven't spoken to a living soul since last night. Give me your cell number and I'll call you when I learn what's going on.' He did – reluctantly, but what choice did he have?

First I called the palace and asked to speak to Sergeant Rogoff. The desk sergeant told me Al was busy at the moment. I asked when he might be free and was told, 'I don't know. You wanna leave a message?' No, I did not, but I had learned what I wanted to know. Al had pulled the graveyard shift last night and would not be in the station house this morning unless he had been summoned. Al was the officer who had responded to our distress call last night and now he was locked up with Lady Cynthia and Desdemona Darling. I didn't even want to think what this might mean.

I called my father's office and got Mrs Trelawney. 'We're all as curious as you, Archy,' she told me when I asked what she knew about a lawyer being dispatched to the police station.

'We got a call from Lady Cynthia about an hour ago and she requested that a lawyer who knew something about criminal law join her at the Palm Beach police station. That's all she said. Your father would have gone but he was with a client. James Ventura, as a matter of fact. That's all I know but you had better get yourself here ASAP.'

Criminal law? I started thinking about what I didn't want to think about as I pulled on a pair of chinos and a lavender Lacoste. Argyle socks and a pair of tan bucks left from my brief tenure at Yale completed my outfit. I left my perch reflecting on James Ventura's visit to McNally & Son. Exit Richard Holmes. Enter James Ventura. I felt like I had just turned a corner and met myself coming the other way.

In the kitchen I told Ursi I was starved but I didn't have much time. 'I can warm you a healthy portion of the Roquefort quiche I prepared for lunch and give you a helping of hash browns and sausages to go with it.'

I didn't find a thing wrong with that. I helped myself to a glass of Ursi's fresh-squeezed orange juice before pouring a cup of black coffee. 'You made all the front pages, Archy,' Ursi said as she busied herself at the stove.

I picked up the morning edition Jamie had left behind and saw myself and Joe Anderson kneeling over the body of Richard Holmes. The headline blared ACTRESS'S HUSBAND SUCCUMBS AT THEATRICAL GALA. Lolly Spindrift got the byline.

'A terrible thing,' Ursi went on. 'Your father knew all about it this morning.'

'I told him about it when I came in last night, Ursi. Have you heard anything?'

'With Mrs Marsden away, I have no connection at

Lady Cynthia's. All I know is what I read in the morning newspaper and what your father told me.'

'You don't know the woman who's taking Mrs Marsden's place while she's away? Her name is Annie.'

'I don't know her, Archy.'

That was unusual. The domestics up and down the A1A were as close as pages in a book and their grapevine one step ahead of the people who employed them. 'Where did Lady C get her from?' I wondered aloud.

'I hope I'm not intruding.' Kate Mulligan was standing in the kitchen doorway. 'I came for a cup of coffee.'

'You're not intruding at all,' I said as Ursi served my breakfast. 'Please, have a seat and join me.'

'If I ate like that I'd be as big as Desdemona Darling. I was shocked when I saw her picture in the paper this morning – and your picture, Archy. I didn't know you were a socialite.'

'I'm not. I just happened to be in the wrong place at the wrong time. It's the story of my life.'

Kate took the cup of coffee Ursi offered her, but didn't sit. 'When Desdemona Darling was a regular at the clubs in Las Vegas, she had a figure that could rival any gal in the chorus. Now look at her.'

'I'm losing my appetite, Kate.'

She laughed, crinkling her nose and setting the freckles there in motion. 'I doubt that. And you didn't tell me you were a director.'

I was painfully aware of Ursi being forced to listen to our conversation from which she would conclude, rightly, that my mother's garden helper and I had more than just a nodding acquaintance. Ursi wouldn't breathe a word of this to my parents but if her pal, Mrs Marsden, was not away she would certainly mention it to her. Such were the unwritten edicts of domestic engineers. And, from Mrs Marsden's lips to Connie Garcia's ears. Did I say Buzz Carr liked to live dangerously? For the present, Mrs Marsden's absence saved me from a fate worse than death. Looking at Kate, I decided to enjoy the day for tomorrow I might be warbling *Un Bel Dì* for a living.

This resolve did not prevent me from feeling a tad uncomfortable when I answered, 'I'm not a director. It's community theater and except for Desdemona Darling there's not a professional actor in the cast. I never expected the show to make the front pages of our local gazettes.'

'It's a shame about Desdemona's husband. They say it was a heart attack.'

'That's what they say.' I refrained from passing on the more current news, feeling Ursi had enough fodder to pass along Ocean Boulevard for one morning. 'Won't you sit?' I asked Kate once more.

'No, thank you. I must get back. If you don't mind, Ursi, I'll take the coffee with me.'

'Help yourself, dear,' Ursi answered as she placed a warm scone and a pot of apricot preserves before me. 'Nice woman,' she added when Kate had departed, 'and your mother likes her.'

'For which we are all grateful,' I said, and seeing an opportunity to do a little missionary work I explained to Ursi, 'I ran into Kate in West Palm the other day and we had a drink together.' Subterfuge is like a bottomless pit. There's always one step further down you can go.

'That's nice,' Ursi said. I went out to the greenhouse to see mother, hoping to get in a few words with Kate in private. 'Good morning, mother.'

'Oh, Archy,' mother exclaimed, looking up from one of her clay pots. 'Kate told me you were having breakfast.' I bent to kiss her as she went on. 'What a tragedy at Lady Cynthia's last night. And you were right there, giving him resuscitation. It's in all the newspapers.'

'Actually, he was beyond being resuscitated, mother, but I was there.'

Kate was puttering around the potting table doing absolutely nothing as far as I could see. I caught her eye and executed what I intended to be a meaningful nod. 'I just stopped by to say hello before going to my labors. Enjoy your morning, ladies, it looks like we're in for a bit of rain this afternoon.' Florida weather is unpredictable, as witnessed by the brilliant morning sun fast giving way to dark clouds scudding in from over the Atlantic. The sun could be back out in two hours or we might not see it again for two days.

'The tourists may not like it but the garden needs the rain,' Kate said, sounding very professional.

'Yes,' mother nodded approvingly. 'That's just what I was saying earlier. You have a good day, too, Archy, and I like your shirt. I have a budding begonia coming in just that color. You know the one I mean, Kate?'

'Yes, Mrs McNally, I do,' Kate answered, picking up her coffee cup. 'I'm going to run this back to the kitchen, if you'll excuse me for a moment.'

'Oh, Archy can take it,' mother volunteered my services.

'Well,' Kate began hesitantly, 'I would like to visit the powder room.'

Poor mother blushed scarlet. With a reassuring pat on the shoulder, I gave her glowing cheek a good-bye kiss.

'I'll carry your cup,' I offered.

'Thanks. But I can manage.' Walking back to the house Kate opened with, 'I got the distinct impression that you weren't exactly thrilled with our conversation in the kitchen.'

'You make it sound as if I were annoyed with you. I'm not. It's just that I've never mentioned our dinner date to the family. Our prattle must have seemed a bit odd to Ursi, that's all.'

'Oh, I see. The boss's son and the lady who helps in the garden.'

'Come on, Kate. It's nothing like that and you know it. What's got into you, anyway?'

'I don't know. Maybe it was seeing your picture in the newspaper and learning you know all those society ladies. I thought you were just a detective.'

'Those society people are my father's clients, which makes them the bosses and me the hired man's son.'

219

We were nearing the kitchen door and I slowed down purposely so as not to end our talk on this note. 'Can I call you tonight?'

'Sure. It's your dime.'

'Don't give me a hard time, Kate. I had a lousy night and this morning wasn't much better. There's a problem with Richard Holmes's death.'

That stopped her cold. 'A problem? What do you mean?'

'I'm not sure myself.' Then I told her everything I knew. 'I'm on my way to the office to see if father has heard anything more.'

'Are you telling me he was murdered, Archy?'

The M word had finally come out of hiding. 'Don't start rumors, Kate, please. It could all be much ado about nothing. I don't know what the day will bring but keep tonight open in case I'm free.'

'Make contingency plans, Archy, in case I'm not free.'

I deserved that.

'Richard Holmes died of arsenic poisoning,' father announced without fanfare as I entered his office.

I sank into a chair. 'Is that official, sir?'

'When I got Lady Cynthia's call this morning I dispatched Saul Hastings to the police station. He called me ten minutes ago with the news.'

'Has anyone been arrested?'

Father shook his head. 'No, Archy. Lady Cynthia and Desdemona Darling were questioned for almost two hours. They've been released and Hastings is on his way back here. We'll get a full report when he arrives.'

'Was the arsenic in the wine the women were distributing, sir?'

'Hastings told me it had to be. It's a very fast-acting poison and according to both Lady Cynthia and Desdemona Darling, he died minutes after drinking the wine.'

What did Joe Anderson say last night? Life imitates art. The media was going to have a field day with this one. Lady Cynthia would have to call off the show. It would be obscence to go ahead with it now. 'Unless his death was self-inflicted, sir, I don't see how anyone could have tampered with his wine. There were at least thirty people present, all watching as the women poured the wine and handed it out.'

'So you told me, Archy. Where were you standing at the time?'

'I was with Lady Cynthia and Desdemona. Remember, Lady Cynthia had just finished her speech. The crowd was all huddled in a group, facing us.'

'And where was Holmes?'

I had to think a moment. 'The patio was lit with lanterns and hurricane lamps. Visibility was poor to say the least.' I was recalling how Al Rogoff had called for the powerful police torch the minute he came on the scene. 'In the front row,' I finally said. 'He was in the front row.'

'Are you sure, Archy?'

'Positive, sir. He came forward seconds after the toast had been given. He couldn't have done that if he wasn't right up front.'

'And who was near him, Archy? Can you recall?'

I saw myself, a little embarrassed, staring at the audience. It was like looking at a picture taken without sufficient light, dark and murky. Then I remembered. 'Binky, Connie and Joe Anderson. It had to be them. You see, sir, they were helping set up the wine table and when the ceremony began they stepped back a few feet and joined the onlookers. They had to be in the front row, too.'

'Of course the caterers removed all the glasses and the wine decanters, so any evidence concerning where the arsenic came from will be circumstantial,' father said in the vernacular of the legal fraternity.

'But scientific,' I put in.

'To be sure,' he agreed. 'And everyone present will be questioned, including and especially you, Archy, thanks to your vantage point. A pity our friend Ouspenskaya contacts ghosts by radio and not television. It would be interesting to see a rerun of last night's events.'

'Ouspenskaya!' The bulb went off. 'Where was he standing?'

'He was there?' father questioned.

'Thanks to Lady Cynthia. He's now her personal rabbit's foot. Did I tell you Richard Holmes told me he had read Ouspenskaya the riot act yesterday afternoon?'

'No, Archy, you didn't.'

'Because when I spoke to you last night it didn't seem relevant to Holmes's death. But now . . .'

'What exactly did Holmes tell you?'

'That if his wife continued to see Ouspenskaya she would have to do so with her own money. Holmes would no longer finance her sessions with the psychic.'

'And he told this to Ouspenskaya?'

'He did, sir.'

'Do you have any witnesses to the statement?'

'No, sir. I don't.'

'Then it's hearsay of the purest nature, Archy. Pity. What do you intend to do now?'

'I'm going to try and see either Lady Cynthia or Desdemona Darling and get a firsthand account of what they learned at the police station. After you speak with Hastings, we'll compare notes. Between us we should be able to put together a comprehensive picture of what the police have learned and are thinking.' Al Rogoff would be my main informant, if I could get to him, but I didn't want to share this with father until I knew how much Al was willing to share with me.

'This puts a different slant on your investigation of the seer,' father said.

'Different, sir?'

'Of course. The death of Richard Holmes. From what you just told me it's clear that Ouspenskaya is our most likely suspect. If he would commit such a heinous crime to keep a paying client, what might he do to someone who was committed to exposing him as a fake?'

This had occurred to me but I didn't agree that Ouspenskaya was the only person who found Richard Holmes inconvenient. 'What about Desdemona Darling, sir? She might have wanted to remain in Ouspenskaya's camp as ardently as he wanted her to stay. If she didn't have the money to do so while her husband was alive, she does now.'

'That would depend on two suppositions, Archy.'

'Did she know that her husband had threatened to cut off Ouspenskaya?' I said.

'Correct. And did she serve him the wine?'

'If she didn't, sir, Lady Cynthia did. And where does that leave us?'

'Ruminating, which we have no right to do. You've met Desdemona. Do you think her capable of such a thing?'

'She's loud and a bit vulgar, sir, but a murderer? I think not. However, I thought my friend Ouspenskaya was nothing but a con artist until today.'

'Watch your step, Archy.'

'I will, sir.' I opened the door, remembered James Ventura and closed it. Turning to father, I said, 'Mrs Trelawney told me James Ventura was here this morning. May I know what he wanted?'

'With all this other business going on I almost forgot to tell you. He wanted you. I told him you would call him. He left a contact number with Mrs Trelawney.'

Déjà vu all over again, in the words of Yogi Berra.

When I left father Mrs Trelawney told me Connie Garcia had been trying to get me all morning. 'No message, Archy, she just left word for you to call her as soon as you got in.'

I rode up to my glorified rabbit hutch but before I had a chance to call Connie, Joe Anderson made an appearance. 'Rumors are flying all over the office, Archy.' Joe looked a bit shopworn after last night's perturbation.

'Who's saying what, Joe?'

'Maggie, Saul Hastings's secretary. She says Hastings was sent to the police station first thing this morning to represent Desdemona and Lady Cynthia. Why did they need a lawyer to help them ID the body?'

'He wasn't representing them, Joe, not in the legal sense. He went to advise them.'

'Cut the bull, Archy. There's something fishy about that guy's death. Am I right?'

Quickly calculating the situation, I figured that the police would issue a statement as soon as they had finished interviewing Desdemona and Lady Cynthia, giving the evening editions their headlines as well as supplying television anchormen with their lead stories. Based on that, I gave Joe a preview of the six o'clock news.

The poor old man looked more upset than had the widow last night. 'Who did it, Archy?'

'For all anyone knows he did himself in, or it was a grotesque accident. Forget it and let the police puzzle it out.'

'Was it in the wine, Archy? Like in the play?'

'It was in something Richard Holmes ingested last night. I think that's all anyone can say right now.'

'It was no accident, Archy. Poison doesn't get passed around at a friendly party like pot or coke. The guy was done in,' Joe stated, looking very distressed by the fact.

'It was a bad night for all of us,' I told him. 'Why don't you go home and get some rest. The mail can wait a day.'

'Thanks, Archy, but I'll be okay. The news is worrying my nerves, that's all.'

'It has us all a bit jumpy. Sudden death from unnatural causes tends to stimulate our imaginations.'

'I didn't imagine that I was standing next to Richard Holmes when the ladies passed out the wine.'

So that was it. 'Who was on his other side, Joe? Do you remember?'

He shook his head. 'Binky, maybe. Or Connie. No – no – it was the beauty they call Fitz.'

'And did you all take your wine from the same tray?'

'Sure.'

'And who served you, Joe?'

'Lady Cynthia Horowitz, that's who.'

16

Before calling Connie I dialed Lolly Spindrift's cell phone number as I had promised him I would and got a busy signal for my troubles. An educated guess told me the police had issued a statement to the press and Lolly was on with his editor, turning a terse press release into a saga.

When reporting, Lolly never lied, but he never told the truth either. He was a master of insinuation and innuendo. Our purveyor of all the news that's barely fit to print would never win a Pulitzer, but that wasn't his aim. Remaining a fixture on the Palm Beach 'A' list, scoring extra dough for society obits, and competing with Phil Meecham for the local beefcake trade were his métiers and he excelled at all three.

Next I called Connie and got her.

'Archy, what do you know?'

If one more person asked me that today I'd jump out the window – if I had a window to jump out of. Has anyone ever jumped out of an air-conditioning vent?

'Brace yourself, Connie. Richard Holmes's heart did not cease to function because of his cholesterol count. He was poisoned.'

I could hear Connie gasp before she cried, 'Oh, my God! Oh, my God, Archy. He knew! He knew!'

'Take it easy, Connie. Who knew what?'

'Ouspenskaya, that's who. He felt something wasn't kosher when he woke up this morning. He had a dream. That's what he said. It came to him in a dream.'

Connie was not the hysterical type but right now she was fast losing claim to that distinction. In contrast, I spoke as slowly as possible, hoping to put the brakes on her babbling. 'Tell me what he said and take it one step at a time, starting from the beginning. When did you see Ouspenskaya?'

Another gasp and Connie exclaimed, 'Every extension on my board is blinking at me, Archy. The world is trying to call Lady Cynthia. This is crazy.'

She was referring to her 'telephone,' which consisted of a panel of red and green lights similiar to something Mission Control would use to send a man to the moon. 'The word must be out,' I told her. 'Pay them no mind, Connie, I'm sure Lady Cynthia is not ready to make a statement.'

'They can all leave messages on the voice mail system,' she answered.

'Good. Now tell me when you saw Ouspenskaya.'

'I didn't see him, Archy. He called me twice.'

She was revving her engine again. 'Connie, take a

deep breath, count to ten backwards and pick up from when you got out of bed this morning.'

She must have heeded my advice because it was a good half minute before she answered. 'I got up late,' she began, decidedly calmer. There was still an edge to her tone but who could blame her for that? 'After last night I thought I deserved it. I got here about ten and Annie, who's filling in for Mrs Marsden, told me Madame had left before nine in her Jaguar. Then I found a note from her on my desk telling me she had gone to pick up Desdemona Darling to take her to the police station. She expected to be back in an hour or so.'

'Fine,' I said. 'Then what?'

'I checked my voice mail like I always do and one of the messages was from Ouspenskaya. He said he wanted to speak to Lady Cynthia and would she please call him.' There was a pause before she groaned, 'Half the lights went out and now they're all lit up again.'

'Forget the lights, Connie, and go on with your story.'

'Don't sass me, Archy. I'm tense enough as it is. He was murdered? Right in front of all of us? How is that possible?'

'I didn't say he was murdered. I said he died of poisoning. The latter is not a necessary result of the former.'

'Like an unwanted pregnancy is not the result of one drink too many.'

I decided not to challenge that one. 'Go on, Connie. Then he called again? When?'

'Not long after I arrived here. That would make it about fifteen or twenty past ten. He was very excited. He wanted to know if I had gotten his earlier message and if Lady Cynthia had returned. I told him she had not.

'Then he said it made no difference because he was too late. That's what he said, Archy. That he was too late. He knew that Lady Cynthia was going to escort Desdemona to the police station. That was decided last night. He called here this morning to try to stop them.'

'Stop them? Why?'

'Listen, Archy. Just listen. It's scary,' Connie maintained. 'He said he had tried to get Desdemona earlier this morning after calling here but she had already left. Her houseboy told him that she had been picked up by Lady Cynthia and so he knew he was too late. I asked him what the trouble was and if I could help him.'

'And what did he tell you?'

'He told me that he awoke this morning with a heavy heart – you know how he talks, Archy – because he remembered a terrible dream he had had during the night. He didn't say what the dream was, just that he wanted to stop Desdemona from going to the police station because something terrible awaited her there.'

Those icy fingers were at work on me again. This Ouspenskaya was playing my spine like a xylophone. 'This could be important, Connie. Do you know what time Ouspenskaya left the message on your voice mail?'

'Sure. I get the date and time verbally at the end of a message. It came exactly one minute after nine.'

'And the second call came after ten?'

'That's right. I got in a little after ten and his call came shortly after that. What does it mean?'

It means, I calculated, that at nine o'clock this morning, when Desdemona and Lady Cynthia were just arriving at the police station, Ouspenskaya knew what only the police knew at that time. When Lolly called me, he said the ladies had arrived at the station house at nine and had been locked up with the police for an hour. That would make it about ten when Lolly called me, just when the press was beginning to suspect something was rotten in Palm Beach. This is when Ouspenskaya made his second call to Lady Cynthia's residence. He knew more about what was happening there than the press on the scene.

Sticking to my spy theory, it meant Ouspenskaya had a plant in our police department. Impossible. That left two choices. Ouspenskaya had the gift or he had poisoned Richard Holmes. But if he had slipped Holmes the mickey he certainly wouldn't be leaving voice messages telling anyone who cared to listen that Desdemona and Lady Cynthia were not going to have a nice day. That left the one hypothesis I still refused to accept. Who told Ouspenskaya, before nine o'clock this morning, that Richard Holmes had been poisoned? The doc who performed the postmortem?

'Are you still there, Archy?'

'I'm here, Connie. Don't take any calls until Lady Cynthia gets back and then consult with her on what you should say. I believe she left the police station a short time ago. Then tell her I'm on my way to see her.'

'You haven't been summoned, Archy.'

'If you don't lower the drawbridge I'll swim the moat, but I have a hunch Lady C will be very happy to see me.'

'I know I'll be happy to see you. What about lunch?'

'With all that's going on do you think you'll be able to get away for lunch?'

'Yeah. I forgot about that. Let's see how it's going when you get here.'

Counting on it going my way, I called Al Rogoff at his 'wagon,' where I guessed he should be by now. I was right. The 'wagon,' as Al dubbed it, is a mobile home off Belvedere Road, where it sits on a solid foundation along with similar residences. A trailer park, if you will. A mobile home resembles what used to be called a railroad flat in old New York tenements. Those that still exist are being sold as co-ops and touted as having old-world charm. The old-world charm comes with a hefty new-world price tag.

Al had a kitchen, bath, living room and bedroom, all in a row. He was his own interior decorator and while not fancy, it was a comfortable bachelor's digs.

'You awake, Al?'

'I am now, pal. I thought I would be hearing from you. Your society ladies are up to their chins with this one. I knew I would lose sleep the minute I got the call to that mansion, and when I saw you there I figured the guy didn't expire of natural causes.'

'Why, Al?'

'Because you're the custodian of God's waiting room, pal, that's why.'

'Thanks a bunch, Al.'

'Like I always tell you, we're here to serve.'

'Can I serve you lunch this afternoon?'

'I'm trying to get a few hours' shuteye, Archy. I got off duty at six this morning and they called me back in at nine. Have a heart.'

'I have more than a heart, Al, I have information for you.'

'I think you're more interested in the information I can give you. How much do you know, Archy?'

'The lawyer, Hastings, called my father from the palace and told him Richard Holmes had been poisoned. That's as much as I know.'

'I don't know much more, pal.'

'Remember, Al, I'm a material witness and I know what's been going on behind the scenes. Catch a few Z's and meet me at the Pelican at three for a late lunch.'

When I didn't get an immediate response I knew I had piqued his interest. 'You already told me Holmes had given Ouspenskaya his walking papers and there was bad blood between them.'

'When did you learn that Richard Holmes was poisoned?' I asked him.

'When I got to the palace, about nine-thirty. Why?'

'Serge Ouspenskaya knew it before nine this morning.'

It didn't take Al long to consider his options. 'See you at the Pelican, Archy.'

'Thanks, Al.'

Lady Cynthia had elected to wear a black pantsuit to view the remains and did not change to receive me. She was seated in a throne-like wing chair holding fast to what looked to be a tall whiskey and soda. 'I generally don't condone drinking hard liquor before the sun is over the yardarm but today is an exception to all the rules. Would you like one, lad?'

'No, thank you, Lady Cynthia.'

She was a tough woman but I must say the events of last night and this morning had her looking her age. I even noticed that she was having a hard time controlling the hand that held her glass, which trembled ever so slightly. If Lady C, who is not a booze hound, was indulging at high noon, I could only imagine how poor Desdemona Darling was dealing with all this.

'What do you know, lad?'

I was thinking of getting a sign proclaiming I KNOW ZILCH and pasting it to my forehead. I said to Lady Cynthia, 'Only what Saul Hastings reported to my father on the phone. What did the police tell you and DeeDee?'

'Not much more. They asked a lot of questions and I must supply them with last night's guest list, including the caterer's crew. After consulting with Saul Hastings, DeeDee and I decided to issue a statement to the press. It's to come from me. Connie is preparing it now. DeeDee will remain incommunicado for the present.'

'And what will the release say, may I ask?'

'You may, lad. It will say that Mrs Holmes is in a state of shock and that both she and Lady Cynthia Horowitz believe the unfortunate occurrence is the result of a bizarre accident.'

Now that should go over like flatulence in a crowded elevator. 'An accident? How could arsenic accidently get into a wine glass at a social gathering?'

'Simple,' Lady C retorted as if expecting the question and being fully prepared to answer it. 'The glasses were supplied by the caterer. One of them was not properly sanitized. I'm thinking of suing.'

This was too much. Even Catherine de Médicis had never made such a claim. These two crones must have intimidated Saul Hastings into not opposing either the press release or its wording and right now the poor man was trying to explain this madness to my father. But I didn't lose sight of the fact that Lady C was no fool and would wager my last pair of cashmere socks that there would evolve some rationale to this lunacy.

'Are you saying, Lady Cynthia, that arsenic was served at the last party your caterer facilitated and one glass was not properly washed? How jolly.'

'You're splitting hairs, lad. That's our story and we're sticking to it.' Lady C backed that up with a hearty swallow of her beverage.

'You and DeeDee poured and served the wine,' I reminded her. 'Did one of you accidently give Richard Holmes the glass that accidently contained a wee bit of arsenic left over from your caterer's last happy event?'

Lady Cynthia didn't like that at all and let me know it. 'Listen, young man, and listen good. We poured that wine in front of everyone present, including you. We told that to the police and invited them to question everyone present, including you, to see if anyone saw anything even vaguely suspect in how DeeDee and I performed. Good lord, lad, we rehearsed what we were going to do before the party. We didn't ad-lib.'

And anyone knowing the drill could have incorporated it into their own malevolent plans. Who and how was the question. There being safety in numbers, the best way to get away with murder was to surreptitiously commit one in front of a dozen witnesses who would automatically become suspects along with the nefarious culprit. I could only think of one person among us last night who had the cunning and daring to pull it off. But did he have the opportunity?

'As director of this year's community theater presentation,' Lady C rattled on, 'I suggest you go along with our view of what happened last night. Solidarity is vital to our success.'

'Our success? You mean you intend to go ahead with putting on *Arsenic and Old Lace*? I don't believe it.'

'The play will go on whether you believe it or not,' Lady C said. 'This unfortunate accident has given us a very high profile and we should strike while the iron is hot.'

She knew of what she spoke. Lady Cynthia had struck six irons while they were hot and had walked away with a king's ransom in gold and a title.

'I think it would be in very poor taste, Lady Cynthia. Especially when you take into account the way Richard Holmes died. The morbidly curious and the more lurid tabloids will flock to see us. The gentry will stay home.'

'Nonsense, lad. Mr Ouspenskaya told me the play will act as a catharsis to this terrible business. Avoiding it would only encourage our wounds to fester. He predicts success and a new career for DeeDee.'

So the oracle had been consulted and the die was cast. No big surprise except that Desdemona Darling wasn't backing out. 'And DeeDee has already agreed to go on with the show?' I questioned, hoping to convey the distaste I had for the decision in general and Ouspenskaya in particular.

'She is,' Lady Cynthia stated as she carefully placed her glass on the service table. 'We're from the old school, DeeDee and I, made like winter wheat that bends with the wind and bounces right back when it's past. Not like today's breed of shrinking violets.

'On the day my last husband died,' Lady Cynthia

divulged, 'I refused to cancel a charity tea for the benefit of humpback whales. The show goes on, lad, and you go with it. Like it or not.' The threat of pulling her account out of McNally & Son was inherent in the statement.

Her last husband was high in a tree snooping on two click beetles going at it when the limb of the sturdy oak holding him *accidently* broke away from the trunk. He had married her for her money and she had married him for his title. As usual, she got the better part of the deal.

'Maybe your guru can tell us how that particular glass got into Richard Holmes's hand.'

'I know you dislike Mr Ouspenskaya because he unearthed your burlesque comic grandfather. Don't be such a prude, lad. Everyone in town knows where the McNally money came from.' I would expunge that when reporting this conversation to father.

'If everyone knows it, what's so remarkable about Ouspenskaya knowing it?'

'What was remarkable was his predicting your involvement in our community theater exercise when no one on this earth knew DeeDee and I had elected to ask you to direct. *No one on this earth*, lad, is the operative phrase, as they say. Elsewhere the future is often clearly visible as Mr Ouspenskaya proved once again today. Connie told you about his call to me this morning to warn of what lay ahead for DeeDee and myself. How can you doubt the man's sincerity?'

'How can you unequivocally accept him based on a

few parlor tricks? Did you know Richard Holmes was my client, Lady Cynthia?'

'He told DeeDee and me last night that Richard had hired you to investigate him. It was very foolish of Richard.'

'So foolish that it may have gotten him killed.'

'Careful what you say. There are laws against libel. And now that Richard is gone I expect you will close your case against Mr Ouspenskaya.'

I wasn't going to tell her what I was up to, so I answered, 'I might order up a séance to see what Ouspenskaya can tell us about Holmes's death.'

'Richard Holmes is newly arrived on the other side. It will be months, perhaps years, before he is acclimated to his new life and until then contact with his shadow is impossible.'

She spoke by rote, as if she had memorized every bit of bilge Ouspenskaya had spewed out on the subject. This tactic was easy to figure out. Both Lady C and the widow must have asked Ouspenskaya to contact the dearly departed to see if Holmes could explain his own sudden demise and Ouspenskaya wasn't going to go near this one with the proverbial ten-foot pole, especially if he knew more about it than he cared to admit. If his paying customers liked the accident theory, so be it. And Archy was going to worry this case until Richard Holmes cast his *shadow* across Ouspenskaya's turban.

'Then we'll just have to wait and see what the police come up with,' I forecast.

'Until then,' Lady Cynthia said, 'you can start thinking about working out a rehearsal schedule and calling a cast meeting to distribute it. They will need a pep talk, lad. That's your job. The theater is bugging me for an opening date. Of course DeeDee must observe a respectable period of mourning after the service, but you can work around her until then.'

'A service?'

'Cremation. DeeDee will take his ashes back to California and inter them in her plot in Forest Lawn. All her husbands are there.'

'I hate to rattle your beads but the police will have to release the body first.'

'I'm aware of that,' she snapped back.

At that moment Buzz Carr, clad in white trunks and his skin glistening with moisture, entered the room. 'Excuse me,' he said, 'I was working out in the pool and forgot my robe. It's starting to rain out there. How are you, Archy?'

'You're excused,' his patron said, eyeing his half-naked form lasciviously. They say in matters sexual men lose the ability but women never lose the desire. Lady Cynthia Horowitz was proof of half the assumption.

Buzz went directly to Lady Cynthia and took her hand. 'Are you feeling better?' he asked her solicitously, sounding sincere.

'I am, my dear. I was just telling our director we are going ahead with the show.'

Buzz was clasping Lady C's hand between both of his. He had been with Fitz last night and more than likely would be seeing Phil Meecham later in the day because men like Buzz Carr can't afford to burn any bridges. Versatility was his long suit and a shot at acting was his last hope to break away from courting women old enough to be his grandmother and men who traded pocket money for favors. With Ouspenskaya a firm supporter of the show and its star, it was in Buzz's best interest to keep the psychic out of harm's way.

'We're all sorry about Mr Holmes,' Buzz said, still in his solicitous mode, 'but Mr Ouspenskaya says we should go ahead and he predicts we'll be a big hit.'

'From his lips to Apollo's ears,' I said, standing.

'Apollo?'

'Apollo was the Greek god of the theater,' Lady Cynthia informed her protégé.

'I'm going to pick up my script from Connie and be on my way,' I told them. 'I'll call you as soon as I've worked out a schedule.'

'See you, Archy,' Buzz bid me adieu. Our Creative Director was silent.

Connie was so busy fielding calls she barely had the time to tell me she couldn't go to lunch. I picked up my script, told her I would call her later and left her to her chosen profession.

On the way out I met Annie, who showed me to the door. I wondered if she, an attractive woman of about thirty, had come to Palm Beach in search of a rich husband as Hanna Ventura suspected was the lure for most of our winter help.

'How do you like working here?' I asked her.

'Fine, sir, except for last night. I hear the poor man was done in.'

'Accident, according to your boss.'

'Either way, sir, I hope Mrs Marsden gets back real soon.'

17

The Pelican Club was practically empty except for a few stragglers who had lingered over their lunches. Mr Pettibone was sitting on a bar stool studying the latest stock quotes and Priscilla, looking ravishing in a red frock that resembled a sarong with shoulder straps, was setting the tables. 'You're too early for dinner and too late for lunch,' she informed us. 'Take your pick but take your leave.'

'Lunch is served till three,' I told her. 'It's a house rule.' I steered Al to my favorite corner table and Priscilla reluctantly followed us.

'They broke a few rules at your fancy ball last night, Mr Director, unless a "suspicious death" is what's happening on the ocean side of the A1A.'

'Suspicious death?' I said. 'Where did you hear that?'

'It came over the local Miami TV channel on a newsbreak about an hour ago. My first society party and I knocked 'em dead with my presence.' Like Connie, Priscilla was perturbed by the news of Richard

Holmes's unnatural death and her glib chatter did little to hide it. 'I see you're tight with the fuzz. Is that for protection or is he going to give you the third degree over your victuals?'

'I thought I saw you in that sea of faces last night,' Al said. 'What's your role?'

'I know I saw you, Sergeant, and I was going to be makeup artist to the stars,' Priscilla answered.

'What do you mean *was*?' I broke in.

'I take it the show will go dark before we had a chance to turn on the lights,' Priscilla explained.

'Sorry, but you take it wrong,' I said. 'The show will go on and I hope you're still on board, Pris.'

'Is the widow still on board?'

'She is. The old gal is made of true grit,' I told her.

'Or there's less to her grief than meets the eye,' Priscilla observed. 'I'd say the play is jinxed, so I'll have to reconsider your offer.'

'I doubt if Henry Lee Wilson will back out,' I teased.

'I don't need to powder his nose to keep him interested. Now what are you having? It's one minute before three, so make it snappy.'

When lunching with Al Rogoff we didn't have to look at the menu to place our order. Burgers, medium rare, along with Leroy's fries, which are made by peeling and slicing potatoes, not reaching into the freezer, and two drafts. 'Could Leroy put together a mixed green salad to go with that?' I ask Priscilla.

'With Thousand Island dressing,' Al added.

Watching Priscilla's trim stern withdrawing, Al observed, 'You know, Archy. She's got a point there.'

'I would say she has several points, Al.'

'More curves than points, pal, but that's not what I mean. She said the actress dame might not be as upset over her husband's death as she pretends to be and now you tell me that she ain't dropping out of the show. Seems odd to me.'

I nodded in agreement. 'Ouspenskaya is advising her to stick with it. He predicts a new career for the lady.'

'At her age?'

'Jessica Tandy got her Oscar when she was eighty,' I informed Al.

'Has this Desdemona ever won an Oscar?'

'No, Al. Her appeal was more to the eye than the ear.'

'What's in it for Ouspenskaya if the show doesn't get canceled?' Al asked.

'I had the same thought. I think he doesn't want to see Desdemona fly back to California with her husband in an urn. There are also several other ladies, including Lady Cynthia, who are with the show and all of them are Ouspenskaya's faithful followers. Why break up the gang? Besides, Desdemona still hasn't found her lost work of art. She's a cash cow.' Before I had a chance to withdraw the unfortunate analogy, Priscilla brought us our brews in pilsners, each with a perfect two-inch topping of white froth.

'Here's mud in your eye,' Al said, hoisting the glass

with a beefy paw. One sip and the pilsner was half empty – or half full if you happen to be an optimist. I'm a firm believer in Murphy's Law. Anything that can go wrong, will. For those who disagree I have two words: *Titanic* and *Hindenburg*.

'I think Ouspenskaya told Desdemona about the phone call he got from her husband, threatening to stop financing Desdemona's patronage.'

'Before we go into that, Archy, tell me how this Ouspenskaya knew about the poison.'

'I wish I could. All I know is what Connie told me this morning.' Here I repeated, almost verbatim, Connie's words.

'And you're sure about the times of those calls?'

'Positive,' I answered. 'The nine o'clock call is a matter of electronic verification, not someone's word. You think the guy has a shill at the station?'

Al shook his head. 'Check this out, Archy. The medical examiner got in about eight this morning. He went to work and reported the results of his autopsy to us at nine, just about the time the actress was giving her statement to the press outside the station house.'

That not only gave me pause, it also did permanent damage to what was left of my sanity, leaving me bothered and bewildered if not bewitched. 'Are you saying Ouspenskaya knew about the poison before the police?'

'Just about,' Al said. 'So maybe he is psychic. It ain't impossible.'

It was more bravado than confidence that had me saying, 'Or he helped Holmes meet his maker.'

'And then announced it the next morning?'

'The guy is nervy, Al. Was the arsenic in the wine?'

'Who knows? It was in Richard Holmes, that's for sure. They say the stuff is quick-acting and the wine was the last thing he downed before he expired, right? Hence, we go by the theory that it was in the wine.'

Priscilla arrived with our mixed greens in a huge teak salad bowl, two salad plates and a bottle of Kraft's Thousand Island dressing. Leroy usually disguises his store-bought dressings in a store-bought cruet but I guess latecomers should be happy with what they get.

Priscilla put three shakers on our table, announcing, 'Salt, pepper, arsenic,' and fled.

'Some sense of humor,' Al griped.

I helped myself to the greens before Al got his hands on the bottle of dressing and deluged our salad. 'Where does one get arsenic, Al?'

'Where do kids get assault weapons to take out their history class? It's a controlled substance but so is marijuana. It's in rat poison and products sold to clean out wasp nests and things like that.'

In spite of the subject matter I applied a few dabs of dressing to my salad and dug in, not realizing how hungry I was until I did so. Pop dressings, like pop music, are irresistible.

'I'm more interested in how it got in the victim's glass than in how the murderer came to possess it,' Al continued.

'So you think it was murder?'

'What do you think, pal?'

'I agree.'

'And you think Ouspenskaya is suspect *numero uno?*'

Al finished the salad on his plate and I told him to take what was left in the bowl and he did. Al Rogoff is not shy.

'Look at it this way,' I said. 'Holmes hires me to prove Ouspenskaya is a phony and expose him. Ouspenskaya is aware of this for reasons I have yet to learn. Next, Holmes calls Ouspenskaya yesterday morning and tells him he will no longer finance his wife's quest for a can of film some joker claims to possess.'

'So he knocks off Holmes with poison,' Al picked up my story, 'and then he calls Lady Cynthia the next morning to tell her all about it. You have to do better than that, pal. And how did he get the arsenic in Holmes's glass? According to Lady Cynthia and Desdemona Darling, Ouspenskaya was nowhere near Holmes when they passed out the wine.'

Priscilla was once again upon us with our order of burgers and fries and a bonus helping of kosher dills and pickled cherry peppers. I asked her to bring us two more drafts.

'Did they say who was near Holmes?' I asked.

Al put down the ketchup long enough to dig a crumpled piece of paper out of his pants pocket. 'Your friend Binky. Your girl, Connie. Some guy named Joe Anderson. Elizabeth Fitzwilliams and a Buzz Carr.

They were in the front row of spectators, along with the victim.'

That tallied with my list except for Buzz, but he had been up front with Lady Cynthia along with Binky, Connie and Joe, so it was only natural that he ended up in the front row and you didn't have to be a rocket scientist to figure out that Fitz was there because Buzz was there. 'Did Lady Cynthia tell you she served Holmes the wine?'

'She did, but how do you know?'

'Joe Anderson told me. He was standing next to Holmes. He's our mail person at McNally and Son, in case you don't know.'

'Don't tell me he's in your show, too?'

'He plays the old codger the ladies try to poison. How's that for a plot?'

'Like *Hamlet*, Archy. A play within a play. But that's a good piece of info. The ladies didn't know exactly who was standing where.'

'The girl, Fitzwilliams, was standing on Holmes's other side. They call her Fitz, by the way.'

'And you saw the ladies pour the wine?'

'Like everyone else, I was watching them, Al, but I wasn't scrutinizing them. I'm sure you remember the patio was in semi-darkness thanks to those lanterns, but even with that disadvantage someone would have noticed if either of them had deliberately emptied a vial of poison into one of the glasses. And how could they know which glass Holmes would take? They put four or five glasses on their trays and moved out into the crowd. People picked their own glass, they weren't told which one to take.'

'If we put Ouspenskaya on a back burner and forget about how the arsenic got in that glass, who else do you think had it in for Holmes?' Al proposed.

It didn't take me a nanosecond to respond, 'Desdemona Darling, because Holmes threatened to cut off her cash flow. Then there's Buzz Carr. He's counting on the show to help his nonexistent career and he's currently shacked up with Lady Cynthia, who's the driving force behind this season's community theater. He would want to protect Ouspenskaya to keep his patron and the show's star happy. But he's a long shot, Al. The guy is a hustler but I don't think he'd have the nerve to say boo to a goose.'

Al polished off the last of his fries and forked up a cherry pepper. 'Suppose the wrong guy got the right glass. Who else in that crowd was carrying baggage?'

'Who wasn't? And you're going to love this, Al. Low sex in high society. Buzz is getting it off with Fitz so Lady C would not lose sleep if Fitz suddenly vanished. Vance Tremaine is also sniffing after Fitz and his wife doesn't like it. William Ventura is also hot for Fitz and Arnie Turnbolt is hot for William.'

'Poor Fitz,' Al mumbled.

'If you saw her, Al, you'd join the bread line. Did I mention that Hanna Ventura and her stepson, William, are usually at each other's throats and that Buzz used to live on Phil Meecham's yacht before Lady C lured him into her nest?'

'You've got more going on backstage than onstage,' Al said, spearing a pickle with his fork.

'It's not unusual for a theatrical company,' I informed him. 'It keeps them on their toes like in the ballet.'

Al produced a toothpick and began chomping on it. Gauche, but it was preferable to the butt of a used cigar. This, incidentally, triggered a craving for a cigarette but I had left my box of English Ovals in the Miata. 'You have no idea how Ouspenskaya knows what he knows?' Al mused.

'My theory is that he operates with a network of spies who report to him, like gossip columnists use stringers and press agents.'

Al responded to this with a wave of his toothpick. 'He arrived in town a few months ago. Are you saying he came with his own network of spies? Forget it, pal.'

I would be happy to forget it if I had another theory to go on. 'How are the police going to proceed on this one?' I probed, hoping for some inside poop.

'We're going to begin by questioning everyone who was on the scene when Holmes was done in. You're on the list, pal, so don't leave town.'

'You have my word. And I think you should know that Lady Cynthia is issuing a press release saying she and Desdemona think the poison got into Holmes's glass by accident. An unsterilized glass supplied by the caterer.'

Rather than laugh, Al said, 'You know what, Archy?

After hashing out everything we know about this case, that could be the most plausible explanation.'

I drove the Miata directly home and, yes, I lit an English Oval along the way. Once in my penthouse lodgings, I dialed the number Mrs Trelawney had given me to contact James Ventura. A very efficient secretary told me I had reached the offices of Ventura Enterprises. That could mean it was anything from a booking parlor to the home-away-from-home of a millionaire who liked to get away from home. When I gave her my name I was immediately connected to James Ventura.

'My father said you wanted to see me, sir.'

'I do, but I'm not looking for a part in your show,' he assured me.

I like a man with a sense of humor to equal my own. 'All the roles are spoken for, sir, and both your wife and your son portray policemen.'

'Does that mean Hanna can't show her legs?' he laughed.

Neither can your son, I wanted to answer, but I didn't want to test the limits of Ventura's sense of humor. 'We'll see what we can do about that. How may I help you, sir?'

'You can start by calling me James, but never Jim or Jimmy.'

'James it is. How may I help you, James?'

'Nothing I can discuss on the phone, I'm afraid. Are you free for lunch tomorrow?'

'I can make myself free,' I said, implying that I had a lunch date I would have to break.

'Good. What about the Amaranth at one?'

The Amaranth is this season's 'in' restaurant. Even more 'in' than when it was called the Arcadia last season. It seemed James liked to travel first class and who was I not to go along for the ride? I've been known to wear white tie and tails to Burger King so putting together a costume for Amaranth did not dismay me in the least. 'I'll be there, James.'

According to Hanna, young William was a loose cannon with a short fuse. I was certain the boy was the reason I'd be making my debut at the Amaranth.

Then I called Kate Mulligan and got her answering machine. 'I'm out for the evening. Please leave a message and I'll return your call in the morning. Thank you.' Was I the first Lothario to get the telephonic equivalent of the cold shoulder? If so, I wouldn't be the last. I did not leave a message.

To give a boost to my ego I donned a pair of cerise Speedos with a matching terry cardigan and stepped into a pair of espadrilles just for the hell of it. One of the advantages of this outfit was that it instantly stopped traffic on the A1A, making for a safe passage from shore to sea. I had my swim, one mile north, one mile back, and returned to my room to enter the latest developments on 'Serge the Seer' in my journal.

The man professed to be in constant touch with those who had crossed over but the last thing I had anticipated when I took this case was to witness one making the crossing – least of all my own client. Pseudo psychics and bogus fortune-tellers seldom, if ever, resort to violence when working a scam. Their art is to foster confidence in the credulous, bilk the mark and exit, leaving behind a few bruised egos now poorer but wiser for their brief encounter with the hereafter. Ouspenskaya had the most obvious reason for doing in Richard Holmes but both his profession's modus operandi and his lack of opportunity logically ruled him out as the heavy.

But was he connected with the murder of Richard Holmes? That is, if Ouspenskaya had not arrived on our island this season, and Desdemona and Richard Holmes had, would Holmes be alive today? How did the arsenic get into that glass and why did Holmes take the tainted glass off Lady Cynthia's tray? You would have to be a magician to do the former and a psychic to know the latter. And I was right back to square one.

I recalled Desdemona Darling's party and found myself once again looking through that kaleidoscopic sea of humanity. Richard Holmes shoving Ouspenskaya away from DeeDee as William Ventura looked on with glee. Penny Tremaine crashing the party and confronting Vance and Fitz; Phil Meecham arguing with Buzz Carr and cursing Arnie Turnbolt when he tried to break it up. I knew the picture wasn't complete the minute I finished my mental sketch but I could not compute the missing element. Experience had taught me that the more I rummaged around my memory, the more nonplussed

I would become. So I let it go and turned my thoughts to matters more ethereal but not less pressing.

The sun was setting, the surf was rising, and I celebrated the passage of Helios and the rise of Luna by lighting my second English Oval of the day and brooding over life, liberty and the pursuit of happiness – my life, my liberty and my happiness. An evensong for Archibald McNally. Twilight had this effect on me. So did a case in which my prey eluded me in every encounter.

I blew smoke rings at the moisture spots on my ceiling (courtesy of the leaky roof) and reflected on the sudden death of Richard Holmes. This encouraged me to reaffirm my resolve never to take a world full of pestilence, violence and happenstance seriously. I would continue to drink every drink and grab every bit of pleasure as if it were the last. However, the certitude left me feeling like the woman of song, Rose of Washington Square, who had no future but oh what a past. At moments like this, I felt that the answer to all life's mysteries, including Ouspenskaya's parlor tricks, was as obvious as my puss in a mirror. So why did I draw a blank at every turn?

Should I re-call Kate and leave a reconciliatory message? Should I call Connie and see if she was free this evening? I ended up calling Binky Watrous and telling him to assemble the cast tomorrow night to receive their rehearsal instructions.

'Where?' asked Binky.

'Call the Creative Director and ask her,' answered I.

Then I dressed for cocktails and dinner with the family. Always a safe bet and never a tab.

'Nice to have you with us,' father said, serving our martinis.

'Thank you, sir.'

'Oh, Archy,' mother gushed, her face flushed with excitement, 'that man's death at Lady Cynthia's was all the talk at our C.A.S. meeting this afternoon. They all saw your picture in the newspaper, trying to resuscitate him. I was quite the star.'

The C.A.S. is the Current Affairs Society, of which mother is a faithful member. They meet once a month and listen to a lecture by experts on such diverse subjects as global warming, political unrest in Tibet and the joys, trials and tribulations of same sex parenting. Mother is the group's former sergeant-at-arms.

'They said,' Mother continued, 'that he was poisoned and your father tells me this is true.'

'I'm afraid it is, mother,' I said.

'How terrible,' she lamented. 'This sort of thing never happened in what I like to think of as the good old days, when you and your sister were just children. The whole world has gone crazy.'

'Have you heard anything new?' father asked me.

'I spoke with my police contact, Sergeant Rogoff, but he didn't have much to add to what we already know. And I called James Ventura, as you requested, sir. I'm seeing him tomorrow.'

'Good,' father said. 'I'll fill you in on what Saul

Hastings had to say later. Right now I think we should engage in happy talk to go along with our happy hour.' As always, father wanted to protect mother and the serenity of our household from the more tumultuous aspects of our business. For this I admired him.

'Cheers,' mother cried and I seconded the motion.

When we went downstairs to dinner we discovered that Ursi had prepared my favorite mixed grill (lamb chops, tournedos, medallions of veal), accompanied by julienne vegetables and crispy roast potatoes. Father produced a fine red Bordeaux for the menfolk and mother, as usual, stuck with her sauterne. We ended the repast with Black Forest cake and coffee.

Mother and father settled in front of the television and I climbed the stairs to my room to work out a rehearsal schedule, pour myself a marc and light my third English Oval of the day – but who's counting?

Jinxed. Priscilla had said our play was jinxed and I couldn't stop the word from running amok in my head as I took the first step in getting *Arsenic and Old Lace* on the boards.

18

James Ventura was a man who had made his fortune early enough to retire to Palm Beach in what he probably considered his middle age, although I doubted he knew many men who were a hundred. His physical appearance made it clear that he could still partake in a bracing game of golf or tennis and, having met Hanna, I knew he was virile enough to enjoy the pleasures of a wife just past the legal age of consent.

There were now silver threads among the black hair and a decided thickening about the waist, but the configuration of his dark good looks made him immediately recognizable as William's father. He wore a lightweight gray business suit and the traditional blue and red silk rep tie. 'I appreciate your taking the time to see me, Archy,' he said, extending his hand as the maître d' seated me at his table. 'I hope this is not inconvenient, but I find the food better than the club's and the diners less inquisitive.'

James Ventura didn't mention the club at which he

found the cuisine lacking and a glance around the room told me the indifferent diners were the regulars on the New York/Palm Beach circuit who made the society columns as well as the front pages of the dailies in both venues. Besides the landed aristocracy of our classless society I spotted titans of industry, politics and letters. The women, wives or powers in their own right, were perfectly coiffured, perfectly haute coutured and painfully thin. In effect, my host was telling me that he was a small fish in a big pond and the sharks had better things to be agog over than the sight of James Ventura lunching with a Palm Beach denizen noted for resolving embarrassing problems with a minimum amount of stress and strain on the aggrieved. Ventura would be amazed to know how many of our luncheon companions had availed themselves of my unique services.

'The pleasure is mine, especially if you're treating,' I said with a smile on my face and a song in my heart. Hey, I wasn't kidding and the man knew it.

'No bull. I like that,' Ventura complimented.

In fact I was feeling rather frisky in my olive green three-button job and black knit tie. It was an outfit I had put together for attending church with those who bore me. I was drawn to the services by the full-figured contralto in the choir whom I was seeing on the side. When she married a naval aviator and moved to Pensacola my faith ebbed. I resurrected the olive green job (no pun intended, please) in honor of today's lunch.

At that moment two Bloody Marys in crystal stem glasses were placed in front of us. 'I ordered them,' Ventura said, 'and told them to bring 'em when you arrived. The tomato juice and fruit make it healthy and save the trouble of ordering an appetizer. Shouldn't overdo at lunch unless you're a construction worker, which my father was before he bought the outfit. Cheers.'

'Cheers,' I said to the control freak, for that's just what James Ventura was, but with a decided difference from your run-of-the-mill control freak – he didn't try to hide the fact. James Ventura was most likely a second-generation American born on the wrong side of the tracks whose father ended up owning the company that had hired him to pour cement. Rags to riches; an American romance as opposed to an American tragedy. I must remember to tell Sofia Richmond that the Ventura money didn't come from Wall Street but from building streets. That aside, it was as good a Bloody Mary as our Mr Pettibone could conjure up and probably would have been my choice of cocktail.

'Do I have to tell you who recommended you, Archy?' he wanted to know.

'No, you don't, and I'd rather you didn't. Discreet is not our middle name, James, it's our first name.'

'That's why I came to you. Too bad about Holmes. They say it was poison. What do you think?'

If we were playing word association on a shrink's couch I would say I was recommended to him by Richard Holmes. 'If the police say he died of arsenic poisoning I think he died of arsenic poisoning. They don't mince words. What do you know about it?'

He almost dropped the glass he had just lowered from his lips. 'Me? I don't know a thing. What do you know? You were right there, giving the guy first aid.'

'They say a picture is worth a thousand words. In this case, all of them wrong. I was merely feeling for his pulse, which I didn't find. I know as much as your wife and son, James. They were both there.'

'Today's papers say it might be an accident. Contaminated glass. It's possible, I guess.'

'They say with Jesus all things are possible.'

It took him a minute to respond and when he did he chuckled loud enough to draw the attention of several sharks and their sharkettes. Two things one must never do in fine restaurants is laugh too loud or eat too much.

'You know my wife, Archy.' It was a statement, not a question.

'I had the pleasure of lunching with her at your home. I went to see her to learn more about our celebrity of the week, Serge Ouspenskaya. Like you said, James, no bull. Your wife's diamond clip was the launching pad for Ouspenskaya's career and both she and Holmes's wife are under the man's spell. I think Richard Holmes came to you for a firsthand account of the lost and found diamond clip, trying to find a flaw in the story, and you discussed the psychic and Holmes told you he had engaged me to investigate the man. Right so far?'

The maître d' was upon us offering menus, which Ventura waved away. 'The lemon sole, poached, with a salad and vinaigrette dressing. You can bring the bread and butter with the meal.'

Like it or not, I was going to have the lemon sole, poached. Fortunately, I liked it. And I had been wondering where our bread and butter was and now I knew. James didn't like nibbling before his meal, therefore neither did I. How did Hanna cope with the man and why did she? The money, to be sure. What fools these mortals be, as Puck had proclaimed one midsummer's night.

'Do you drink wine?' Ventura asked.

'Indeed, I do,' I told him.

'Bring us a nice white,' he told the maître d'.

'Make that a nice *côtes de Provence*, whatever year you have in the cellar,' I got in before the man escaped and returned with something outrageously expensive and not worth the cork that contained it.

'You know about wine, Archy,' he said, seemingly pleased that I did.

'I know a little bit about a lot of things, James . . .'

'And nothing about Serge Ouspenskaya,' he cut in. 'You're correct. Holmes told me he had hired you and the night before he died he told me you had turned up nothing on the guy to date.'

We had finished our drinks and obviously were going to go dry until the wine got here. The ice water before me looked tempting but I feared it would rust my windpipe. 'Do you want me to continue my investigation of Ouspenskaya, James? Pick up where Holmes left off?' Maybe I could add to the meager advance Richard Holmes had given me. The pater would be proud. Alas, it was not to be.

'Not me, Archy. I have no beef with the guy. Look, he did find that clip that set me back a few bucks and if he amuses the ladies, why not?'

'You have no problem paying for his consultations at five hundred bucks a consult?' I insisted.

'I have no problem because I won't let Hanna have one. Too bad Holmes didn't do the same with his wife but when you're married to a famous actress I guess you don't make the rules. No, Archy, my problem is not with Ouspenskaya's sittings. It's when he cancels them that has me worried.'

On that interesting note the bus person wheeled over the tripod holding a bucket of ice in which our wine was chilling and deposited two wine glasses on our table. The waiter right behind him did the decanting as we watched in silence, and when done he poured a dollop into Ventura's glass. Ventura sipped and nodded his pleasure, which I found amusing, and then my glass was filled. '*Cent' anni,*' I toasted.

'You know Italian, too.'

'As I told you, I know a little bit about a lot of things but I don't know anything about canceled séances and I'm all ears. Why should they bother you, James?'

The poached sole arrived with a salad that looked as if the Romaine and Boston Bibb leaves were picked an hour ago and chilled in vinaigrette dew. I tend to babble in the tongue of P. Shelley when good food is served as a feast to the eye as well as the belly, as it should be, and as was our lunch.

'Hanna goes to all of them when she's invited, which is often, thanks to the diamond clip. She's a one-woman press agent for the guy. She went to one last week. I think it was Wednesday night, at Fanny Seymour's place. You know Fanny and Ed Seymour? Hanna and Fanny run around together.'

I assumed that Fanny Seymour was the woman I had seen with Hanna the day I cased Ouspenskaya's office. She was at Lady C's party, too, and now I knew why. If I wasn't mistaken her husband was a member of my cast. I told this to James Ventura.

'Hanna got home after midnight,' James went on. 'The next day at the club I heard some women talking about Ouspenskaya. One of them said she had been invited to a sitting last night but it was canceled. So where was Hanna?'

'Did you question your wife?'

'No. I gave her the benefit of the doubt. My doubt that the woman I heard had the date right. Or maybe she was talking about another psychic – the town is full of them, and I wasn't listening that carefully. I'm not a suspicious man, Archy. Don't trouble trouble before trouble troubles you is how I see it.'

'And it did?'

He put down his fork. 'She went to another sitting two nights ago. That Lolly Spindrift was there. I know because he wrote it up in his column yesterday and listed all the guests. Hanna was not among them. That's when I came to see you.'

The meal was as superb as the conversation was dispiriting. The waiter refilled our glasses. When he withdrew I asked, 'Do you want me to find out where your wife was on those occasions?'

Looking down at his plate he answered, 'Yes.'

'Why don't you ask her? There could be a logical explanation for this.'

'Give me two for instances, Archy.'

I thought about this while sampling my second glass of wine. It was as good as the first, but I couldn't come up with even one for instance.

'I'm waiting,' Ventura said.

'I don't like domestic cases, James.' And neither did the police. Al Rogoff says that when called on a domestic squabble the couple kiss and make up six times out of ten and then threaten to sue the police for breaking and entering. And I rather liked Hanna. Based on our no bull understanding, I boldly asked, 'Do you think she's seeing another man?'

'I would be lying if I said it didn't cross my mind.'

The bus person approached to clear away our lunch, eliciting a pause in our discussion. I imagine those who serve are used to the *conversations interruptus* their presence evokes. Our waiter, once again, was on the bus person's tail and asked if we wanted to see the dessert menu. I was delighted to learn we would.

'I ask,' I said when we were once again alone,

'because I must tell you that your son makes it a point of telling anyone who cares to listen . . .'

I was stopped with a wave of Ventura's hand. 'I know, Archy. I know,' he moaned. 'William was very close to his mother and very unhappy when I married Hanna. It's no secret that Hanna was part of William's crowd down here and I think he was more embarrassed than angry over our May/December romance, and still is. I should toss him out but I can't do that to my own son, and I should box his ears but he's too old for that. I think it's best to ignore him and let time pass. He'll get over it.'

Silence, if not denial, seemed to be Ventura's way of dealing with the evils that beset the human race. I hated to buck the trend but felt I must. 'I think you should simply ask Hanna where she was on the nights in question.'

'It might prove awkward, Archy.'

'Why?'

'Suppose this thing is just a passing flirtation? Hanna is young and young girls are hopelessly romantic. The point is, I'm willing to forgive and forget if that's all it is. A few clandestine meetings for the thrill of it and then it's over. But if I confront her, and it's nothing more than that, it will cause a rancor between us that will never heal. You see why I need your help?'

I saw, but I still didn't like it. What I didn't see was the dessert menu. Before I had a chance to peruse the *carte*, Ventura signaled our waiter and ordered raspberry sorbet for two. It wasn't my favorite but then I wasn't paying the bill.

'I thought you would be especially interested in helping me, Archy, because of Ouspenskaya.'

'I don't see the connection,' I said.

'Both times Hanna lied, she was supposed to be with Ouspenskaya. Are other Palm Beach matrons using him as a beard, and does he know it?'

The plot not only thickened, it damn near congealed. I took the case along with the raspberry sorbet – not very keen on either.

When I got back to my office I called Lolly Spindrift. 'You attended a séance with Ouspenskaya the other night and wrote about it, is that right?'

'Right,' he said. 'If you want to mix and mingle with the Palm Beach elite, that's where you'll find them. The man is what's happening this season and my readers can't get enough of him. I hear he's booked weeks in advance. Are you still in hot pursuit?'

'My ardor has cooled,' I fibbed, 'and Ouspenskaya is not the reason for my query. I want to know if you left out anyone when reporting on the night's participants.'

'Many things are possible, Archy, but Lolly Spindrift forgetting to drop a name is not one of them. Why do you ask?'

Lolly was no fool and I had to tread lightly with this one. 'There's a rumor making the rounds that a big pol attended a Palm Beach séance on the grounds of anonymity and I want to verify the story before I cast my next ballot. I don't want this year's budget determined by Abe Lincoln.' From small fibs, mighty prevarications grow.

'Interesting. I'll remember to keep my eyes peeled. Now tell Lolly who claimed to be there and wasn't – and why?'

'At least give me a gold star for trying, Lol.'

'I'll give you all the gold stars you want if you tell me the true reason for this call.'

'Sorry, but I can't.'

'Has it got anything to do with Richard Holmes's untimely demise?'

'It does not, Lol. Cross my heart and hope to die,' I vowed without fear of reprisal.

'Only the good die young, Archy. Are you buying the accident theory being put out by the Brewster sisters? Can you believe it? The pair announce taking over the parts of the fictitious poisoners, pour the wine and a gent drops dead. There's been nothing like it in polite society since Lizzie Borden went ape with an axe. I can't reach *les girls* for comment. What's your take on it?'

'I'm keeping an open mind, Lol, but I do have a nice item for you,' said the spider to the fly.

'Really?' said the fly suspiciously, 'like what?'

'The play will go on as scheduled.'

He gave that some thought before asking, 'With the cast as announced by Lady C on the fateful night?'

'With nary one substitution,' I insisted. 'Desdemona Darling is a trouper of the old school, Lol.'

'She is a cow,' Lolly unkindly responded. 'Can I confirm this with your Creative Director?' he wanted to know, hoping to get an exclusive with Lady C on Holmes's death.

'I'm the director. You can take my word that the show will go on with Desdemona Darling in the lead.'

'It's weird, Archy.'

I could think of worse things to call it, but refrained. 'We live in weird times, Lol, a time of sudden death and indecent romance, to coin a phrase.'

He didn't have to mull that one over for long. 'It's my phrase you're coining.'

'So it is. Can I know who's being indecent?'

'In this town? Everyone! And I said I would tell you if you told me why one of your lawyers had arrived at the station house that morning to assist Desdemona and Lady C. Remember?'

'I did call you as soon as I learned the answer, but your line was busy. You must have had the police press release by then.'

'So we owe each other nothing,' Lolly stated.

'Tell me as a favor and I'll owe you.'

'Listen, Archy, it was something I picked up by chance from not too reliable a source. I mean I got it secondhand.'

No surprise there. 'You get everything secondhand,' I said.

'Secondhand from reliable sources. That's different. I don't want to make waves unless I know it's true.'

This was a revelation. The only thing that liked to make bigger waves than Lolly Spindrift was the *QE2*. A few days ago he was willing to tell all. Now he was having second thoughts. Who was he protecting? 'Okay, Lol, but will you answer one question?'

'Tell me what it is, and I'll think about it.'

'Is one of the parties one of my wannabe thespians?'

He gave this a lot of thought and I waited patiently for a response. When it came it was a simple, 'Yes, one of them is.'

In our game of give and take why did I get the feeling that Lolly Spindrift got more than he gave?

19

It was after three when I got off the phone with Lolly Spindrift. Kate usually arrived at our house at ten and left about three, when mother went in for her nap. There was a good chance that she would be back in her condo in West Palm at this hour. Now that I could once again bill my time I decided to ride over to Currie Park and, if she was still speaking to me, ask Kate a few more pointed questions about the art of magic and fortune telling.

Over our Tex-Mex dinner she had admitted to knowing several psychics in her Las Vegas days. Since checking out the accommodations on Clematis Street I wanted to know what, if anything, she knew about the man upstairs. It was my new client who had pointed out the connection between Ouspenskaya and Hanna's mysterious outings, therefore I had no compunctions about ambling along in the Miata with Ventura's meter ticking.

As I drove I thought about my new assignment, looking for something besides the fee I would earn to be cheerful about and coming up snake eyes with every try. Hanna was young, pretty and trying to make a difficult marriage work while doing battle with a hostile stepson who lived in. If she was seeking solace elsewhere I didn't want to be the one to blow the whistle. Be that as it may, I had taken the job and I had an obligation to my client. I would call it as I saw it but hoped, as Ventura had suggested, that the diversion was nothing more than a passing flirtation.

The suspicion that his wife was using Ouspenskaya as a beard, possibly with the seer's consent, was too intriguing to pass up and gave me a starting point for my investigation, which, to my advantage, took up where my last case left off. The boy, William, also had to figure in this débâcle. He watched his stepmother like a hawk, looking for just such an indiscretion to report to his father. Either William didn't know what was going on or he was waiting for Hanna to pass the point of no return before going public. My job was many things, but never dull.

Kate was still in her gardening clothes, minus the Top-Siders, when she opened her front door. 'I didn't call,' I said, 'because I was afraid you'd refuse to see me.'

She smiled that fetching smile and stood back to let me in. 'Someone called last night but rang off without leaving a message,' she answered, closing the door. Except for her shoes, which lay on the floor in front of a cushioned chair, the place looked uninhabited and even more austere in the bright light of day than it had the other evening.

'Guilty,' I admitted. 'I called to invite you to dinner but if you weren't here, what was there to say?'

'Oh, but I was here and I would have picked up the moment you mentioned dinner,' she said with a mischievous look in her bright eyes. 'If you had called to make excuses not to see me, I would let you believe I was otherwise engaged.'

'You're a devious young lady,' I scolded, taking her in my arms and planting a kiss on her freckled nose. In her stocking feet the top of her head just cleared my shoulder. She returned the embrace until my lips sought hers and then she pulled back, putting me at arms' length. 'You smell of the good earth, Kate,' I quipped.

'Your mother's good earth. And you smell like something very expensive,' she rejoined, sniffing the air between us.

'Royal Copenhagen,' I announced.

'If that's Royal Copenhagen, I'm the queen of Denmark.' The woman was sharp and wanted people to know it. 'Would you like a drink? I have the brandy and the snifters.'

'Too early for anything that potent and I've just come from lunch.'

'That accounts for the snazzy suit. What about coffee?'

'I'll take a cup of coffee,' I accepted.

'It's instant,' Kate called, heading for the apartment's

galley kitchen. With her back to me she didn't see me wince. Raspberry sorbet and instant coffee. Only the memory of the lemon sole kept my stomach from revolting. 'Have a seat. It won't take a moment.'

When she returned with our coffee on a tray along with cream, sugar and sticky sweet rolls still in the box they came in, she put the load down on the glass and chrome coffee table and perched on the edge of the couch. I put a drop of cream in my coffee, assiduously avoiding the sugar and rolls.

'Were you going to take me to dinner at your Pelican Club?' Kate asked, helping herself to both the sugar and a roll.

I almost dropped my cup and saucer. 'Where did you hear about the Pelican?' I asked, as if I didn't know.

'Your mother, of course. She loves to talk about you. I also know about your silk berets and your expulsion from Yale. You naughty boy.'

Hoping to elude committing myself to being seen at the Pelican with Kate Mulligan and having it reported to Consuela Garcia, I said with great concern, 'Did mother tell you why I was booted from Yale?'

'She didn't seem to know, but was certain the school was being unfair. Were they, Archy?'

I feigned a sigh of relief and quoted Sofia Richmond. 'Yesterday is a memory, gone for good forever / while tomorrow is a guess / what is real is what is here and now / and here and now is all that we possess.'

Kate laughed and licked a sticky finger. 'The blarney

stone must have landed on your head, McNally. Why did you come here this afternoon? I would imagine a director would have more pressing things to do when his actors begin taking their roles a bit too seriously – like posting closing notices.'

'The show will go on, Kate. Desdemona Darling insists.'

'When you've buried as many husbands as she has the ritual must wear thin. Do you know anything more about the poisoning than is in the papers?' Kate asked. 'I refuse to believe it was an accident.'

I managed a sip or two of the coffee before returning it to the table. 'I agree and I know as much as you do.' Not wishing to get into a discussion of Holmes's death and the decision to go on with the play I said without preamble, 'Remember our discussion about psychics and how they ply their trade? You told me you knew a few in Las Vegas.'

Kate finished her coffee and putting down the cup she leaned back and shrugged her shoulders. 'I knew them in passing. There was a café that never closed, like everything else in Vegas, where the minor acts hung out to see, be seen and swap stories. That's as much as I know about them. And I get the feeling we're back to playing cat and mouse, Archy, and I don't like it. Is this about the guy who was at the party where Desdemona's husband was poisoned?'

Kate Mulligan shot so straight I felt like a fink. 'It is, Kate, and I couldn't discuss it the other night because

I was working on a case, but now that Holmes is dead so is the case.'

She sat forward, facing me. 'You mean you were working for Desdemona's husband?'

'I was, and if you'll hear me out I'll tell you all about it.' I took out my box of English Ovals. 'Mind?' She shook her head. I lit up and recited the continuing saga of 'Serge the Seer,' leaving out only Desdemona Darling's reason for seeking help from the psychic. When I was finished Kate patted the cushion next to her in an inviting gesture. Being a gentleman, I acquiesced.

She rested her head on my shoulder and I placed an arm around hers. She did smell of the good earth, and soap and water, and sticky sweet buns. 'Freddy McNally and Lolly Pops,' she giggled. 'Show business is in your blood, Archy. I knew we were kindred spirits the moment I laid eyes on you.'

'If you want to keep your job I wouldn't mention Freddy to mother and especially not to father,' I cautioned.

'I get the picture,' she said. Thinking over what I had just told her, Kate commented, 'It's easy to guess how he knew about your grandfather, but how he knew that Holmes was poisoned almost before the police is baffling. How do you figure it?'

'I have no idea short of him having a connection at the station house,' I admitted.

'You don't seriously believe that,' Kate stated.

'Not for a moment,' I answered. 'His office is one

floor above Temporarily Yours. I had him under surveillance and checked out the building.' I thought the
better part of valor was not telling her I had entered
the lobby only after I had seen her coming out of the
building.

'I know,' she said. 'If he wears a turban I've seen
him in the elevator.' I was very conscious of her body
nestled against mine and feared it was beginning to
become noticeable. 'I've also seen his name in the local
press. He's very popular with the ladies who like to be
entertained and can afford it. What do you want from
me, Archy?'

I kissed her and this time she didn't resist, but
rather encouraged me. 'According to his followers he's
done some pretty remarkable forecasting. Locating lost
objects seems to be his specialty. I thought you might
be able to tell me how he does it.'

She ran her fingers through my hair and I thought
of a line from my favorite Jean Harlow film – 'I'd love
to run barefoot through your hair.' Come to think of it,
Kate was barefoot, but this not being a Harlow film,
or any film, I held fast to my tasseled loafers. 'Sorry,
Archy, but I can't,' Kate answered. 'I could tell you
how to pull a rabbit out of a hat but how your Mr
Ouspenskaya knew where to find that diamond clip
is beyond my ken.

'The few so-called psychics I knew out west were
actually mind readers. Some people have a natural
talent for it and practice it with amazing results. They
work places like Las Vegas, New York, Miami and

New Orleans for obvious reasons. The tourist crowd. Even a novice can spot a couple on their honeymoon, the recent widow on the make, college kids on their own for the first time and illicit lovers on a spree. Their stories are painfully similar. The psychic makes a few very educated guesses and boggles the minds of the hayseeds. His predictions are always far enough into the future so that he never has to face the consequences of a wrong forecast.'

'Do they ever use a shill?' I asked, hoping she would never stop combing my hair with her fingers.

'Definitely,' Kate proclaimed, 'especially with the lounge acts. The shill works the bar, chatting with people to get as much information out of them as he or she can without causing suspicion. The psychic knows a lot about his audience before he sets foot on the stage.'

In other words, I thought, they employed a spy. As Kate had just explained, it was easy to see how it could be accomplished in a public place with a built-in audience. Ouspenskaya didn't have the convenience of either. 'How often do you visit your home office, Kate?' I asked.

'At least once a week,' she told me, 'to pick up my check and see if there are suitable jobs available. I'm with your mother only four hours a day, so I have time to pick up a few extra bucks if the job and the hours dovetail with my meager talents and time.'

'Pretty fancy digs for a part-time employee in need of extra bucks,' I couldn't help noting.

'What? Oh, the apartment. I don't own it, Archy, I rent. I had a little nest egg from my chorus girl days and combined it with my severance pay from my married days to buy my little car and head east. There's not much left so I have to supplement it as best I can.'

'I didn't mean to be inquisitive . . .'

'But it's the nature of your business,' she finished, restraining my roving hand. 'Unless you plan on spending the night I suggest we untangle and part. I have to shower and give some thought to dinner – or do I make my debut at the Pelican tonight?'

I untangled rapidly and told Kate that my director chores made that impossible. 'I have to hand out the rehearsal schedules and give the obligatory pep talk. Given our particular circumstances, that won't be easy.'

Kate began to gather up the remains of our coffee and return them to the tray. 'I'm sorry I couldn't be more helpful,' she was saying, 'but now that you lost your client I imagine anything you learn about Ouspenskaya will be purely academic.'

'You might say that, but I'm a tenacious cuss and can't stop fiddling with a knot until it yields to my ministrations. Would you do me a favor?'

She was on her way back to the kitchen but stopped in her tracks. 'Me? How?'

'When you visit your office keep your eyes open for Ouspenskaya and his clientele and let me know anything that strikes you as out of the ordinary.'

She continued to the kitchen and I followed her. 'Are we going to play Nick and Nora Charles or Nero Wolfe and Archy?' Kate laughed with great pleasure at her own wit.

Maybe she had something there. Ouspenskaya knew me and everyone I associated with and watched my every move. If he used a spy, why couldn't I? Kate was discerning and game for adventure. She had worked lounge acts with a magician and shared billing with clairvoyants. I bet she could spot a scam through a brick wall. 'Why not?' I said. 'Are you up for a little sleuthing?'

'Don't be silly, Archy. I was just kidding.'

The kitchen was very narrow and we were very close. 'Hear me out,' I begged.

'I hear better when I have room to breathe,' she pleaded.

I gave her room, but not much, and continued cajoling her. 'All I want you to do is visit his office and inquire about a consultation. You can say you work downstairs and are curious. It's perfectly logical and legal.'

'What will this prove?' she wanted to know.

'I want to see how he treats someone who walks in cold. Someone he has never seen before and knows nothing about. Also, what he charges if he's willing to do a consultation. It's that simple.'

The cups were in the sink and the sticky rolls were placed in the refridge. 'I'll have to think about it,' Kate said. 'I'm not an actress.'

'We'll talk more about it tomorrow night,' I told her.

'Over dinner at the Pelican Club?' she said hopefully.

I returned home in time for my swim and to add a few notes to my journal, deciding to merge my new case with that of the pseudo psychic. Then I called Binky who had just returned from walking his patients and was informed that the Palm Beach Community Theater was meeting at the home of Lady Cynthia Horowitz, Creative Director, at nine.

On a hunch I called Desdemona Darling and got Jorge. His accent told me that he might be of Philippine extraction but he was hatched in New Jersey. He said he would tell *La Signora* I wished to speak to her. Give unto me a break.

'Archy,' she bellowed when she came on, 'I knew my director wouldn't desert me even if everyone else has.'

'I want to know if you'll be at the meeting tonight,' I said. 'I'm handing out the rehearsal schedules.'

'I wanted to come, but Cynthia doesn't think it would be proper and I'm sure she's right. It's not that I'm insensitive to what happened. I loved Richard. But I hate sitting on my hands and brooding. It never did anyone a lick of good.'

'I agree, DeeDee, but perhaps it would be better if you rested for a week or so before starting rehearsals. We can work around you.'

'It's a long way around,' she roared.

I held the telephone a good six inches from my ear but didn't miss a syllable. 'When is the service for Richard?'

'I won't know that until the police officially release him. They questioned Cynthia and me for hours at the station house and they told us to stay available for more questioning. That's a polite way of telling us not to leave town.'

'They're going to question everyone who was at the party that night, which means our entire cast and crew plus the catering people. It's their job, DeeDee, and can't be avoided.'

'Some publicity for our show,' she sighed. 'It's the kind of press you can't buy and don't want.'

'Out in Hollywood they say there's no such thing as bad publicity,' I reminded her.

'Tell that to Fatty Arbuckle, Archy.'

She had a point there. 'I'll leave your schedule at Lady Cynthia's. The call is four evenings a week, Monday through Thursday, leaving the weekends free. I broke down the scenes and characters so people will know when they must attend. I think we'll need four weeks but as the theater hasn't given us our opening date I can't say what Monday we'll begin.'

'What time are you meeting tonight?'

'Nine,' I answered.

'Why not come by here first and drop off my schedule?' DeeDee proposed. 'We can have a cocktail and a nosh and you can lie to your star and tell her how happy you are you'll be working with her. It's standard procedure where I come from.'

It was just what I wanted to hear. 'It's the best offer I've had in years, DeeDee. Should we say seven for seven-thirty?'

'Let's say seven for seven, Archy. I'm no camel.'

I wanted to tell DeeDee that I would mix my own drink but that would be pushing the envelope one push too far. I put together an outfit that suggested authority with a hint of mystery. Black pants with pleated front. White silk turtleneck. Madras jacket. Designer sneakers. In lieu of a hat I placed a pair of dark glasses atop my dome and was set to take over the reins of the community theater, a company consisting of one unnatural death and a dozen suspects.

Father was assembling the paraphernalia for the evening cocktail hour when I stopped by the den on my way out. Mother had not yet arrived, which was just as well, as I didn't want to report my meeting with James Ventura in her presence. When I finished my summation father nodded pensively but I didn't know if that was because of Ventura's plight or the dark glasses nesting in my hair. The cheaters had his eyebrows and eyeballs bobbing up and down in perfect sync. Amazing.

'I thought as much,' father said, 'when I spoke to him. What do men who marry children expect, Archy?'

'A little more lead in their pencil at best and fidelity at the very least,' I answered honestly.

'Don't be vulgar, Archy.'

'Sorry, sir. It's just a manner of speaking.'

When I told him my plans for the evening he asked

if I had learned anything more about the demise of Richard Holmes. 'Nothing, sir, but I'm hoping his wife will shed more light on the subject. You've heard about the accident theory?'

'Hastings told me. How do you think it will play?'

'Like a snowball in hell, but I don't know how the poison got in his glass and why he chose that particular glass when the tray was presented to him. Al Rogoff thinks the accident theory might be the only explanation.'

Father had finished lining up the vodka, vermouth, olive jar, liquid measuring glass and stirrer. Now he proceeded to place ice cubes in the silver pitcher, one at a time. Was a precise number of ice cubes as vital to his ritual as the ratio of vodka to vermouth? I believed it was.

'Hastings said Lady Cynthia told the police she believed she had placed four or five glasses on her tray. When she got to Richard Holmes, there was only one glass left. In other words, Archy, he had no choice.'

And that made the cheese more binding. 'So the point is not why did Holmes take that glass, but why didn't anyone else? The more we learn about the distribution of the wine the more of an enigma the case becomes.'

'You thought of the possibility that if it is indeed murder, the intended victim might not have been Richard Holmes,' father offered.

'I did, and I discussed it with Al Rogoff. We're still left with the two essentials. How did the poison get in the glass and how did the murderer expect to match the glass with the victim? It's a conundrum, sir.'

'Are you working on the case with Al Rogoff, Archy?' father asked.

'Unofficially, as usual. Thanks to my position with the community theater I'll be tongue-and-groove with all the suspects for the next month, at least. I intend to keep my eyes and ears open, sir.'

'And watch your back, Archy. Poison is a coward's weapon.'

'And a woman's weapon,' I added with a glance at my watch. Mickey's hands were telling me I would be late if I didn't leave immediately. 'I'm off to the wars, sir.'

'One thing more, Archy,' father said. 'The police will question everyone who was at the party that night. Should they require a lawyer to be present at the interrogation, we can be of service.'

Remarkable man, Prescott McNally. 'I'll keep that in mind, sir.'

'Something else, Archy,' he suddenly remembered. 'Yes, sir?'

'I prefer the silk berets. Even the one in puce.'

'I'll remember that, sir.'

I met mother coming downstairs and paused long enough to give her a kiss. 'Why, Archy,' she exclaimed, 'you look just like a movie star.'

'Bless you, mother. Bless you.'

20

Jorge, impeccable in his black trousers with their razor-sharp crease and white shirt with its starched collar, led me to *La Signora*, who received me in the great room. Wanting a few dozen partygoers, the room looked cavernous but served to render its sole occupant less imposing than her bulk otherwise demanded and pathetically vulnerable, if not demure. It was a scene a director of film noir might create to elicit pathos for his character. I'm sure this did not escape Desdemona Darling's notice.

For our meeting she chose one of her formal muumuus in black with a white satin border around the collar and cuffs. 'My condolences,' I said when I entered. She was seated in a club chair and opened her arms to me as I approached. I bent to kiss her cheek and became engulfed in a bear hug. Theater people become kissing cousins in less time than it takes them to become mortal enemies – which is a very short time, indeed.

'Oh, Archy,' she cried, 'you don't know what I've been through. I was just coming to terms with the fact that Richard was dead when the police told me how he died. Can you believe it? Poison, just like in the play.' She touched her eyes with a crumpled handkerchief, careful not to disturb the dusting of face powder that covered her flawless complexion.

I assumed she refrained from complimenting my outfit and the dark glasses affixed to the top of my head because she was accustomed to being surrounded by movie stars. 'I know how you feel,' I said. 'We're all in a state of shock. Are you sure you want to go on with the play? No one, including Lady Cynthia, will fault you if you back out.'

'I'm sure, Archy,' she began, then as if suddenly remembering her manners she exclaimed with great fanfare, 'Help yourself to a drink. All Jorge can mix is a tequila daiquiri, which tastes even worse than it sounds.'

A credenza held the necessary bottles, mixers, ice bucket and glasses. 'Can I freshen yours?' I asked, indicating the glass that sat on what I believe is called a TV table – a tray on a folding stand – within arm's reach of the actress.

'Just add some vodka,' she said, 'it's gone a bit watery.'

If it started out as vodka over ice it was going to become vodka over vodka. I put together a light vodka and tonic for myself and replenished Desdemona's drink. 'Pull over a chair so we can talk without shouting,' Desdemona ordered. 'Whoever furnished this room didn't have intimate conversations in mind.'

Taking her drink from me she continued, 'I'll go on with the play. I'm a child of the big studio days in Hollywood where we contract players fought each other for every scrap of publicity. There are a few I can mention who were jealous of the attention Lana got when her daughter killed poor Johnny. I'm ashamed to say it, but I can't resist being the centerpiece of this drama, on and off the stage. It's in all the L.A. papers and it's on the television news every night. The Golden Girl,' she said with reverence, 'they still call me that, Archy. The Golden Girl.'

She seemed to have forgotten the lesson of Fatty Arbuckle but then *ars longa, vita brevis*. The memory of her golden days as the Golden Girl, plus the booze to be sure, plunged Desdemona Darling into a nostalgic reverie. 'I had my pick of men, Archy, from Aherne to Zanuck and all the stops between. Even royalty paid their respects but we went undercover because the prince was married. Ty Power was our beard. Dear Ty. He needed a few beards of his own as I recall.' She couldn't resist the risqué innuendo even when it was apropos of nothing under discussion.

'Men like Cynthia's Buzz were a dime a dozen back then.' Once started there didn't seem any way to stop her. 'You know Buzz is making time with that Fitz girl and why the hell not? Cynthia knows but she keeps her mouth shut because a bird in the hand, as they say. But I could take him away from both those ladies, just like that,' she assured me with a perfectly executed snap of her crimson-tipped fingers for emphasis.

'I told Buzz that my Hollywood connections could get him past the studio guard and into makeup for a screen test.' She laughed with great gusto. 'He wanted to know if I would rehearse with him on the side. You know, a little private tutoring. I'm thinking about it.' More laughter.

I had dragged over a matching club chair – it wasn't easy – and positioned it so that the portable table was between us. This being more or less of a condolence call I skipped any toast before sampling my drink. Desdemona didn't seem to notice as she ranted on. With all the rehearsing that was going on in private, I wondered if I wouldn't be declared redundant before I heard one of my actors recite a line. Didn't these old biddies ever give up? No, they did not. That's why they make the news lesser mortals read about – and dream about.

'But now that Richard is gone I think I'll let Cynthia and Fitz do battle over Buzz,' she pledged. 'I don't want it to look like Richard's death was more convenient than tragic.'

DeeDee's having finally brought up the subject of her husband's 'accident,' I followed up with, 'What exactly did the police tell you?'

'They said Richard was poisoned.' Again a snap of the fingers to drive home the point as she reiterated, 'Just like that, they said it. Must have been in the wine because that's the last thing he drank before he keeled over. You know it's always the spouse they suspect in cases like this and while they didn't come right out and accuse me, they grilled me for over an hour. It wasn't until Cynthia told them that she served Richard the wine that they let up on me.'

'Did they interrogate Lady Cynthia?'

'Only until that lawyer your father sent over showed up. Then they eased off on both of us. I owe you for that, Archy.'

'It was my father's doing, DeeDee, and I'll pass on your gratitude. What happened next?'

'They told us to stay in touch as if we would beat it as soon as they released us. Beat it to where? Brazil? The police see too many movies, Archy.'

'You described everything that took place from the time Lady Cynthia made her presentation until the wine was distributed?'

Desdemona sipped her vodka before assuring me that she had. 'Now they're going to question everyone who was present to . . . to . . .'

'Corroborate your story,' I finished for her.

'That's it. Corroborate. You were there, Archy, and so was everyone else. How could we lie about what happened?'

'You couldn't, and we'll all back your story. Are you and Lady Cynthia sticking with the accident theory?'

'Do you have a better solution?'

I didn't but I resented people asking. Jorge appeared with two table stands. Silently unfolding them he placed one before each of us before scurrying out only to reappear a moment later with a tray bearing the contents of the horn of plenty. This he rested on the stand before Desdemona. Running out again, he returned with a similar tray for me.

Desdemona's idea of a nosh was what many would call a banquet. Swedish meatballs; mini-sandwiches stacked to form an edible pyramid; prosciutto, sliced paper thin, wrapped around sesame breadsticks; pickled corn; lox on mini-bagels; hard-boiled eggs, quartered – and a partridge in a pear tree. If her husband's cholesterol count was larger than his bank balance, hers must take on the proportions of the national debt.

'No fuss, Archy,' she nudged verbally, 'just pick at what you want.'

Graze would be a more appropriate way of putting it. A fork and small plate were also provided and following Desdemona's lead I fixed myself a smorgasbord.

'You know,' she said, nibbling daintily, 'that Mr Ouspenskaya knew what we would encounter at the police station. He called Cynthia to warn us and then tried to get me here, but we were already on our way to the police station.'

'Did Jorge tell you Ouspenskaya called here after he tried to get Lady Cynthia?'

'Oh, yes,' she said. 'He wrote it down like he does all the calls. It was a few minutes after nine that morning. Isn't it amazing, Archy?'

Grazing, I didn't answer immediately, which prompted Desdemona to get in, 'You think he's a fake, don't you?'

Picking up a prosciutto-wrapped breadstick I gave

my standard response to the Ouspenskaya query. 'I'm an agnostic in things spiritual. Only if there was no humanly possible way he could have gotten that information am I ready to believe it was whispered to him in a dream.'

'But how could he possibly know?' she contested.

'Someone at the medical examiner's or the police station could have told him,' I explained.

'But that's impossible,' she persisted.

'Sorry, DeeDee, it's improbable, but not impossible. There's the rub.'

This contentious conversation did not arrest her appetite. 'I know Richard hired you to investigate Mr Ouspenskaya,' she admitted.

'I know you do, DeeDee. It's no longer a secret.'

'And what did you discover?' she challenged.

'Nothing,' I said. 'I lost my client before I had a chance to do my job.'

'You would have come up empty-handed if you had gone on, Archy. Believe me, he's for real. I've consulted a lot of so-called psychics in my time and none of them could do what Mr Ouspenskaya has already proven he can do.'

If we were letting it all hang out I saw nothing wrong in confessing, 'Your husband told me why you consulted psychics, DeeDee.'

She flushed ever so slightly but looked me right in the eye when she answered, 'I thought so. Richard had a big mouth.'

I put my plate down, resisting the temptation to

help myself to more. 'It's now none of my business and your secret is safe with me. What worries me is that your husband told Ouspenskaya he would no longer finance your consultations. The man was not sorry to see Richard drop dead. The police will have to know this, DeeDee.'

'Are you saying I wasn't sorry to see Richard die for the same reason?' she shot back.

'I'm not the police and I have no right to question you or make accusations. I'm just trying to caution you of what may lie ahead.'

She held out her glass and asked me to freshen it once again. 'Better put some ice in it this time,' she stated.

I did as requested and helped myself while in the process. When I served her libation she told me, 'Mr Ouspenskaya is advising me in this matter.'

That riled me enough to snap at her, 'If he's so great how come he hasn't found what you've been searching for all these years?'

It took her so long to respond I thought she had lapsed into either a trance or an alcoholic stupor. Her famous blue eyes seemed to be focused on something visible only to her. Was I going to be witness to a metaphysical epiphany or a vodka-induced blackout?

When she finally blinked, a rapturous smile appeared on her face and she said with perfect lucidity, 'Oh, but he did find it.'

With that bombshell, Desdemona Darling closed her

eyes, rested her chin on her satiny collar, and began to snore rhapsodically.

The cast members of *Arsenic and Old Lace* weren't any more animated than the show's star I had just left to the ministrations of Jorge. Richard Holmes's death had knocked the P & V out of them and replaced it with apathy bordering on fear. Only Connie chose to comment on my dashing appearance. 'I prefer the silk berets,' she told me, 'even the one in puce.' It appeared that everyone was out of step except mother and me. In a fit of pique I removed the glasses from the top of my head and placed them in my jacket pocket. *Ars gratia artis* was not to be the maxim of our community theater.

I noted that we were missing two members, Priscilla Pettibone and Joe Anderson. Connie reported that Jasmine, Priscilla's mother, was down with the flu and unable to fill in for Priscilla at the Pelican. As makeup consultant Priscilla's presence this evening or at rehearsals was not necessary. Hank Wilson didn't look as if he would agree.

Binky informed us that Joe Anderson was reconsidering participating in the show. That was a low blow because Joe was perfect for the role and, besides Desdemona, the only cast member with acting experience. 'He thinks the show is jinxed,' Binky whispered in my ear.

There was that word again. 'Keep that to yourself, Binky. It's the stage manager's job to boost morale, not debase it.' Joe seemed to be more upset over

Holmes's death than the widow. I would have to have a word with him and see if I couldn't talk him into persevering.

I must say I was proud of the way Binky was handling his duties. He gave out the scripts, verifying everyone's phone number as he did so and even adding their cell phone numbers to his big black book. He had had business cards printed with his name, title and contact numbers. These he had placed in each script. If nothing else, the cast and crew would be in constant communication.

We were gathered in Lady Cynthia's drawing room where folding chairs had been set up along with a podium. I didn't think for a moment that Lady C had rented the chairs from a funeral parlor, however, their occupants looked more like professional mourners than amateur actors about to put on a comedy. Our Creative Director was at the podium, clad in one of those sleeveless printed shifts that were all the rage this season. Her Capezio slippers were testimony to her age if not the current fashion, but why let go of a good thing?

Lady C was also sporting her famous tennis bracelet, which was as touted in Palm Beach as Mrs McLean's Hope Diamond had once been in Washington. Buzz was at her side, more to keep him from sitting next to Fitz than for any expedient purpose. Neither drinks nor food were in the offering as befits a business meeting. Lady Cynthia was a tough broad, as Al Rogoff would say.

Unable to avoid the issue, Lady Cynthia began by discussing the 'accident' that had claimed the husband of Desdemona Darling. 'Desdemona will not abandon us and I trust her brave resolution will encourage one and all to emulate Desdemona's devotion to the cause of community theater.' Really! They had all signed on for a lark and right now they looked dedicated to nothing more than keeping themselves alive.

As she spoke I canvassed the room. Things I would have paid scant attention to before Holmes's death and my newfound interest in Hanna Ventura suddenly became paramount. I was a psychiatrist in search of hidden meanings, all of them with a sinister bent.

Why was Hanna sitting next to her self-proclaimed nemesis, William Ventura?

Why had Fitz banished herself to the rear of the assembly where she looked forsaken without Buzz at her side? And why wasn't William filling the void?

William was flanked by Hanna and an empty chair, so where was Arnie Turnbolt? Tête-à-tête with Phil Meecham, that's where, and both of them slightly apart from the group as a whole. Did they know something they were loath to share with their cohorts?

The Tremaines were sitting up front, keeping their eyes glued to the podium.

The two men forming a trio with Hank Wilson would have to be Ed Rogers and Ron Seymour. I would soon learn which one was Seymour and invent an excuse to discuss his wife's aborted séance with Ouspenskaya.

With thoughts of bypassing the security guard and going directly to makeup for his screen test inflating his pretty head, Buzz wasn't giving two hoots in hell for the deceased and how he got to be that way. Before facing a camera, Buzz would have to run the course, bypassing Lady Cynthia, Fitz and Phil Meecham in order to 'rehearse' with Desdemona and fulfill his destiny.

Our lucky mascot, Ouspenskaya, was not with us. Just as well. The luck he had dispensed at our last outing would last us a life-time, especially Richard Holmes's lifetime.

Sudden thought: If Lady C had served wine this evening, how many would have declined the offer?

When the Creative Director had finished her homily it was my turn in the barrel. Being a *director* director rather than a Creative Director, I thought I would tell them what they had come to hear.

'I just wanted to add briefly to what Lady Cynthia said about the unfortunate death of Richard Holmes,' I began, pricking up all ears. 'In order to determine how the poison got into Richard Holmes's wine glass we will all be questioned by the police in the very near future.' I could feel rather than see Lady C's wrathful glare.

'Just tell them what you saw and try, if possible, to recall who you were standing next to at the time.' With this, heads began to turn and fingers began to point. It was the biggest show of enthusiasm they had exhibited all evening.

To placate Lady Cynthia I said, 'The cause of the accident must be determined to help prevent such a thing from happening again.' In support of father I said, 'If you should choose, you may have a lawyer present when summoned.'

Then I told them I had just come from a visit with Desdemona and that she was resting quietly. I explained the schedules Binky had distributed, adding that we would begin rehearsing four weeks before our opening which had yet to be determined. I suggested that they learn their lines before rehearsals began, stopping short of encouraging them to form workshops to do so. There was enough of that going on already.

Because living theater was what we were all about I infused a dash of theatrical lore into our first conclave. 'Joseph Kesselring, the author of *Arsenic and Old Lace*, thought he had written a very serious and gruesome drama. When it made the rounds, producers rejected it on the grounds that both the premise and the characters of the drama were so insipid, audiences would laugh it off the stage. It took those two geniuses of modern theater, Howard Lindsay and Russel Crouse, to discern that if the drama made people laugh it wasn't unproduceable, it was a comedy. Lindsay and Crouse did indeed produce the play, laughing all the way to the bank.' I got a polite spattering of applause.

I ended with, 'You're going out there unknowns, but you're going to come back stars.' It did not get a laugh.

All in all it was a somber and sober meeting, which

did not speak well for a company on the eve of presenting a comedy. When I was done no one had any questions nor were they inclined to hang around and chat.

Buzz asked me if I thought he should call Desdemona to see if he could be of assistance. I answered in the negative, drawing a smile from Lady Cynthia.

I introduced myself to Ed Rogers and Ron Seymour, who both fled after shaking my hand.

Fitz gave me the obligatory peck on the cheek. Phil Meecham, as usual, cornered Buzz. Arnie Turnbolt told me that the old Warner Bros. version of *Arsenic and Old Lace* was on a waiting list at all the local video rental shops. 'You're competing with Frank Capra,' he warned. Then the three of them left together to regroup at Ta-Boo' or the Chesterfield, was my guess. Would Buzz be joining them?

Hanna gave me a quick wave before departing with the Tremaines, followed by William. My para turned instantly noid. Was she avoiding me? Did her favorite psychic know about the meeting between her husband and yrs. truly and leak it to her? If so I would tear up my license to snoop and take up needlepoint.

Binky and I walked Connie to her office to pick up her things and I told them the truth about my meeting with Desdemona Darling. 'She's going to be trouble,' was Connie's educated guess. 'And did you get a look at her bedroom?'

'I most certainly did not. Why do you ask?'

'Remember the night of her party when she told me

to put your megaphone in one of the bedrooms? Well, it was her bedroom I put it in and I couldn't help notice the framed photos on her dressing table. Five of them. All men. Didn't she have five husbands before Richard Holmes?'

'That she did,' I said. 'Lady C has flags, Desdemona has framed photographs. I wonder which I like least.'

'Do you think there are six framed photos there now?' Binky asked.

'I would say it's too soon,' I told him. 'But what do you think Richard thought of her rogue's gallery?'

'Maybe he didn't spend too much time in her bedroom,' Connie offered.

On the way out we ran into the housekeeper, Annie, and Binky paused to have a few words with her. When we reached the parking area I could just about make out Hanna and William in the light of the overhead floodlights, conversing. As we approached they broke off and got into their respective cars, and drove away. Interesting?

I saw Connie to her car and waited for Binky. When he came out I chided him for hitting on the help.

'I wouldn't do that, Archy,' he pleaded. 'I know Annie from work. She's with Temporarily Yours, too.'

Interesting?

21

It's a funny thing about cases. There are those you can work on for days, even weeks, following every lead and compiling all the facts, but when you sit down to put the pieces together you discover that none of them mesh to form the picture on the cover of the puzzle box. Juxtaposed is the case you take on in the morning and that night a single clue tells you all you need to know, even if it's not what you want to know.

But in either case it's often that bit of nuance – a seemingly inconsequential event, a word spoken in haste, a wry glance – that signals the beginning of the end. A young man stops to say a few words to a young woman. Two profiles silhouetted in the orange haze of a floodlight part at the sound of approaching footsteps.

Binky's astounding news, coming before I had a chance to digest Hanna and William's abrupt parting and DeeDee's earlier revelation, had me defying Lady Cynthia's cardinal rule – NO SMOKING anyplace on her ten acres. In the words of the late Diana Barrymore, 'It was all too much, too soon.'

'I thought you gave those up,' Binky, who is as predictable as our planet's orbit around old Sol, droned.

'My dear Binky, *jure divino* compels me to abandon my English Ovals but *jure humano* makes the break arduous. In clichéd English, the mind is willing but the flesh is weak. Now drive directly to the Pelican Club and await me at the bar.'

'Who's buying, Archy? *Jure divino* or *jure humano*?'

Good grief! Either walking his patients or rubbing shoulders with the theatrical crowd had Binky crowing like a stand-up comic. 'Last to arrive buys the drinks,' I proposed.

I crawled along in my Miata because I wanted to think and because Binky deserved a nightcap for diverting my attention from the mystical to the factual – the obscure to the obvious – the pits to the cherries.

Mrs Trelawney called Temporarily Yours and told them of our need for temporary help with mother's garden. Did she mention that mother and father were going to cruise the Caribbean? Probably, because Mrs Trelawney likes to chat. Did she know what cruise lines were being considered? Probably not, but one step at a time will get us there.

Serge Ouspenskaya got his start in Palm Beach society when he called Connie Garcia and offered his services as a psychic before anyone knew Lady C was in the market for a psychic for her 'who-done-it?' gala. Did Mrs Marsden leave for vacation before the party and was Annie of Temporarily Yours ensconced in the house when the decision to use a psychic was made?

To be determined. But Annie was there when Lady C and DeeDee discussed the Lake Worth Playhouse and, more to the point, when they discussed bringing me into the community theater as director.

At lunch with Hanna Ventura she had stated very clearly, 'Margaret is new.' Margaret being the Venturas' housekeeper. Where did Margaret come from and was Margaret employed in the Ventura home when the diamond clip went missing and so conveniently reappeared? That would be easy to check on.

Did other Palm Beach households boasting remarkable losses and finds attributed to Ouspenskaya employ help from Temporarily Yours? When Ouspenskaya directed Mrs Haberstraw to that desk drawer did a temp parlor maid, secretary or flower arranger lead the way?

It would appear that Temporarily Yours and Serge Ouspenskaya had more in common than just an address. Binky and, I hoped, Kate Mulligan were proof that Temporarily Yours was a legit business with perhaps a few of Ouspenskaya's plants among the ranks. If so, were the owners of Temporarily Yours aware of the infiltration? It never occurred to me to ask Binky to pay a call on Ouspenskaya when I learned of the agency's proximity to the psychic's offices because Ouspenskaya knew of my relationship to Binky thanks to the community theater.

But I did ask Kate to spy for me, and in doing so had I tempted a mole to become a double agent? I couldn't think of one thing I had confided to Kate Mulligan that had come back to haunt me in the guise of an Ouspenskaya prediction. Therefore, would I think twice before I discussed anything but food, wine, women and song with Kate? You bet your tushie I would. *Getting into bed with the enemy* is common practice in the worlds of commerce and espionage, but leave it to Archy to transcend the metaphorical into the literal.

To be sure, this was all speculation based on a chance comment by Binky Watrous. The only thing I knew for certain was that Desdemona Darling had told me Ouspenskaya had found her can of film. Was this wishful thinking, tipsy chatter, or the truth? If the latter it could validate Serge Ouspenskaya and invalidate all of the above.

I could add to this evening's educated guesses my hunch that Hanna and William Ventura were the best actors in our troupe. This observation was based solely on a chance glimpse of the pair in Lady C's parking area under the light of an electric lamp, not a full moon. In both cases I was shy on facts but I now had two working hypotheses to prove or disprove.

When I arrived at the Pelican the only person at the bar was Mr Pettibone, polishing glasses. The Pelican is open from noon to midnight, but generally the last of the diners and drinkers are gone by eleven and the clapboard house is dark below stairs and lit above where the Pettibone family dwells in comfort.

'Good evening, Mr Pettibone. Where's Binky?'

'I haven't seen him all evening, Archy,' Mr Pettibone informed me.

If I had walked I couldn't have gotten here much later, so where was Binky? The boy couldn't win a bet even when his adversary threw the game. Binky Watrous, I often thought, could be depended upon for two things – catching colds and missing planes. 'He should be here momentarily, I hope, but while I'm waiting, Mr Pettibone, what can you tempt me with?'

He recommended a little-known brandy with great pretensions. 'It will lift you for an hour and then gently drop you into a dreamless sleep. Guaranteed.'

'Sold,' I declared. 'And how is Mrs Pettibone? I hear she has a touch of the flu.'

'That she has and she won't stay in bed like she should. The doctor has given her a little something so we'll *all* get some rest tonight.'

Here, Binky entered the Pelican and joined me at the bar. 'Did you come by way of Boca?' I questioned.

'I was stopped for speeding,' Binky announced. 'The officer made me take a breathing test to see if I was drunk.'

'And?' I said, anticipating the worst.

'I passed,' Binky told me and Mr Pettibone, who had paused in his work to listen to Binky's narrative.

'Good for you, Binky. Join me in a brandy,' I invited.

'I'll have a beer,' he answered. 'I told the cop I was hurrying home to my invalid grandmother.'

'And?'

'I failed. He gave me a ticket.'

Consumed with guilt I called off the bet and offered to pay not only for the beer but for Binky's summons as well. This brought a smile to his face but even when Binky smiled he looked on the verge of tears. 'Now tell me,' I began, 'when did you learn that Annie worked for Temporarily Yours?'

'Just today. I went to the office to collect my check and she was there for the same reason. She's not a bad looker, Archy.'

In the world according to Binky Watrous, sex determines comeliness. If it's female, it's not a bad looker. 'Indeed not,' I agreed, eager to move on. 'And have you befriended any other employees at Temporarily Yours?'

My brandy and Binky's beer were placed before us along with Mr Pettibone's blessing. 'To your health, gentlemen.'

We raised our glasses in salute to our well-wisher before Binky answered me. 'No, Archy. Annie is the only one I've talked to. Why do you want to know?'

'Curious. What did you and Annie talk about?'

'Richard Holmes and how he was poisoned at the party. What else? That's all everyone is talking about. Annie can't wait for a new assignment.'

'Think, Binky. Did she question you about anyone in the community theater and me in particular? Anything at all, even if it seemed like a perfectly ordinary question at the time.'

Putting down his beer, Binky turned to me and said, 'What is this, Archy, a case?'

There is nothing Binky likes better than a case, especially when I ask for his assistance in the proceedings. We are not the Sherlock and Watson of the pulps, perish the thought, but more akin to Charlie Chan and Number One Son of the old B flicks. I would consider taking in Binky as a partner if we could afford the additional cost in liability insurance such a move would entail.

'It was a case,' I confessed. 'Holmes hired me to investigate Ouspenskaya but, as you know, I lost my client.'

'Are you investigating his death?' Binky asked.

'No, I'll leave that to the police. I'm still curious to learn how Ouspenskaya works his magic. I've thought for a long time that he has informants and I'm guessing that Annie is one of them.'

Shaking his head, Binky disagreed. 'I don't think so, Archy. She's new in town and if she can find work after the season winds down she might settle in. I hope she does.'

Ouspenskaya was also new in town and so was Margaret and so was Kate. I hated to include Kate in my list of suspects but I had no choice, did I? 'Did Sally Duhane interview you at the agency?' I asked Binky.

'How do you know Sally?' he asked with genuine surprise. 'Archy, have you been nosing around Temporarily Yours? Why?'

'I was checking out Ouspenskaya's digs and noticed he was in the same building as the agency so I paid a call on your employer to see what they were all about. Perfectly legit, Binky, I assure you.'

'I don't believe you.' Binky's innocence seemed to have gone the way of his mustache. Where was the boy who never doubted my word even when I did? 'You're trying to connect Temporarily Yours with Ouspenskaya, Archy, right?'

'I'll not say nay to that one. The agency is like an octopus with tendrils in the best homes.' Including my own, I might have added. 'It wouldn't be the first time the help tattled on their employers for thirty pieces of silver. Well, did the Duhane woman interview you?'

'No,' Binky stated. 'Sally Duhane is the receptionist and I think the owner or one of the owners. Kyle Romaine does the interviewing.'

I motioned for Mr Pettibone to refill Binky's glass. 'Is Romaine about your age and height, Binky? Dark hair and slim?'

'Thanks, Archy,' Binky acknowledged when his fresh beer was drawn and served. 'That sounds like Kyle. You've seen him?'

'When I was at the agency I saw him come in from the adjoining room. Is that where the interviews take place?'

'Yeah, Archy. There are just two small interview rooms but as far as I know Kyle is the only one who does the interviewing.'

'And you don't recall him asking you anything odd or unconventional when he conducted your interview? I mean was he feeling you out for any extracurricular activities he might want to send your way?'

We were interrupted by Priscilla in jeans and a man's

shirt with the tails hanging out, who had emerged from the kitchen bearing a plate of something that looked like Lincoln logs. She served her father before offering them to Binky and me. 'And what do we have here, pray tell?' I inquired.

'Mozzarella,' Priscilla named her offering, 'dredged in seasoned breadcrumbs and sautéed in olive oil and butter. Leroy is thinking of putting them on the menu.'

'I've had them,' Binky said, helping himself. 'They're delicious.' Binky frequents fast-food bazaars where such items abound.

A rolled-up pizza? It sounded like instant *agita* but when has that ever stopped me from indulging?

'How was the meeting?' Priscilla asked.

'Uneventful,' I told her.

'No one died, if that's what you mean,' Binky rejoined, scooping up another fried cheese delight. I had to admit they weren't bad but felt they went better with a beer than a pretentious brandy.

'I hope you're sticking with the show,' I lectured Priscilla, trying to unstick my fingers from the mozzarella wrap.

'I'm still thinking about it,' she said. 'Did Hank ask for me?'

'As a matter of fact, he did not. Out of sight, out of mind, young lady, so you had better make your intentions known,' I pressed on.

'Absence makes the heart grow fonder, Mr Director.' With that, Priscilla picked up her tray and departed.

'For every adage,' Mr Pettibone stated thoughtfully,

'there is one to countermand it. Look before you leap,' he tossed at me.

'He who hesitates is lost,' I returned the volley.

'Seek and you shall find.'

'All things come to he who waits.'

'For every man there's a woman,' Binky proclaimed.

Mr Pettibone and I gave this some thought but could come up with nothing to douse Binky's hopes. 'You win, Binky, but I wouldn't count on it. Now drink up so Mr Pettibone can put the Pelican and his family to bed. And do me a favor, please.'

'Sure, Archy. What is it?'

'Keep your eyes and ears open around Temporarily Yours.'

'You can count on me . . .' Binky paused in midsentence and then vociferated, 'That's what Kyle said, Archy. Now I remember.'

'What did he say, Binky?'

'When he sent me to the animal hospital he told me to keep my eyes and ears open and report anything of interest about the operation and the personnel because it would be helpful to the agency to better service them.'

Interesting?

Alone, alone, all all alone in my crow's nest. I undressed, washed, brushed and donned my silk dressing gown. Begging Noel Coward's pardon, I dispensed with the ascot. Then I poured myself a marc which had no claim to pretention to banish the memory of Mr Pettibone's brandy, and in lieu of music I lit an English Oval to soothe my savage breast. Settled, I entered my newly formulated hypotheses in my journal and ruminated upon their validity.

If Ouspenskaya wasn't connected with Temporarily Yours, I would pop the question to Connie Garcia in May. (And May it never happen.) I doubted if all the agency's employees worked for Ouspenskaya. The operation must consist of patsies, like Binky, and paid informers.

And which was Kate Mulligan? Should I drop a few choice items into Kate's pretty ear when next we cohabitated to see how long it took for them to be recycled into an Ouspenskaya radio broadcast? The thought aroused more than my interest. Distrust an aphrodisiac? I banished the thought before it led me astray.

Desdemona Darling and her can of film. Did she have it and did it and/or Ouspenskaya have anything to do with Holmes's death? I had given Al Rogoff all the information I had relating to Desdemona's search for her lost work of art and Ouspenskaya's involvement with it, so let the police ruminate over that one. I had enough on my plate.

Before I turned out the light I turned my thoughts to Hanna and William Ventura. They could very well be the subject of the indecent romance Lolly Spindrift didn't want to discuss. Lolly had said his information was secondhand and his source could have been some-one who caught the two in a compromising situation as I had in Lady C's parking lot. I thought Hanna protested too much about William's intolerable behavior from the day I met her.

Mother and stepson. It wasn't unprecedented. Once upon a time a very talented Hollywood director married an Academy Award–winning actress half his age. Not long after, she divorced him to marry his son by a previous marriage. The fact that Hanna and William lacked originality did not make my job any easier, and so be it. When I assumed the leadership of Discreet Inquiries father did not promise me a rose garden.

My folly in agreeing to direct for the community theater had begun with Desdemona Darling's party. Then, I recited a line from Coleridge's 'Ancient Mariner' to describe my grand entrance. Now, believing I was nearing the end of my voyage, I crawled into bed knowing the journey, like the old mariner's, would render me *A sadder and a wiser man.*

22

I was up early, but not early enough to breakfast with father, who had already left for the office when Ursi prepared my coddled eggs on buttered whole wheat toast and sausages with chunks of chilled diced pineapples. When I declined a freshly baked blueberry muffin (Leroy's mozzarella stick lingered in more places than my memory) Ursi asked me if I was off my feed.

'No, Ursi, just trying to keep in sparring form. Like Don Quixote I'm off to do battle with a windmill.'

'I never saw a windmill in Palm Beach,' Ursi observed.

'It's just a figure of speech, compliments of Mr Cervantes.'

'Cervantes? I don't know him, Archy.'

'I would venture to say, Ursi, few in Palm Beach know him either. But you do know most of the families that comprise the upper echelons of our island.'

'I know the people they employ,' Ursi corrected me.

'And do you know that Kate Mulligan works for an agency called Temporarily Yours?'

'Yes, I do, Archy. She's mentioned it.'

Finishing my second cup of coffee, I implored our Ursi, 'Do me a favor, please, and call around to your friends and see if you can learn how many other households in town are using temp help from that agency.' Given an excuse to trade gossip put a smile on our Ursi's face. 'And be discreet,' I cautioned unnecessarily.

On several other occasions I have used Ursi's below-stairs connections to my advantage. By implication rather than a direct order I knew my request had instantly alerted our loyal housekeeper to keep her thoughts to herself when near our part-time gardener.

I paid a quick visit to mother in her greenhouse because I was eager to drive off in my Miata before the yellow VW pulled into our driveway. I wanted to be armed with as much information about Temporarily Yours as I could ferret out before my next meeting with Kate Mulligan.

I met Jamie in the driveway where he was replenishing Hobo's water supply. 'The next time you speak to Max, the Ventura gardener, would you ask him how long the girl called Margaret has been working for the family and if he knows where she came from?' 'Uh-huh,' Jamie agreed. Hobo barked.

'Also, was Margaret there when Mrs Ventura's diamond clip was lost and found.'

'Uh-huh,' Jamie agreed. Hobo barked.

'And when you speak to Roland over at the Tremaines,

ask him the same thing. Have they employed any temporary help lately, and if so, who supplied them.'

'Uh-huh,' Jamie agreed. Hobo barked.

Employing domestic engineers to thwart Serge Ouspenskaya was tantamount to fighting fire with fire.

When I got to my office the first thing I did was call Connie.

'Lady Cynthia's residence. Connie Garcia speaking.'

'Archy McNally speaking,' I responded.

'Archy? Lady C just asked me to call you. She heard from the Lake Worth Playhouse this morning. They've given us an opening date and confirmed a two-week run.'

Great. Just what I didn't want to hear. Everything was suddenly happening at once. Another indication that my cases were coming to fruition. That first big break always came on like a snowball rolling down a mountain, gathering bulk and momentum on the descent. From experience I knew that I had to keep my eyes on the approaching avalanche if I didn't want it to land squarely on my head.

'What's the date, Connie?'

She gave it to me and a glance at my calendar told me that according to my schedule rehearsals would begin on Thursday. Today was Wednesday. I had one more day to wrap up both 'Serge the Seer' and the Ventura cases before I started emulating Frank Capra. The joy of unmasking Ouspenskaya was tempered with the sorrow of what I might have to report to James Ventura. And would I be missing two cast members when that ship hit the sand? Make that three cast members if I couldn't talk Joe Anderson out of leaving us in the lurch. The avalanche was fast approaching.

'We have permission to rehearse in the Stonzek Studio where our play will be presented. It seats about seventy but Madame is now trying to get the main theater for our showcase. She thinks Desdemona's name and the publicity over Richard Holmes's death will draw an audience from Miami to New York. What do you think, Archy?'

I think Lady Cynthia Horowitz has all the tact of a bloodhound on the scent. 'She's right but she won't get the main house. We're in the height of the season and I'm sure it's been booked solid for months. The only reason we have the studio is because they're kind enough to block out a few weeks for the community theater every year.'

And it was just as well that we were confined to the small house. Between Desdemona's size, the incompetence of the cast and my inept direction, the fewer people who saw our *Arsenic and Old Lace*, the more likely the chances of the community theater surviving the débâcle. Sorry, Buzz – you had better reclaim your berth on Phil Meecham's yacht.

'Madame has been known to stop the rain before her Fourth of July bash so don't count her out,' Connie forewarned. 'I'll tell Binky to start contacting the cast to give them the time and place. According to your schedule you want everyone present the first evening for a cold reading. Is seven o'clock okay, Archy?'

'Fine, but right now I'd like to know if you remember when Mrs Marsden took off to see her daughter.'

'Why, Archy?'

'I'll tell you if you tell me.'

That got a giggle: 'I'll check my diary. Hold on.' Connie's diary was not a lovely book of soft Moroccan leather but a hardnosed computer that sucked in floppies and spewed out information. If the suffragette movement failed to herald the end of civilization the computer would. 'Here it is,' she announced, giving me the date.

'Now tell me, Connie, was this before or after Madame's 'who-done-it?' party?'

'I know Mrs Marsden was here when we began preparation for the party but she left before the event.'

'How long before?' I asked.

'Are you writing a book, Archy?'

'No, I'm closing one. How long before the party?'

'A week,' Connie said. 'Yes, a week before. I remember Madame was upset and told her she couldn't go until we had a replacement. That's when Mrs Marsden came up with Annie.'

'Annie is from Temporarily Yours, the temp agency Binky is with. Binky ran into Annie at the agency by chance yesterday,' I told Connie. 'Now I know Annie was in residence when it was decided to bring in a psychic to jazz up the party.'

'I assume all this has a point,' Connie complained.

'Oh, it does. That mysterious phone call you got from Ouspenskaya, offering his services, was compliments of Annie.'

'What?' Connie cried.

I was rounding third base but not yet home to score the winning run. That would take another interrogation. 'I think so, Connie, but I'm not positive, so not a word to Madame or anyone else for the time being.' Feeling expansive, I said, 'And, Connie, you gave me the lead on this one when you told me about the Palm Beach law of supply and demand. Remember? Madame's spies dish her the dirt and she keeps them on her A party list. Ouspenskaya's spirits are flesh and blood.'

'You know, Archy,' Connie reflected, 'now that I think of it, every time I went into the kitchen for my coffee break Annie always joined me for a cuppa and a bit of gossip. Me and my big mouth.'

If hindsight were foresight I'd be out of business. 'You never told me this, Connie.'

'Why should I? It was just girl talk. Nothing to interest you.'

'On the contrary, Consuela. Girl talk is the only thing that interests me. I hope we can get together over the weekend.'

'He who only hopes is hopeless, Archibald.'

If there was a retort to that one it was not on the tip of my tongue.

'By the by, Archy,' Connie went on, 'the police are stopping by today to question me and Buzz and Annie. I'm very nervous.'

'Just tell them what you saw,' I advised. 'And, Connie, if you can, try to learn what Annie has to tell them.'

Father was seated at his desk reading *the Wall Street Journal*, a periodical I eschew in favor of the financial counseling of Simon Pettibone. Mr Pettibone keeps a 'phantom' portfolio of stocks and bonds, closely watched by Pelican Club members. Beginning with a modest investment of ten thousand dollars, Mr Pettibone's 'investments' were now worth one million dollars. It was rumored that not all of Mr Pettibone's portfolio was wishful thinking.

'Come in, Archy,' father invited.

'Good morning, sir. I wonder if I might ask you a few questions?'

Raising one eyebrow, father answered, 'Me? I trust it has nothing to do with the Ventura case. I'm not up on local gossip, be it PBF or PBR.'

The initials stood for Palm Beach Fact and Palm Beach Rumor, an abbreviation I coined some years back that has since become assimilated into our local jargon. Father's use of the idiom, so contrary to his character, always amused me. 'What I want to know, if you can remember, pertains to the time you asked Mrs Trelawney to arrange a gardener to tend to mother's plants in her absence.'

'Certainly. She called the agency who sometimes supplies temporary help for the office. They sent us Kate Mulligan, with whom mother is very pleased.'

'Did you at any time talk to anyone at the agency or was Mrs Trelawney the sole contact?'

'What is all this about, Archy?'

'Indulge me, sir. There is a reason for my asking.'

Nodding, father stroked his mustache as he thought back. 'Yes,' he answered. 'I did speak to someone there. I remember telling you so.'

'A Ms Duhane, perhaps?'

'I don't recall the name but I do recall that I thought it very efficient of them at the time. You see, they wanted to speak to me directly so that they could get a better idea of exactly what I was looking for in the way of assistance. The personal touch, I believe it's called. This gave me the opportunity to tell them about mother, her garden and our home. The result was the charming Kate Mulligan.'

'And did you tell this person about your proposed cruise?'

'I did,' father said, beginning, I believe, to ascertain where all this was leading. 'As a matter of fact I had just picked up the brochures from the travel agent and I might have mentioned the choices of cruise lines out of Fort Lauderdale.'

'I'm sure you did, sir. And the end result, besides Kate Mulligan, was that you told Serge Ouspenskaya everything he regurgitated for my benefit the night of the séance at the Tremaines.'

Father was silent for some time, showing his chagrin by tugging on his mustache. Prescott McNally does not

like to be made a fool. Then he reflected, 'The help supplied by the agency report to him everything they learn from those they are sent to assist.'

'That's correct, sir.'

'Does he own the agency, Archy?'

'That I don't know. But I believe you spoke to a Ms Duhane, who is the agency's receptionist and perhaps a principal of the firm. If she passed the information you gave her on to Ouspenskaya, we can assume he recruits his creatures with the full knowledge of Temporarily Yours.'

I proceeded to outline for father everything I now knew about Ouspenskaya's operation, naming Annie, and detailing my suspicions of the woman working for the Venturas.

'And Kate Mulligan is a spy in our home?' father concluded from my account.

'I don't know that, sir. Binky Watrous works for Temporarily Yours and he is certainly not a mole for Ouspenskaya. Judging from some of the intimate details that come Ouspenskaya's way, I think the charlatan has a roster of paid spies besides picking up any and all information he can garner from the unsuspecting employees. In the meantime I recommend being on guard around our Kate Mulligan.'

'To be sure,' father said, 'however, mother . . .'

'I know. Mother is apt to rattle on while puttering among her begonias, but I don't think she's privy to anything that goes on here, sir.'

'No, she isn't. And until we know more we will

keep this from her, too. I don't like this one bit, Archy. Mother is very fond of Kate Mulligan.'

So am I, but I didn't think father wanted to hear that.

'What do you intend to do now, Archy?'

'I've got a few feelers out, which should tell me how many more informers Ouspenskaya has planted about and after that I'm going to try to learn the relationship between the man and the agency. When I'm done I'm going to tell Ouspenskaya's fan club to get themselves a new idol. The party is over.'

'A good piece of work, Archy,' the sire extolled in a fit of largesse. This, as always, was as much praise as Archy would ever get from Prescott McNally. But who's complaining?

I encountered Joe Anderson outside father's office, pushing his mail cart and looking a bit sheepish at the sight of me. 'I left your mail on your desk, Archy,' he said, moving on.

'Just a moment, Joe,' I called. 'What's this I hear about your leaving the show?'

He paused and turned to me. 'I don't know as I want to do it,' he said.

'May I ask why?'

'You may, but I don't have to tell you.'

That was true. 'Does the death of Richard Holmes have anything to do with your decision?'

'I'll admit it shook me up.'

'They say it was an accident,' I maintained.

'Really? So why did the police contact me to set up an interview?'

The police were certainly on top of things. I would have to call Al Rogoff to learn the results of the interrogations.

'If you had been at the meeting the other night you would know that the police are going to question everyone present at the time of Holmes's death. It's strictly routine.'

'And are you going along with the accident theory, Archy?'

People kept asking me that question because it was the question everyone in Palm Beach was asking each other. No, I didn't think it was an accident but, as DeeDee had said before so rudely dozing off, 'Do you have a better solution?' No, I did not.

'It's police business, Joe. Let them decide if his death was misadventure or otherwise. We begin rehearsals Thursday night at the theater. A cold reading from start to finish. Can I count on you being there?'

As if he had not heard a word I said, Joe answered, 'A few weeks back Richard Holmes came here to see you. Everyone in the office was talking about his visit. What did he want, Archy?'

I could see no reason to skirt that one. 'The truth, Joe, is that he wanted me to investigate Ouspenskaya, the popular psychic. Desdemona Darling couldn't get enough of Ouspenskaya's forecasts at five hundred dollars a pop. She wanted Ouspenskaya to locate something for her.'

Joe smiled and shook his head. 'Like a film she didn't want anyone to see?'

'You know about that?'

'Me and a few million others. Desdemona Darling was just one of many actresses rumored to have gotten into the big time via the casting couch and smoker flicks. A popular scandal magazine in the fifties ran a piece listing all the suspects, Desdemona among them. It also said she frequented psychics to locate any prints that still existed so she could destroy them. The psychic she was seeing at the time gave the magazine the exclusive.'

'Nice crowd,' I noted. 'Between us, Joe, DeeDee told me Ouspenskaya found what she was looking for.'

'Good. So everyone lives happily ever after.'

'Not Richard Holmes, I'm afraid. Do you think his death has anything to do with Ouspenskaya's supposed find?'

Joe began to push the mail cart toward the next stop. 'Like you, Archy, I'll let the police puzzle it out.'

'Will you be with us tomorrow night?' I said to the back of his head.

'I'll probably be there. I left your mail on your desk, Archy.'

'You already told me that.'

23

When I got back to my office the phone was ringing. It was Connie, breathless with excitement. 'Archy, after your call I remembered that when Desdemona Darling and her husband arrived here they asked Lady Cynthia to recommend an employment agency to supply them with domestic help.'

'You mean Jorge didn't come with them from California?' I asked.

'He did not,' Connie said. 'What's interesting is that Madame told them to talk to Mrs Marsden and if Mrs Marsden got Annie from Temporarily Yours she must have been familiar with the agency. Did Mrs Marsden suggest Desdemona call them?'

'I think she did, Connie, and I'm sure Jorge came from Temporarily Yours, too.' And another mystery bites the dust. Jorge was privy to conversations between DeeDee and her husband, and when Richard Holmes called to make his appointment with me, Jorge overheard that, too. I told Connie I had a few more leads to verify and then I would pay a call on Lady Cynthia.

I left the office and drove back to our citadel on Ocean Boulevard. The yellow VW was in the driveway, but the station wagon was missing, therefore I was surprised, and elated, to find both Ursi and Jamie in the kitchen. Mother was out in the station wagon with Kate Mulligan. The McNally luck was alive and well in Palm Beach on this lovely afternoon, and I was on a roll.

Success being a natural tonic I accepted Ursi's invitation to nibble on a turkey club sandwich as she related to me the results of her morning phone-a-thon. An offer of a turkey club told me that while I was feasting on DeeDee's smorgasbord the McNallys were enjoying a turkey dinner. Now, Ursi sliced generous slabs of cold white meat from the bird's breast and, along with bacon, sliced tomatoes, lettuce and three pieces of toast, buttered and lavished with mayonnaise, she put together a jaw-breaker only Dagwood Bumstead (and Archy McNally) could truly appreciate.

It seems that several homes Ursi had contacted employed temporary help this season: from housekeepers to cooks, parlor maids, chauffeurs and bartenders and waitpersons for social events. One of the names Ursi mentioned was Haberstraw – of the divorcing Haberstraws.

Jamie tempted me with a bottle of beer as he reported in as few words as possible what I had already taken for granted. Max didn't know what agency Margaret came from but she was in the Ventura home at the time of the diamond clip fiasco. Roland said the Tremaines had not taken on any temporary help, but then Ouspenskaya had nothing to broadcast to Penny Tremaine the night he resurrected Freddy McNally.

I had enough ammunition to call upon Lady Cynthia and inflict a profound blow to her pride – it would take an atom bomb to destroy it.

Annie gave me a curt nod when she opened the portal to me. 'Good day, Annie. It was nice knowing you.'

'Uh?' said Annie. (Had she been spying on our Jamie?)

Lady Cynthia looked like a million bucks in a beige linen Chanel frock – Coco, that is, not Mr Lagerfeld – that must have set her back a half day's interest on one of her money market accounts back when a dollar was worth ten of today's and a pack of smokes cost two bits. I opened with a flourish of an invisible plumed bonnet. 'Lend me your ear, Madame. I come to bury Caesar, not to praise him.'

'Really, Archy,' Lady Cynthia chided. 'Being asked to direct the community theater has gone to your head. Better stick to snooping.'

'Oh, but I have been snooping and I'm here to pull the plug on Serge Ouspenskaya's shortwave apparatus. You better sit down, Lady Cynthia.'

'I am sitting, lad. Now out with it or out with you.'

If father was chagrined at having been duped by Ouspenskaya, Lady C could best be described as livid. It did not go well with beige. The word 'bastard' was but one of the more colorful names the lady attributed to her former mentor. When it came to expletives, our Creative Director was at her creative best. As she picked up the house phone to summon Annie, I made my exit.

On the way out I passed Annie on the way in. 'Like ships passing in the night,' I said in passing.

I stuck my head into Connie's office and gave her the news. 'Unless Mrs Marsden is expected back today, you had better get on the horn and find a replacement for little Annie. Temporarily Yours is permanently out of business.'

Connie reached for her computer keyboard. 'I hope I can locate a domestic agency on the Web.'

'He who only hopes is hopeless,' I reminded her.

'Get out of here, Archy McNally.'

I drove to the office building on Clematis Street and took the elevator directly to the fourth floor. The layout was very similar to the floor below with the elevator opening directly onto a large reception room. Unlike the agency, the space was furnished more like an ornate living room than a modern office. Flocked wallpaper, settees, side tables, lamps, Oriental carpeting and a sound system emitting music to charm cobras out of wicker baskets.

The young man seated in one of the lounge chairs, clipping his fingernails, was the same young man I had seen conversing with Ms Duhane on my visit to Temporarily Yours. 'Kyle Romaine, I presume.'

'Who wants to know?' he snapped back, pocketing his clippers.

'Archy McNally,' Serge Ouspenskaya said, entering from the adjoining room. 'I was expecting you.'

Without his turban and Nehru suit he was indistinguishable from the thousands of prosperous businessmen who spend the winter vacationing in Florida. He had a full head of dark hair and the olive complexion was more a result of the sun than his progenitors.

'I just got off the phone with poor Annie,' Ouspenskaya went on. 'I take it the jig is up, as they used to say. Please, have a seat, Mr McNally. I can't offer you anything as we don't keep liquor on the premises. It's bad for business.'

The consummate actor to the end, he didn't appear the least distressed at the collapse of his venture. I sat as Kyle looked at me askance but didn't say a word. When Ouspenskaya settled into a lounge chair he continued, 'Congratulations, Mr McNally. Can I know how you did it?'

'Binky Watrous ran into Annie downstairs,' I said. When I learned that she was with Temporarily Yours I began to count heads. I knew for a fact Kate Mulligan was with the agency and learned from my father he had talked personally to Ms Duhane when he applied for temporary help.'

'Actually, he talked to Mrs Ouspenskaya, my wife. This is Alexander, our son. Families that work together stay together.'

He was conceding with all the aplomb of a guy who

really believed that it wasn't winning that counted but how you played the game – and with a warped sense of humor.

'Annie led to Jorge and so on down the line,' I told him. 'Did Margaret put the diamond clip Hanna had neglected to deposit in the safe back on the discarded dress?'

'If you wish to believe that, Mr McNally. I acquiesce to defeat but I admit to nothing.'

Didn't the Nazis use that same line? 'I think you made your first serious slip when you described my meeting with Hanna Ventura. Remember Narcissus?'

'I'm afraid I do, Mr McNally. I'm sometimes too clever for my own good. I can't help pushing the game to the edge of the abyss.'

'And falling in,' Alexander said, sassing his papa.

'Who asked you?' his papa rebuked. Turning to me Ouspenskaya went on. 'My mother was a gypsy. Her name really was Ouspenskaya. I didn't take my father's name because I never knew it. Neither did mama. She wanted a child but not a husband. Mama was a fortune-teller. Some said she really had the gift. Whatever talent I have in that direction I learned from her. When I went out on my own I worked Hollywood. Very fertile ground. I had a legit act in Las Vegas for a while and even traveled with a circus.'

I started at the mention of Las Vegas but Ouspenskaya gave no indication that he noticed.

'I got the idea for this operation when I returned to California. I imagined Palm Beach would be as fertile a venue as Hollywood and I was right. I contacted a broker here and he told me a temp agency was for sale. A good omen. The owners were desperate to get out and agreed to a lease deal with an option to buy. I recruited a number of hopeful starlets and actors who were down on their luck and, Horace Greeley notwithstanding, we headed east.'

'You know we've done nothing illegal,' Alexander put it. 'There's nothing the police can charge us with.'

'I think Mr McNally is aware of that,' Ouspenskaya told his son.

Technically, they were right. Ethically, they should be tarred, feathered and run out of town. 'Where do you go from here?' I asked by way of a gentle hint.

'My mother used to say that the gypsies, like the European Jews, always hoarded string. Do you know why, Mr McNally?'

'To tie up packing boxes for quick moves,' I answered.

'Exactly. I think we will go back to southern California where we have a home and plan our next move. This wasn't a bad run, Mr McNally. Between the legit business downstairs and the gullible ladies of Palm Beach we turned a neat profit.'

'You're a criminal and a social cancer,' I told the miscreant.

His son didn't like it but Ouspenskaya gave no indication that he was offended. 'I am many things, but I have never resorted to violence. I speak of the death of Mr Richard Holmes. The police have been here to question me. I don't like the police, Mr McNally. When they put their nose in, it is time for me to get out. So, your exposé is redundant. We would have been out of here in a matter of days even without your help.'

'You think Holmes was murdered?'

'Who knows? Who cares? That the police are asking questions is enough for me to call it quits.'

Was this the truth or was he saving face? And did he know more about Holmes's death than he cared to admit? I didn't want to antagonize him any further because I wanted information only he could give me. 'How did you know Holmes was poisoned almost before the police did?'

He smiled his patronizing smile and answered, 'There are some tricks a true professional never reveals.'

'Then I have to assume you poisoned him. He was cutting off his wife's allowance, which was your bread and butter.'

'Assume what you will, Mr McNally, but remember what I said. I never resort to violence. There's no profit in it.'

And I believed him. 'Desdemona Darling told me you found what she was looking for. True?'

This took the actor by surprise and his facial expression told me what I wanted to know before he told me. 'It's always nice to know I've succeeded where others have failed. Was she in her cups at the time of the disclosure?'

'She'd had a few.'

'That's what I thought. Now if you'll excuse us, Mr McNally, we have to gather string and load the covered wagon.'

'One last thing,' I said, rising. 'Kate Mulligan. Is she part of your operation?'

I was treated to the smile once more and only common sense kept me from wiping it off his face with my fist. Besides, Alexander looked lean and mean – and younger than me by ten years.

'You will have to ask her, Mr McNally. Those in my employ that you have discovered I can no longer protect, but I will never tell you who the others are. They might want to remain in Palm Beach and good luck to them. You see, there really is honor among thieves.'

What I wanted to do now was get back to Ocean Boulevard, don my swimming togs, and jump into the Atlantic to cleanse myself of the Ouspenskaya family stink. As I emerged from the building a cat crossed my path and I knew, instantly, that Kate Mulligan was one of Ouspenskaya's informers. Follow carefully this line of thought association, a process faster than a speeding bullet.

A while back I was hired to locate a kidnapped cat. (In Palm Beach this happens.) The case led to murder as my cases sometimes do, and the prime suspect, the victim's husband, maintained his innocence because he had called his wife in the presence of father and me, then found his wife dead when he arrived home. This seemed to prove that his wife was alive when he was with us, and murdered before he got home.

Not true. He had murdered his wife before leaving

home and in our presence he made the call and spoke, most likely, to his answering machine. Father and I heard only one side of the conversation. The murderer's side. We believed he had spoken to his wife because, at the time, we had no reason to doubt it.

Serge Ouspenskaya called Lady Cynthia at nine the morning she and Desdemona went to the police station and left a message on Connie's voice mail. The message simply stated that Ouspenskaya wanted to talk to Lady Cynthia and would she please call him. He had said nothing about a disturbing dream or that the women would encounter trouble at the police station. When he called back after ten that same morning, he said his earlier call was to warn Lady Cynthia of trouble because by then he knew what the police had found. How? I told him, that's how.

Walking with Kate back to the house from mother's potting shed, I told her that Richard Holmes had been poisoned. It was then shortly after ten. Now I needed Ursi to confirm that Kate had immediately contacted Ouspenskaya.

I was relieved to see Kate's car gone from the driveway and the station wagon returned. She had gone for the day – and forever if I had anything to say about it. I went directly to the kitchen and put the question to Ursi.

Our housekeeper had to think a while before answering. 'Yes, Archy,' she said, 'I remember that day. You and Kate came in from the garden. I remember because as soon as you left, Kate asked to use the phone. She said she wanted to make a call in private. I told her to use the phone in the den.'

When Tony Newley belted out his classic, 'What Kind Of Fool Am I?,' he said it all, didn't he?

I had my swim and debated whether or not I should confront Kate Mulligan one last time when I received a call from James Ventura. 'I hope you don't mind me calling you at home, Archy,' he said. 'They told me you had left the office and I wanted to speak to you before this evening.'

'Not at all, James, it's the reason I gave you this number. What can I do for you?'

'Hanna is going out tonight, to rehearse for the play with Penny Tremaine,' he informed me.

'That's possible, James. We start formal rehearsals tomorrow, but some of the cast may be getting together to bone up.'

'Have you seen the *Arsenic and Old Lace* film, Archy?'

'Yes. Why?'

'Both Hanna and Penny are policemen, or policewomen. I don't think they have any lines, or at most a sentence each. For this they need to rehearse all evening?'

'I see your point,' I said, reluctantly. I hate trailing people, especially lovers. 'What time is she leaving, James?'

'Seven.'

'I'll get on it,' I said.

'Did you hear about Ouspenskaya?' he asked.

With the speed of light, I thought, the news had traveled up and down Ocean Boulevard. 'I heard, James.'

'We got rid of Margaret. You know, I never cared for her.'

It was too late to rent a Ford Escort, so I would have to borrow mother's Ford wagon – and would need another swim when this was over.

24

I waited for Hanna a safe distance from the Ventura home. When she pulled out in a smart black Corvette, I followed her to A1A. Most cars head in that direction so I had no fear of her paying any special attention to me. We went north on A1A which, as usual, was busy so all I had to do was join the herd. When she turned off for Lantana, I got the craziest idea that I knew where she was heading – and I was right.

Hanna pulled up outside the home of Dr Gussie Pearlberg. There were several other cars parked in the vicinity and leaning against one of them, obviously waiting for Hanna, was none other than William Ventura. Mother and stepson entered the home and office of Dr Pearlberg. What was going on? A cocktail party, an orgy or – blessed mother of Sigmund Freud – a group therapy session?

I had met Dr Pearlberg, who is a psychiatrist, through Al Rogoff. This wonderful woman, who was eighty if she was a day, had on occasion provided the police with psychological profiles of serial murderers and rapists. I never consulted Dr Gussie, as I call her, for my own neuroses, which I know to be incurable, but had introduced her to father, who often recommended her to clients in need of psychiatric help.

I waited the fifty-minute hour for a group of about eight souls to emerge, get into their vehicles and depart. Hanna and William spoke to each other for a moment before doing the same. When the coast was clear I got out of the Ford and rang Dr Gussie's bell.

'You?' she said in her raspy voice. Dr Gussie has a two-pack-a-day habit.

'Me,' I answered. 'How are you?'

'Alive, last time I checked. What do you want at this hour, Archy?'

'I know you can't talk about your patients, Dr Gussie . . .'

'That's right, I can't. So where do we go from here?'

I followed her into her office and I could see by the chair arrangements that she had been conducting a group session. 'Listen to the story of my life before you toss me out,' I begged.

'That's what I do all day, young man, for a hefty fee. You can't afford me.'

'I don't need your services,' I said, 'I'm very well adjusted.'

'Which means you've come to terms with your shortcomings.' She lit a cigarette, unfiltered, and following the doctor's lead I pulled out my box of English Ovals and joined her. 'Those things will kill you,' she cautioned.

'How old are you, Dr Gussie?'

'None of your damn business, young man. Now what are you doing here?'

Having no choice, and counting on her professional discretion, I filled her in on James Ventura's fears.

'Foolish man,' Dr Gussie said. 'He's got sex on the brain. It happens at his age. Well, he has nothing to worry about. Hanna loves him, but then there's no accounting for taste, is there?'

Dr Gussie saw no harm in telling me that Hanna had come to her seeking advice for her (Hanna's) problem with William. Dr Gussie invited Hanna to join one of her group sessions with those who had similar problems. 'I called William myself,' Dr Gussie admitted, 'and got him to come to one session. He's a good boy, Archy. His father marrying a girl who was William's peer was very traumatic for the boy. He rebelled and lashed out at the object of his frustration. Not unusual. Tonight was his third session with us and he's making progress. You know, he really likes Hanna.'

'But why didn't they tell James what they were up to?' I asked.

'I told them not to,' Dr Gussie said. 'First, because he might want to join the group and that would negate any good the sessions were doing for both Hanna and William. With him listening, they would clam up. Second, because if it didn't work James Ventura might think there was no hope and give up on either his wife or his son. But William is doing fine.'

I was so happy to hear this I could have kissed Dr Gussie. In fact, before I left, I did. She said, 'Don't do that, young man, unless you mean to follow through,' and I think she meant it.

Feeling good, I decided to call upon Kate Mulligan one more time. Dr Gussie would shout 'masochistic' but I thought of it as putting closure to a low point in my career.

Kate didn't seem overly surprised to see me standing in her doorway. 'Some guy wrote that love means never having to say you're sorry,' she wisecracked.

'He was either a fool, or never in love.' She let me in but didn't invite me to sit.

'I'm almost fifty years old, Archy, with one face-lift, two careers and two marriages behind me. The first was to a blackjack dealer in one of the big casinos. A famous film actor played at his table one night and lost his shirt. To compensate, the guy walked off with my husband. After the magician, I met Ouspenskaya at that all-night cafe I was telling you about. He made me an offer I couldn't refuse.'

'Oh, but you could have,' I told her.

'Don't be a jerk, Archy. I'm not the type that settles down. You live in your lovely home, in this lovely town, with your lovely parents and lovely friends, and you can't understand why people like me do what we do. To keep the wolf off our backs, mister, that's why.'

'Nice people die of gentle starvation,' I told her, half meaning it.

'Screw you, Archy McNally.'

'My only regret, Kate, is that mother will miss you.'

'Really? My only regret is that I never got to have dinner at the Pelican Club. Does that make us even?'

My spirits had risen and fallen so many times this day I felt like a yo-yo in the hands of an overwrought school-boy. When I got back to our lovely house (unquote), mother had retired but I found father in the den reading Dickens. It was at times like this when I envied the man his ability to withdraw from this time and place into one more to his liking. He removed his glasses when I entered after knocking. 'Good evening, Archy. What do you have to report?'

'We will need a replacement for Kate Mulligan, sir.'

'I will inform Mrs Trelawney of that fact.'

'The Ventura case is closed, sir, to everyone's satisfaction. Would you like to hear about it?'

'I don't think so, Archy. Would you like a drink?'

'No, thank you, sir. It's been a long day. I think I'll retire.'

'Good night, then.'

'Good night, sir.'

Not crazy about Dickens, I withdrew into an English Oval and a marc. It was still early enough to make a few calls, and I did.

When I reached James Ventura I asked him if I could talk freely.

'Sure, Archy. Hanna is back home and watching the tube with William. Imagine that.'

'I can imagine it,' I said. 'I have very good news for you, James. Very good news, but it's top secret. Do I have your word to keep it strictly between us?'

When I reached Connie she reported that the police had released Richard's body and the cremation service would take place tomorrow. 'Very private,' Connie told me. 'Just Lady Cynthia. And Desdemona is furious with Ouspenskaya. The news is all over town.'

'Would you like to have dinner with me tomorrow night, Connie?'

'I thought you'd never ask. The Pelican?'

'Heavens no,' I protested. 'What about the Alcazar Lounge at the Breakers?'

'What?' she cried. 'The Breakers? What have you done, Archy?'

'What do you mean?'

'I mean you don't buy me an expensive dinner unless you've done something you're feeling very guilty about and want to say you're sorry by flashing your plastic around the Breakers. What is it, Archy?'

'Love means never having to say you're sorry, Connie.'

'Who said that?'

'A guy who was either a fool, or never in love.'

I slept a dreamless sleep and awoke a *happier* and a wiser man – but then the old mariner didn't know Consuela Garcia.

25

On Tuesday I visited Al Rogoff at his 'wagon' and was treated to a Bud straight out of the can to the accompaniment of Vivaldi on the stereo. We sat in Al's padded captain's chairs at an oak dining table positioned in a corner of the living room.

I told him about Ouspenskaya's operation and he agreed that even if anyone brought charges against the man they would be almost impossible to prove.

'These guys are the original Teflon kids. The people they dupe are too embarrassed to report them or appear in court to testify against them,' Al explained through a cloud of smoke coming from his Sunday two-buck cigar.

'He's getting ready to leave town,' I said. 'Are you going to let him go?'

'No reason to hold him,' Al responded.

'Which means Ouspenskaya is exonerated from any wrong-doing in the death of Richard Holmes.'

'We questioned all your fancy friends and came up with nothing,' Al said, rising to get another Bud out of the fridge. In his stocking feet he moved with all the grace of a grizzly. Was his addiction to the ballet wishful thinking? 'Ouspenskaya was nowhere near that table when the wine was being poured and no one saw either Lady Cynthia or Desdemona Darling slip anything into one of the glasses. Then we come up against the same old brick wall – how could anyone know which glass Holmes would take? The case is not officially closed but unless we come up with something new, like a confession, it'll end up on the "Death by Misadventure" shelf and it won't be alone.'

And that, I thought, was the end of that.

The stage was bare but our stage manager had come early and thoughtfully set up folding chairs for the cast and a card table for the director to sit behind, facing his charges. Had Binky found his forte? The venue seemed to give my players a severe case of stage fright. They crossed and uncrossed their legs, opened and closed their scripts and looked at the auditorium wistfully, perhaps imagining what it would be like when all the plush seats were occupied. In short, the full consequences of their rash decision to volunteer for the community theater were upon them – and me.

The groupings were very similar to when we had met at Lady Cynthia's last week. Hanna and William sat together, looking comfortable in each other's company. This gave a boost to my cynical heart. Fitz was up front with Buzz at her side, and why not? In the play they were about to be married. Penny and Vance

Tremaine sat together, and why not? They *were* married. Arnie Turnbolt and Phil Meecham, again, sat side by side. They weren't married but they had a lot in common – namely their sights set on William and Buzz, respectively.

Hank Wilson, Ed Rogers and Ron Seymour were now joined by Joe Anderson who, thankfully, had decided not to leave the show. Binky, Connie and Priscilla sat with me at the table. 'I want to observe their faces,' Priscilla told me, 'like an artist studies a blank canvas.' The only 'canvas' she seemed to be observing was Hank Wilson's.

Our Creative Director had already announced that she would be a no-show and to add to the first-night jitters our star arrived almost thirty minutes late. She made a grand entrance down the theater's center aisle, her pearl white muumuu shimmering about her as she moved. That, need I say, was a lot of shimmering. She was carrying what looked like a bottle of booze.

'Dear ones all,' she unoriginally proclaimed as she mounted the steps to the stage. She kissed first me, then Binky. Connie and Priscilla were spared. 'Sorry I'm late but I was searching for this crystal decanter.' She held the bottle up for inspection. 'Our first prop, as it's called. You saw it last in the hands of dear Dick Powell pouring me a sweet liqueur in *Broadway Blonde*. I've taken the liberty of filling it.'

Given what had happened to her husband this was in the worst possible taste. Also, most of the people she was addressing were not born when *Broadway Blonde* played their local Bijou and who, besides myself and June Allyson, remembered Dick Powell? But every little gesture has a meaning all its own and Desdemona Darling knew them all. Instead of giving the 'prop' to our stage manager, Desdemona carried it to her seat and placed it carefully on the floor beside her. She extracted her script and a plastic cup from her leather satchel and cried, 'Let the games begin.'

Oh, brother!

I read the lead-ins and the actors read their parts. These folks, who couldn't keep their mouths shut in church, became tongue-tied stutterers. I didn't have to worry about Arnie Turnbolt 'doing' Peter Lorre. Poor Arnie could only sound like himself and, as the nutty doctor, that was just fine.

In contrast, Desdemona was superb and the more she sampled the 'prop' the better she became. The velvet voice of her screen years was also evident as she recited her lines, drawing smiles of pleasure from the cast and crew. The Broadway blonde of a bygone era was still a pro.

We broke after the first act and people got up to stretch, giggle embarrassingly and, I think, regret that they didn't think to bring along anything stronger than the designer water in plastic liter bottle some toted. I hoped Desdemona had not set a precedent.

Priscilla ran off to observe Hank at close range. Desdemona, I noticed, alighted next to Joe Anderson and the two seemed to be enjoying a private joke.

Binky, Connie and I pow-wowed at the table. 'Your job,' I said to Binky, 'will be to fill the prop decanter with grapefruit juice as soon as you can get your hands on it.'

'How do I get my hands on it?' Binky wanted to know.

'When it's empty, she'll have no further use for it,' Connie answered.

Just when I was beginning to think I could pull the whole thing together and present good amateur theater, Joe Anderson fell out of his chair, Desdemona screamed and the crystal decanter hit the floor and shattered.

Oy vey!

Al Rogoff and I have several places where we rendez-vous to converse, and often commiserate, in private. One of them is the parking lot of the Publix supermarket on Sunset Avenue. This Wednesday afternoon we chose, by prearrangement, the outdoor juice bar in Lake Worth. I picked up a large pineapple juice and Al opted for papaya. Were Desdemona with us, would she have demanded a rum chaser?

We carried our drinks back to the Miata. I don't like sitting in police cars in public places. It invites rubbernecking.

'One thing I gotta say about your smart-ass friends, Archy. They're consistent.' Al began chomping on a cigar butt to go with the papaya.

'Poison,' I mourned.

'The same stuff that did in Holmes.'

'How did it get in Joe Anderson's stomach? Tell me that, Al.'

'The same way it got into Holmes's glass – osmosis. Look, Archy, the actress says Joe was drinking water from a paper cup he got from the cooler backstage. When his cup was empty she filled it with wine so they could have a drink to the good old days, was the way she put it. And that's it. Joe Anderson is history. The wine, as you know, was mopped up as soon as you all vacated the theater.'

Vacated? If the theater was on fire they couldn't have dispersed any quicker – with Priscilla yelling 'jinx, jinx, jinx' all the way to her car.

'The wine was clean, Al,' I said. 'We all watched Desdemona consume at least half the decanter before we broke after the first act. So why isn't she dead?'

'Funny thing, Archy. That's what she keeps saying. She's convinced someone is out to get her but they keep missing by a few feet.'

'I never came up against anything like this,' I told my policeman confidant. 'Two men poisoned in front of a room full of people and no one knows how it was done.'

'I have to tell you something, Archy. Several people we questioned said that Binky Watrous bragged that he would get Joe Anderson's job when Joe checked out. Binky was also present when Holmes got his. The thinking is that maybe Binky got it right the second time.'

The pineapple juice actually soured in my belly. 'Al, you can't honestly believe that Binky . . .'

'I can't. But my people aren't writing it off. Everyone present both times had opportunity – now we discover one of them had opportunity and motive. That's two strikes against Binky Watrous.'

It was close to five when I returned to my office. The pile of mail on my desk reminded me of Joe's last words to me in the McNally Building. 'I left your mail on your desk, Archy.' And I still hadn't gotten around to opening an envelope. I would miss Joe, but he was gone. Binky was very much with us and I was going to make damn sure he stayed with us. But how?

The envelope on top of the pile caught my eye. It was addressed in large printed letters and post-marked from St Louis, Mo. An advertising gimmick, I surmised, and almost tossed it in the wastebasket. Picking it up, I opened it instead.

It was a photograph from an old magazine, yellow with age, but I recognized Desdemona Darling at a glance. The caption read, 'DESDEMONA DARLING BEING PRESENTED WITH THE GOLD AND ONYX RING MADE ESPECIALLY FOR HER HIT FILM, *MATA HARI HARRIGAN*, BY STUDIO BOSS MARVIN MASON.'

Scribbled in the photo's white border were the letters KIRK.

DeeDee's blackmailer was trying to tell me something. But how did he know who I was or how to reach me?

How did the wine get in Richard Holmes's glass and Joe Anderson's stomach? And if Serge Ouspenskaya had left town, who was manipulating the icy fingers that once again began to crawl up my spine?

I felt so light-headed I had to sit for fear of fainting and yrs. truly is not the fainting kind. *Mata Hari Harrigan*? It never played the MoMA but if there was one person who knew more about old movies than Archy McNally, it was Arnold Turnbolt. I reached for the phone.

'*Mata Hari Harrigan*,' Arnie shouted. 'Where did you dig that one up?'

'Do you know anything about it, Arnie?'

'It's pure camp, Archy. It was made just before World War Two and Desdemona plays guess what? A spy. The gimmick is her ring, made especially for her by the FBI after they recruit her. Can you believe it, Archy? It had a big onyx stone that she reverses on her finger and with a little pressure the stone opens like a door to release a sleeping potion into the glasses of unsuspecting . . .' He paused for so long I thought our connection had been broken. 'Good God, Archy! Good God! Do you think . . .'

'Not a word, Arnie. You hear me? Don't breathe a word of this.'

'But, Archy . . .'

'Not a word or I'll tear up your autographed photo of Vera Hruba Ralston in her ice skates.'

I dialed Connie. 'Just one question. Is Desdemona Darling still with Madame C?'

'She is. Madame is trying to talk her into staying another night. She's in a bad way, Archy.'

Connie didn't say who was in a bad way – Lady Cynthia or Desdemona – and I couldn't hang on long enough to ask. The time for cogitating was over. I had to act – and fast.

I called the palace and got Al just checking in from his tour. 'How much would you give to learn who killed Richard Holmes and Joe Anderson?' I asked the sergeant.

'How much you asking, pal?'

'Assistance in breaking and entering.'

'What?'

'Meet me at the Publix ASAP, Al, and I'll explain everything. Promise.'

We left Al's car in the Publix lot and drove to Via Del Lago in the Miata with the top up. To keep Al's hands clean and his job secure, it was agreed that he would stay in the car and instruct me on how to get into the house. If anyone came down the street Al would duck out of sight. Given the size of a Miata and the size of Al Rogoff, this was easier said than done.

'Go 'round back and try the patio door first,' he instructed.

'Why?'

'Because nine times out of ten it's the one door people forget to lock.'

And, as is often the case, Al was right.

In the eerie light of a winter sunset I made my way

from the patio to the great room, then to the hall where I had watched Connie disappear with my megaphone in happier times. The first door off the hall was the master suite. As soon as I entered I saw the framed photographs on Desdemona's dressing table. I was hoping the table drawer held her jewelry. If not, I would find that ring if I had to take the place apart.

Something struck me as I approached my target. The photographs. There were four of them. Connie said there were five. One of each husband, not counting Holmes. All four were leading men of the silver screen a half century ago. The missing photo wasn't the object of my search but when I opened the drawer I saw it lying face down. When I turned it over I found myself looking at a very young Joe Anderson. It was autographed *Joseph Kirkland 'Kirk' Anderson*. Her first husband, the cameraman of her naughty flick and her tormentor. The missing piece of the puzzle slipped into place and the picture was complete. That night, right in this house, what I had failed to remember was that Joe Anderson was saying goodnight to Desdemona when she nearly passed out, causing Ouspenskaya to rush to her side and Holmes to lock horns with the psychic.

She must have recognized Joe, or 'Kirk,' the moment he walked into the house that night. Her acting expertise had carried her through the evening but one can only imagine what Joe had said to her in parting.

Joe knew Desdemona wanted him dead but got her husband instead. That's why he wanted out of the show. He sent me the clipping to tell me how she had

done it. He told me twice on Monday that he had left
the mail on my desk. If I had seen it that day, maybe
Joe would still be alive.

I heard a sound behind me and turned, expecting to
see Al Rogoff. It was Desdemona Darling, and she was
holding a gun pointed straight at me. 'I've killed two
men to protect my secret and they say there's never a
second without a third. I have a permit for the gun
and you are an intruder. I'll say I didn't notice your
car parked on the street.'

She was as calm, cool and collected as only the
criminally insane can be. 'Joe was your husband,' I
said, still holding the photograph.

'Number one. He was sore when I left him for a more
advantageous union. That's why Joe never made it out
west. He didn't know how to wheel and deal.'

'Did Richard know who Joe was, too?'

'Sure. I told him. That's why Richard wanted me to
dump Mr Ouspenskaya.'

'When did Joe start sending you the letters?'

'Not long after I left him. Now tell me what you're
doing here.'

'Strange, I was going to ask you that.'

An indication of her frenzied state of mind was that
she told me. 'Cynthia wanted me to stay with her
another night. I came here to get a change of clothes
and spotted your car. Tough luck, Archy.'

'I'm here because I got a communication from Kirk.
It mentioned a ring from a film called *Mata Hari
Harrigan*.'

'Kirk won't be sending any more letters, and Archy won't be reading any more letters.' Her blue eyes were like glass and from across the room I could see the sweat beading her forehead. Desdemona needed a drink and I needed time.

'I now know how you put the poison in the wine glass at Lady Cynthia's party. With your *Mata Hari Harrigan* ring.'

She let out a howl. 'That's how I did it. But I didn't want to do it. I went to see Joe after the party and pleaded with him to give me the film. He refused. He was still jealous because I left him and became famous. So jealous. He said he would keep the film as long as he lived and keep me guessing when he would give it to the tabloids. So he had to die, right?'

'But how did you know Joe would take that glass?'

She shook her head and for a moment I thought she was going to drop the gun – she didn't. 'Oh, it got all screwed up. Just when I got the stuff in the glass Cynthia came back from her rounds and took it off the table and put it on her tray along with four others. What could I do? I ask you, what could I do? Scream? Anyone could have gotten it and poor Richard did.'

'But even if you kept the glass how did you know Joe would take it off your tray?'

'Oh, that was easy, too. Cynthia let them select a glass from her tray. I handed them out from my tray, one at a time. I would keep my eye on the right glass and when I got to Joe I would give it to him. But it got all screwed up. All screwed up.'

'Joe knew it was meant for him,' I said.

'Sure he did. I went to see him again. He showed me the can of film. He said I could have it and he would keep his mouth shut if I married him.'

'Married him?' I was incredulous.

'Sure. He still loved me. Maybe that's hard for you to believe, but he did. He was crazy jealous all these years and he still wanted me.'

'So how did you poison him at the theater?'

She laughed and was beginning to sway on her feet. 'You're all a bunch of fools. I drank that wine and made sure everyone saw me drinking it, including Kirk, or Joe as you call him. Before the break I filled my cup for the last time and put the poison in the decanter. Then I poured one for Joe. Neat, eh?'

'And Joe was foolish enough to drink it?'

'Why not? He saw me drinking from the decanter and I was fine. So when I suggested a toast to our wedding, he went for it. Poor Joe.'

'You agreed to marry him?'

'How else was I going to get him to take a drink?'

Poor Joe, is right. For fifty years he had been so besotted with love and jealous rage for the starlet he had won and lost he failed to see that she had turned into an oversized egomaniac with a severe drinking problem.

When he thought he had won her back, did he regret the letter he had left on my desk? After making his final rounds on Tuesday, he knew I had not read my mail. Had he planned to come to the office early the next morning and remove the incriminating epistle before my arrival? Probably. Had Desdemona let Joe live she would have been in the clear and I wouldn't be staring down the barrel of a loaded gun.

Here, I played my final card. 'I could use a drink myself, DeeDee. How about you?'

'You think I'm stupid. Turn around. I have to shoot you in the back like I didn't know who you were.'

I did as I was told and now I was the one with a wet forehead.

Who would have thought Archy McNally would go down in Desdemona Darling's boudoir, clutching an autographed photograph of her first husband?

I heard a groan and when I turned, gingerly, I saw Al Rogoff holding Desdemona's neck in the crook of his elbow. Her gun went off and made a neat hole in the bedroom ceiling.

'Why didn't you wait until she shot me?' I groaned.

'Because I would never have forgiven myself, pal.'

26

A search of Joe Anderson's apartment in Juno Beach turned up a tin can designed to hold a reel of movie film. It was empty, as are most of the closets that contain our personal bogeymen.

Desdemona Darling hired a 'dream team' of Hollywood lawyers to help prove her insane at the time of the two murders. Given Desdemona's acting ability, especially in the glare of a spotlight, father thinks the prosecution will have a tough time refuting the defense's plea.

A member of mother's garden club graciously volunteered to tend the begonias in mother's absence. 'I'm relieved,' Mother admitted to me. 'I hated to tell your father, but Kate Mulligan didn't know very much about gardening in general and begonias in particular. I just didn't have the heart to fire her.'

I replied by kissing mother's rosy cheek.

'All's well that ends well,' I quoted to Binky Watrous, 'and there's a job opening at McNally and Son with your name on it.'

'I know, Archy,' he nodded sadly, not exactly ecstatic over the prospect of fulfilling his dream.

'Just think, Binky. Job security, medical benefits, a pension fund, two weeks' paid vacation, the Duchess off your case, and all the coffee you can drink.'

'I just wish poor Joe had retired in a more conventional way. It's wrong to profit from a crime.'

Binky is as honorable as a comic book superhero, but without the four-color poster boys' built-in defense mechanisms. This sometimes worries me. 'Cheer up and take solace in the motto *ad astra per aspera*.'

'What does that mean, Archy?'

'To the stars, through difficulties. It happens to be the motto of the state of Kansas, and everyone knows you have to pass through Kansas in order to reach Oz.'

From the column of Lolly Spindrift. Palm Beach. The Ides of March.

Our very own Archy McNally pulled off a coup de théâtre last night at the Lake Worth Playhouse where, under his direction, Arsenic and Old Lace *was presented by the Palm Beach Community Theater. The community theater's own Creative Director, Lady Cynthia Horowitz, scored a hit in the starring role of that delightful murderess, Abby Brewster. Another society matron of note, Penny Tremaine, ably supported Lady Cynthia as her equally charming but also lethal sister, Martha Brewster. Other stalwarts of our island in the sun, including Hanna Ventura, Vance Tremaine and Phil Meecham, excelled in supporting roles. And special kudos to Arnold Turnbolt, who had them rolling in the aisles with his portrayal of Dr Einstein; stage manager Binky Watrous, who also portrayed one of the police officers; and Director McNally himself in the role of Mr Gibbs.*

Honorable mention to cast members Ron Seymour, William Ventura, Ed Rogers and Henry Lee Wilson. Everyone looked so well, thanks to makeup consultant Priscilla Pettibone, and remembered their lines, thanks to prompter Consuela Garcia.

But I have saved the best for the last. Not only did Buzz Carr and Elizabeth 'Fitz' Fitzwilliams charm the audience as the play's young lovers, they also drew the eye of a noted Hollywood producer who has offered to screen-test the duo for his next epic! People are recalling names like Tracy and Hepburn, Bogie and Bacall, McQueen and MacGraw, wherever the couple appear. Lady Cynthia Horowitz will give a reception the night of the play's closing to celebrate its success and the good fortune of Buzz and Fitz. WOW!

Give unto me a break.

A selection of bestsellers
from Hodder & Stoughton

McNally's Dilemma	Lawrence Sanders 0 340 76712 X	£5.99 ☐
McNally's Trial	Lawrence Sanders 0 340 63956 3	£5.99 ☐
McNally's Risk	Lawrence Sanders 0 340 60437 9	£5.99 ☐
McNally's Luck	Lawrence Sanders 0 340 59241 9	£4.99 ☐

All Hodder & Stoughton books are available at your local bookshop or newsagent, or can be ordered direct from the publisher. Just tick the titles you want and fill in the form below. Prices and availability subject to change without notice.

Hodder & Stoughton Books, Cash Sales Department, Bookpoint, 39 Milton Park, Abingdon, OXON, OX14 4TD, UK. E-mail address: orders@bookpoint.co.uk. If you have a credit card you may order by telephone – (01235) 400414.

Please enclose a cheque or postal order made payable to Bookpoint Ltd to the value of the cover price and allow the following for postage and packing:
UK & BFPO: £1.00 for the first book, 50p for the second book and 30p for each additional book ordered up to a maximum charge of £3.00.
OVERSEAS & EIRE: £2.00 for the first book, £1.00 for the second book and 50p for each additional book.

Name . . . .

Address . . . .

. . . .

. . . .

If you would prefer to pay by credit card, please complete:
Please debit my Visa / Access / Diner's Club / American Express (delete as applicable) card no:

Signature . . . .

Expiry Date . . . .

If you would NOT like to receive further information on our products please tick the box. ☐